ME DYING TRIAL

PATRICIA POWELL

ME DYING TRIAL

BEACON
150

BEACON PRESS

BOSTON

Beacon Press
25 Beacon Street
Boston, Massachusetts 02108-2892
www.beacon.org

Beacon Press books
are published under the auspices of
the Unitarian Universalist Association of Congregations.

This book is printed on acid-free paper that meets the uncoated paper
ANSI/NISO specifications for permanence as revised in 1992.

Library of Congress Cataloging-in-Publication Data

Powell, Patricia, 1966-
Me dying trial / Patricia Powell.
p. cm. — (Bluestreak)
ISBN 0-8070-8365-8 (acid-free paper)
1. AIDS (Disease)—Patients—Fiction. 2. Gay men—Fiction.
3. Jamaica—Fiction. I. Title. II. Series.

PR9265.9.P68M4 2003
813'.54—dc22
2003057942

For Aunt Nora

Acknowledgments

A first novel is never just the accomplishment of the author, but of all those who have influenced her from the very beginning until its publication. Thanks to my English and Creative Writing teachers: Margaret Spencer, Robert Polito, Meredith Steinbach, Michael Ondaatje and Kate Rushin and Jonathan Strong who have become dear, dear friends.

For their unending support, love and advice over the years, many thanks to Sherrard Hamilton, Joan Becker, Noel Johnson, Darryl Alladice, Silas Obidiah, Stephen McCauley, Winifred Powell, Nevin Powell, Selwyn Cudjoe, Shay Youngblood, Kiana Davenport, Carleasa Coates, Elizabeth Hadley-Freydberg, and, of course, Teresa Langle de Paz.

Introduction

I remember the first time I met Patricia Powell. I was a new student in Brown University's Creative Writing program, from which she had just graduated. We were both invited to a party at a faculty member's house, my first, her last. Over the course of the evening, almost everyone at the party told me I had to meet Patricia. Soft-spoken yet not aloof, she's a hugely talented writer, they kept saying. And she was from the islands, just like me.

Finally, I did walk over to say hello, and at the end of our conversation I asked Patricia if she had any advice for a new writer, at least a new student in a writing program.

"Just do what you do," she said, "and at the end, if you have one friend left, you're lucky."

I have never forgotten this piece of advice. Indeed, it has served me well over the years. What I heard her saying to me then was that writing, like living, takes some measure of courage. Our work requires it, even demands it, and we can deliver no less. Only when I read her magnificent first novel, *Me Dying Trial*, did I realize just how extremely talented and courageous a writer Patricia Powell is.

Me Dying Trial introduces us to Gwennie Glaspole, battered mother of five, whose escape into the arms of another man brings about the birth of her fiercely independent daughter, Peppy. But like all summaries, this does little justice to the scope of Gwennie's arduous trials, her Herculean efforts at getting an education, and of *Me Dying Trial*'s well-paced and exquisite narrative. For *Me Dying Trial* is a book that seduces with its small caresses as well as its larger strokes. And though the broader narrative draws you into its beguiling web, it is the small details that keep you there: the tickle of a blade of grass against the back of a leg, the basin of hot water that is the only salve for bruises, the lilt of voices speeding up to argue, then slowing down ever so lightly to address a beloved child.

Like all of Patricia's work, *Me Dying Trial* digs deep to unravel its own silences. The growing drama, Elizabeth Barrett Browning tells us, does away with the simulation of painted scenes and uses the soul itself as its stage. Here, Gwennie's soul is laid bare through her abuse, her migrations, and her encounters with changes in her own landscape and her children's lives. Secrets hover over these characters like ghosts, or a child's grin, but it takes some effort to see and acknowledge them for the physical and mental anguish they might cause. Though issues of history, culture, gender, and class are often spoken of as though they were separate entities, we cannot separate them quite so easily in an individual life for they always bleed into our personalities to make us who we are. Gwennie can only escape just so far before realizing, as Patricia has said of her own life, that she is like a turtle, carrying her home on her back. If survival is the ultimate goal, then at what cost? Is independence ever really possible for one who is so tightly linked to others? The complex role of community is one of the elements I most cherish in this novel. What would any of us be without our Aunt Coras, who lovingly take us in when our mothers must surrender us for a while? Gwennie's survival ultimately depends on her community, but along with that support come many burdens that make the shell on her back just as heavy as a stone and brick house.

Though stirring and luminous, Patricia's writing never escapes the realities of these very complicated lives. *Me Dying Trial* is a communal as well as personal narrative, an oral as well as written tale, a stage for many souls. It is also one of the most heartbreaking and beautiful novels I have ever read. Its subtlety hides all its ingenuous seams, yet it is extremely well crafted. At times it reads like a dream. Other times like a nightmare, one from which we hope its characters will awaken, but into which we fear any or all of them might sink again.

As I finished this novel, I was reminded of Janie Crawford from Zora Neale Hurston's groundbreaking *Their Eyes Were Watching God*, who, upon her return to a hometown where she's slighted and scorned, tells her friend Pheoby, "you got tuh go there tuh know there." Perhaps we have not been where Gwennie has been, but through Patricia's lyrical and remarkable narration, we feel very deeply what she has been through. This intimacy between writer, reader, and character is in part what makes Patricia Powell a captivating storyteller and one of the most exciting writers living and writing on the island that is the Caribbean-American hyphen.

Edwidge Danticat
Miami, Florida

Family Tree

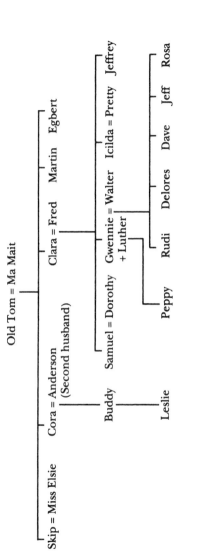

Old Tom = Ma Mait

Skip = Miss Elsie

Cora = Anderson
(Second husband)

Clara = Fred   Martin   Egbert

Buddy

Leslie

Samuel = Dorothy

Gwennie = Walter   Icilda = Pretty   Jeffrey
+ Luther

Peppy   Rudi   Delores   Dave   Jeff   Rosa

PART ONE

I

Friday evening, and the old country bus was ram-packed with market women and school children as usual. At every corner, the bus would bend over so badly, all the baskets with yam, banana, fish and breadfruit mad to fall over, not to mention the people – pack like fresh sardines on top one another. Gwennie hang onto the railing, her bag with the potato pudding she bake overnight clutch tight underneath her arm. Through the tiny square windows of the old bus, she could see the shops sailing by, canefields with stalks bowing in the wind, the cemetery with break-down tombs, Aunt Emmy's house, the old church, the pond . . . Gwennie yank the string and the bus rattle and squeal to a full stop rolling all the dry coconuts down the aisle and on top of people's corn toes. She tread her way careful, pushing pass sweaty market women, big baskets and boxes until finally she jump off the bus.

Outside, she brush the market smell and bus grime from her blue pantsuit and walk up to the brown gate. Nothing ripening-up yet, only sweet-smelling yellow blossoms on the trees lining the gate and plenty bees flying round. The ground was still damp from the rainy season, and the weeds spring up tall in Grandma's garden choking the roots of her fern and morning glory. Tomorrow, sure as rain, Grandma going to send her to pull them out. A little wisp of grass tickle the back of her leg, and absently Gwennie use her foot, scratch the spot. It tickle again, and as she turn round to see what it was crawling up her leg, her face meet with a large grin covering over Luther's face.

'But look at me dying trial! Luther, you here playing games. There it was. I thought it was bees or something.'

Luther laugh. 'Jesus, Miss Gwennie, you deaf just like an old horse. You know how long I been standing up here?'

Gwennie look up in his face. She like the way the little sprinklings of grey at his temples make him look older than his twenty-five years. But then him would laugh, and the two dimples pinching his cheeks and the gap in his front teeth would remind her that she at least five years older. 'Couldn't be that long. I just come off the old bus.' She brush her suit again.

'I was under the orange tree', him point, 'shading from the sun. It sure is a hot one today. Can't talk long though, I have to get back to the bridge now.'

'How's that coming along?'

'About four more weeks left before it ready.'

'Bet you don't want to leave. Not with all that good food mama cooking. Look how you stout-up and everything.'

Him laugh again. 'You better stop teasing me, Miss Gwennie. And why stay here anyway, all the good women gone. Not much choice from what left.'

'You not looking hard enough, man.'

'Maybe.' A faraway look come into his eyes, and as him stare into the hills surrounding the little district, Gwennie had to wonder how come she never set eyes on him long before two months ago, or even before she marry Walter. Him was such a gentleman: kind, church-going and everything. Even with the children, him was real good. Whenever she bring them down to visit Grandma, him was always playing with them, taking them out on Grandpa's old donkey June, telling them Anansy stories and buying them all kinds of nonsense. Last time she come, him even teach her to play dominoes. And after few games she was giving him big-big six love.

'Well, I must get back to the bridge, Miss Gwennie. But I will see you.'

Her good-bye stuck in her throat, and she watch until his shirt-tail turn the corner and she couldn't see him anymore. She brush her pantsuit one more time, pick up the bag with the pudding, lift up the latch and step through the gate.

Grandma was sitting in the front room as usual, her little scraps of cloth all over the place. Her head was bent forward and she hummed, swaying back and forth, the rhythm going with each stitch.

'Who that humming so sweet that hummingbird ownself would shame to hear it?' Gwennie walk silently into the room.

'Gwennie! But see me dying trial,' Grandma cry out loud, dashing down the material and hobbling over to her daughter. 'But how you mean to frighten me so? Every day I think about you, child, wondering when you coming to look for us. How the worthless man – Walter? You

2

pappy worried sick about you. Him plan was to come and see you since I can't do the walking sake of the foot. How you do, child?'

Gwennie hug her. 'Doing okay.'

'How Dave and the bad knee?'

'Doing much better.'

'That poor pickney,' Grandma mutter, seating herself and picking up the sewing again. 'Fall down mash-up his knee cap. If I did just have me own way, I would bring him to the science doctor meself so him can sprinkle a little water over the pickney's head. You'd be surprise to see how quick him get better. I keep telling you . . .'

'You know his father,' Gwennie say to her. 'You know him don't believe in those things. How's your leg?'

'Same way,' Grandma slap her hips. 'Real bad these days with all that rain. They just pull right up. Only the good Lord can heal it, medear, nothing else.' She show Gwennie the material. 'Making underpants for your papa.'

'Him out working, cutting cane as usual?'

Grandma nod. 'You know nothing will stop him. Is harvest time for the cane crop now, so him working harder than usual. Doctor say his blood pressure okay, but him complain of headaches all the time. When is not one thing, is the other.'

'I just see Luther,' Gwennie say, sitting next to her on the bed, watching the stubby fingers with the break-off fingernails grip the needle and make straight perfect stitches with the thread.

'Yes, medear. You papa have to tell him that even though him only staying for a little while, this is a house of God. Him can't be bringing in young gals from out the street in here as him please.'

'What him do now?' Gwennie ask her.

'All the time young gals from about the place just push open the gate, not even close it back so the dogs won't go out the street, and come right in, asking for him. I get tired, man.' She kiss her teeth and push up the cat-like spectacles leaning on her nose. 'When him just come,' Grandma slap her knee, 'every Sunday, him get up early and have prayers with us. These days, huh, him come in all hours of the night.' She stick out her two lips and start to hum.

Gwennie never say anything. She remember that even when she engage to Walter, she still couldn't come in after nine. Her very wedding day when she take careless quarrel with Grandma, Grandma slap her jaw and tell her, 'I don't care how old you be. You must have respect.'

3

'Him good about the boarding fee, though,' Grandma tell her. 'Always pay up on time, and respectful too. Not a bad fellow a tall.'

II

She never see him again that evening, and as cock crow the next morning, him gone.

'Don't stay round much,' Grandpa tell her. 'Him is the foreman, so they keep him busy.'

'Walter gone back to church yet?' him ask, as them sit down outside on the verandah peeling and eating sugarcane and the little pudding Gwennie did carry.

She shake her head.

'That man is a hard man,' Grandpa say, his face sad. 'Remember how the church used to pack when him go to preach? Everybody want to hear to his sermon. And Lord, him could preach.' Grandpa shake his head, eyes far back remembering. 'Now him curse and drink white rum like a blinking jackass. What a shame.'

Gwennie look up in the old wrinkle-up wrinkle-up face. People say they were two of a kind, soft-spoken and just plain good-natured. She wish him never have to work so hard tending animals and cutting sugarcane all the time. All of a sudden she notice how him quiet-up, not saying a word. Gwennie start wonder if him was turning fool-fool, if him forget altogether that them talking. But Grandpa only in deep thought.

'How him treating you, better?'

'As usual. Sometimes him okay, other times . . .'

'My, my! That man is something in truth. What is wrong with my son-in-law? But, you know, as I always tell you, take your things and your three children and come stay with us. Mile Gully School always looking for good teachers. No matter if you don't have your certificate. They will still take you. This house never too small for me children and grand-children. Take your things and come.'

Gwennie sigh deep. She wanted to go, bad-bad too. But she couldn't put up with the eight o'clock bedtime every night, the prayers, church service, night service, and Bible study, three and four times a week. She couldn't put up with the coming in early after she go out to any night function, and that she couldn't come and go as she please without telling them what time she coming back. She was a big woman, not a pickney.

And the way Mile Gully's people love to know and carry people's business, she couldn't put up with them a tall. Them would must want to know what happen to the lovely romance between she and Walter that cause them to pick up themselves and take off like breeze go get married. Now she come back with her face heavy, them was sure to laugh behind her back. Not saying that life rosy living with Walter, for only God alone know how bad she want to leave him. God alone see the bruises and the way Walter possessive and treat her and the children. But it not so easy picking up and laying down roots elsewhere.

'I don't know why you won't stop having them,' Grandma tell her over and over. 'Stop, man,' she would say pushing out her two lips. 'If him treat you so bad, stop. Go to doctor. Make them put you on something. Or tell him to go to hell.'

'But I tell him,' Gwennie would say to her, a little bit weak. 'All the time, I tell him. But him don't care.'

'Because you too soft and him know that. Huh, I would set out for that wretch, get scissors or something, and God help me. What I wouldn't cut . . .'

But Gwennie know better than to take any more of Grandma's advice. She find out now that she no match a tall for Walter when him come home drunk. Last time she lick him with the piece of board Grandma tell her to keep under the bed for protection, him drag it out of her hand and knock her with it instead. She still have all the black-and-blue marks.

III

She see Luther that evening though, and him was his old playful self as usual.

'Miss Gwennie, how about a game of dominoes?' him whisper through the crack of her door after she already put on her night-clothes and say her prayers.

'Sure.' She creep out of bed and tip-toe out the room and down the hall so Grandma and Grandpa wouldn't hear from next door.

'Last time you give me six-love. Huh, tonight I going to show you who is the man,' him laugh, setting up the game on his bed.

'We will see,' Gwennie say, looking about the room and noticing how bare and untidy it was, with his trousers fling over the door, his shirt hang limp from a nail. 'We will certainly see who the man is,' she say again, sitting next to him on the little single bed.

'You going up back Sunday as usual, Miss Gwennie?'

She look hard at the dominoes in her hands and nod her head.

'They having a party up the street. Bet you couldn't tell when last you shake your foot?'

It was true. When she and Walter first get married, most every Saturday night them gone to party. Then one night him and another man catch up in a fight. Him claim that the man dance with her much too long. So from that night, them don't go out much. And then since the babies start to come, one right after the next, she just lose the urge.

'Me is a big respectable married woman, Luther. What you think people would say?'

Him suck his teeth. 'If you spend all your time worrying about other people, you won't get any place. So you better come.' Him nudge her, upsetting the dominoes in her hand, causing them to scatter on the bed.

'See what you do.' She nudge him in return, upsetting his hand as well.

'Well, what you say, yes?'

She hesitate. If Walter find out, him bound to quarrel with her. Just like that other time when she did go to that party with Isaiah. Walter and Isaiah used to be best friends. Work and teach side by side at the same Agricultural school. Now Walter don't even talk to the poor man.

'Come on, Miss Gwennie, man.' Him nudge her again, and this time his arm stay next to hers.

And she could've moved his arm, for she never like the way her belly was starting to tremble, but the warmth from his arm seem to send little tinklings up her back and she like that. And them stay like that for a while, his arm on hers, and the little tinklings running up and down her back. Then his hand start run lightly up and down her side and she could've gone back to her room, but all of a sudden it was feeling real nice to be snuggling up next to him.

And so when her night-clothes start come off, piece by piece, she never do a thing but moan and ease up closer and closer to him, for it was so

6

much nicer than the rush Walter always in. Them did have to take time and not make much noise, for Grandma sleep light. But not even that could stop them from having them own little party right there in the room on the little single bed, pouring rhythms and sweat into one another, moanings and expressions of love better than any juke box.

After the heat wave pass, she realize that the last time it feel so good was when she and Walter was courting. Luther never roll over and fall asleep, instead him caress and hug her, and in no time was ready again. But she tip-toe back to her room, and pretty soon the snoring from next door put her straight to bed.

She never see him at all Sunday morning at prayers, and Sunday evening when time come for her to go back home so she can prepare for school the next day, Gwennie pick up herself and go off to the party with Luther. Grandpa couldn't understand why Gwennie need go out to dance after such a lovely sermon at church, but Grandma never say a word. When Gwennie tell her she going out, she just push up her two lips in the air and start to hum.

Gwennie never dance with Luther much, for she never want to raise any eyebrows. Plenty of her old-time school friends were there, so she chat with them and dance with them husbands most of the time. When she finally dance with Luther, she never like the way him always hold her close, and the way him always want to dance only to slow songs, especially with so many people looking. And that funny look that come into his eyes when she dance with the other men remind her of the way Walter would look at her.

Them never stay long at the party though, for Gwennie did have to get up early and catch the bus back. So them walk back towards the house holding hands when nobody could see them anymore. Everything was dead-quiet through the graveyard except for them shoes whispering on the night-dew grass. Not even one night-bug was out chirping. And so when the moon slip behind the cloud, anybody who see the two shadows kissing-up in the cemetery that night could dip them finger in blood and swear it was Lucie and Charlie, the couple who pass on last March when them car meet up with the four o'clock train on the way back from them wedding. And this time when her stomach tremble, she just pull him closer so him could press way the little tinklings. And the grass did feel real cool on her back as Luther ease her down on the night-dew, and it was just as blissful as the night before.

IV

Him was gone as usual the next morning when she board the old bus with the market women and school children again. But her mood was good, and the bus ride sail by quick. At school, instead of dragging as usual, the day sail by real fast too. And sometimes she would just find herself, with her two hands holding up her jaw and her eyes fix nowhere in particular, thinking about the night-dew last night, and the juke box the night before. Other times she find herself giggling, and it was only when her students start to look at her funny-funny-like that she finally straighten up herself.

But the minute she reach home, the giggling start up again. Her children notice it first thing, and couldn't spell sense of this newness that come over them mother. Walter was inside cooking dinner when she go into the kitchen. She tell him 'Evening', and him just look at her and grunt as usual. But instead of worrying up herself half to death over the way him talk to her, like she do almost every time him don't talk to her when she talk to him, Gwennie pop out with a little giggle. For after Luther, Walter look stupid-stupid-like to her now. Walter turn round, look at her, kiss his teeth and walk out the kitchen. Poor man couldn't understand why she grinning so much when him never give her any joke.

For the rest of the week him never say another word to her. Usually, Gwennie would sit down with her hands holding up her jaw and fret and worry-up herself over how this man won't talk proper to her, now she just hum and sing when she pass him. But by the middle of the following week, in the middle of all her happiness, Gwennie couldn't help but notice something troubling Walter. One evening she hear him ask the older boy, Rudi, if his mother did tell him why she never come home last week Sunday evening. Another time, she see him break and throw away one of the little blow-blow toys Luther send for the little girl, Del.

Since she did start teach the two boys to play dominoes and cards, one evening Walter come home and catch them playing. Hell break loose in the house that night. Walter grab up the dominoes and the cardpack, and what him never send flying through the door, him turn on the stove and burn.

Then him start the quarrelling. 'Gwennie, you don't have anything better to do than to sit here and teach you sons to gamble. What kind of mother you be?'

Gwennie never answer a word. She and the two boys just sit down and look at him, eyes and mouths open wide.

'Make I catch any more blasted domino and card playing inside me house and we will see what happen. I don't want me sons to be blasted gamblers.' And him storm way into his room and don't speak again for the remainder of night.

But Gwennie know it wasn't the gambling so much that was bothering him. It was the fact that she know how to play cards and dominoes and him never teach her.

So that was the end of the domino and card playing tournament. Night time after the two boys, Rudi and Dave, and the little girl, Delores, gone to bed, and since Walter just go straight to his room these days after him eat dinner, she would just sit out in the living room by herself. Sometimes she clean the floor and dust, sometimes she do a little sewing: make dresses for Delores or just patch up her sons' uniforms since them romp rough at school and often tear out the underarms.

Sometimes she crochet one or two doilies for her bureau or for Grandma's centre table, so her figurines can look pretty on it. But most of the time she just sit down on the little stool inside the kitchen, her hands holding up her jaw, and re-run the whole weekend with Luther in her head, the way him talk sweet words to her, the way him love to use his tongue and lick-lick her neck, her shoulders, her ears. And then when she think about it long enough till the little tinklings start to move around in her belly, she just sigh deep, get up, stretch and go to her bed.

At night when she crawl in next to Walter, no matter how late, him would always be laying down there awake, not saying anything, but his eyes would be wide open looking up at the cracks and the little water marks in the ceiling. Depending on how dominant the tinklings she would roll over next to him and try touch-touch him up, for these days she notice that him not quite as demanding. And even though she was kind of glad, for most times she tired, it start to bother her. She start to wonder what him lay down there and think all hours of the night when him not sleeping. She know him can't read her mind, but what if him run into anybody from Mile Gully and them tell him about she and Luther? Walter come from the little district just right across the other side of the bridge. The people from Mile Gully know him well. It wouldn't be too hard for him to find out if people was going to be doggish and walla-walla them mouth about she and Luther.

9

With that song, Gwennie start up prayer meetings with God at night. And she would lie down there and ask Brother Jesus if him could please not let Walter find out, for only the Heavenly Father up above could help her if him ever know. Him alone know what Walter capable of doing to her, and she really wouldn't like to find out. Then she would cry, Amen, roll over next to Walter, and start to touch-touch him up. She could tell him wasn't use to it, for him would just lay down there not moving. But after she start use some of the lickings and rubbings Luther use, him start to relax.

V

When word come from Grandma that the bridge finish and she sorry bad, for the little boarding money so helpful, it was like somebody come in and take out a whole piece of Gwennie's inside, and she never know how to put it back. And it wasn't so much his leaving or the fact that Gwennie never know a God-a-heaven thing about this man – where him come from or anything – but she have a funny feeling that the baby stirring round in her stomach and widening out her hips belong to Luther, and him wouldn't know about it.

So that damp look start appear round her face, and Walter recognize it too, for it was just like when them use to fight like puss-and-dog everyday. The children recognize it too, for them stop ask her stupid-stupid questions, and even the little girl, Del, wouldn't cry as much and give trouble. Even the children at school notice it and start to do their homework and come to class early.

When she visit Grandma a few days later, she linger bout the gate waiting for the laugh. Then she would go into Luther's old room looking for something, a picture so she could show the baby widening out her hips what him look like, a shirt, anything. And Grandma notice the damp look on her face and the way her body look frail even though she expecting.

'Walter bugging you again?' Grandma ask her.

'No,' Gwennie mumble, starting to cry.

'Then what is the matter?'

'Nothing.'

And she mope round the house the remainder of the day.

When Walter see her throwing up all over the place, him figure that maybe she pregnant, but him wasn't too certain, for she seem thinner than usual. But him help around the house and with the children plenty, trying to please Gwennie and help dry up some of the dampness. Him did grow to like the giggle-giggle Gwennie who come munching up to him at night. Him wasn't ready to let her go yet.

Gwennie would write Grandma, asking her if she could please check again and see if she put down Luther's address careless-careless about the place, or if she remember anything about where him live or come from. But Grandma couldn't remember a thing. And the dampness just take over Gwennie's whole body and cause her to become thin and sickly.

But when the little girl finally born and Gwennie notice how her grin and dimple cover up her face just like Luther's, some of the dampness start to go away, and she could allow herself to remember the tinklings in her belly, the moanings and the cool grass. But then she start to notice too that as the dampness ease away, little by little, the more the grin and the dimples resemble Luther's. Grandma see the grin and figure out right away where it come from. Sometimes Gwennie see her looking at the baby, her face puzzle-up. Then she would look off into space. But them never say a word to one another. Grandma just purse up her lips and hum.

While the grin wipe away some of the dampness and bring comfort, it bring fear too. Everyday Walter would pet and coo the little baby, yet not notice that her hairline shape different from everybody in both his and Gwennie's family. And after a while, Gwennie start notice too that Walter was looking hard at the little grin and dimple, and everytime him look, his forehead wrinkle over. So Gwennie start to keep the baby out of his way as much as possible, but it never spell sense to hide it from him, for it was Walter's house and, supposedly, his daughter too.

So Gwennie try figure out how much of Luther, Walter did see. It was only the once though. She and Walter did meet him the same Thursday evening when them bring the children down to visit Grandma. Luther was just moving in and Grandpa introduce them. She still remember the handshake for his hand was strong and sturdy. But she couldn't remember if him was smiling or not. She know him was in a hurry to look at the bridge before nightfall, and it would spell sense not to be smiling-smiling if you hurrying, but she couldn't remember.

And so the fear of whether or not Walter recognize the grin on the little girl's face ride Gwennie day-in and day-out. Cause her to take up praying all hours of the day. And so everytime the baby grin, it was like a nightmare. And the nightmare gallop and kick until Gwennie find herself in Grandma's bedroom weeping and wailing, with the room door lock and the curtains draw tight. And all through the weeping and wailing and moonlight and cemetery and lickings and lovemaking, Grandma never say a word. A few times Gwennie notice her opening up her mouth to cry out unto her Heavenly Father for guidance and strength so she can listen good to what Gwennie saying, but it just dry up right back in her voice box, and so she never bother say anything, she just purse up her mouth and look at Gwennie.

After Gwennie finish cry and blow her nose into the lining of Grandma's old frock, Grandma ask her: 'So when you going to tell the man that is not his pickney you have?'

But it seems like it was the wrong question, for Gwennie start up the weeping and the wailing again, but it never matter to Grandma.

'Me love, I sorry to hear it. But you spread your own bed so you might as well lie down inside it. The pickney is the dead stamp of Luther. Any old jackass can see that. As fool-fool as Walter be, him not that stupid.'

'But him don't know Luther?' Gwennie chime in.

'Yes, but that not going save you. Everybody down here know him. And you know that people down here just love to dip them mouth into people's business. As you turn round, them would start the talking, for that pickney can't hide. She look like Luther too much.'

'What me going to do?'

Grandma look at her and sigh deep. 'Huh, you shoulda think about that when you was laying up in bed with this man. But I don't know, me baby, I don't know.' Then she start the humming, and Gwennie who was resting her head on Grandma's lap, pick up the tune. And the two of them sit down in the room and hum out the entire four verses of 'He Died For Me, Yes Christ Jesus Died For Me.'

After the hymn finish, Grandma clear her throat. 'Well, gal, you can tell Walter or you can wait till him find out. Whichever way, it going to be hell. It make sense if you tell him down here with me and your father present, for him wouldn't be so out-of-order to knock you in the presence of you father. Another thing is you can give the baby to your Aunty Cora to raise, if Walter don't want it inside the house when you tell him. I can't say anything more, child. You choose best. May the good Lord up in Heaven look down and help you.'

So with that song, Gwennie go home to her husband and her children. And that night after everybody gone to bed, she sit down in the kitchen on the little stool in the corner and write her Aunty Cora a long letter, the whole time peeping over her shoulder to see if Walter looking. She tell her Aunty Cora about how Walter beat and abuse her, how him take her money and keep other women with her, how life hard and miserable with the man. She tell her Aunty Cora how she want to leave him, but she afraid to just pick up herself and her children and go back to living in Mile Gully, the very same place she marry to escape from.

Then she tell her Aunty Cora about Luther, how his chest big and his arms strong, how his two dimples pinch his cheeks and his grin cover over his entire face. She tell her Aunty Cora how the man teach her things, take her places, and make her feel like real young gal, how him make her feel like somebody. Then she write about the moonlight, the dance and the cemetery, and how the little girl is the dead stamp of him. At the end of the letter, Gwennie ask her if she could please take the baby for only God alone knows what Walter might do. Gwennie fold the letter, hands trembling, lick the envelope, tack on the stamp and hide the letter in the book of Proverbs so she can post it in the morning.

That night when she roll over on the posturepedic mattress, Walter was wide awake as usual looking up at the cracks and watermarks. Cold sweat wash over her. Her heart pump hard. Tonight she never feel like praying though, she just feel weary, she feel beat. And so she lay down there next to him rigid and cold, her night clothes wet with sweat and her heart pumping out loud through her chest. And she lay down there like this, him breathing deep and even, and she in an upheaval.

VI

Gwennie never have many friends. And whether that was to her good luck or her bad luck, only God alone can tell. The one lady she befriend when she and Walter just move up to Porous, gone off to live with her sister in Canada. Walter never used to like her a tall. Used to tell Gwennie how she no good, how she cheap, how she borrow-borrow money and don't like giving it back, how she love carry-carry people's business, and him couldn't understand why a big respectable married woman like she, Gwennie, would want to keep company with this woman.

And so whenever Julia come by the house, Walter could never find anything him put down. Him always asking Gwennie to do this, to do that, to do everything. But it wasn't only Julia, him would do the same thing when Gwennie's family come to visit or when Trevor, her school teacher friend whom she meet after Julia leave, come visit. Walter didn't give one blast that Trevor already married and wasn't looking any more woman. As long as somebody interested in his wife, that alone mash up every thing.

She remember how she never use to pay him much mind when him start to do it at first. It was only when Grandma bring it up.

'Now, Gwennie, you is a big woman, and I can't tell you how you to run you family life, except that you and Walter must have respect for me and your father. But why the hell him have to call-call you every minute and interfere every time I sit down to talk to you. If you can't tell him to acquire little manners, then I will do it.'

But for some unspoken reason, it still never bother Gwennie much until that day with Trevor. And from that day something lost inside her belly for Walter. It was a Saturday morning, high day, when Trevor drive up and park his car outside the gate. The children were around the back playing. The baby was sleeping. Walter was inside the kitchen listening to racehorse on the little transistor radio and marking down the ones winning. Trevor did just come back from Miami, bringing with him a little present for Gwennie. Gwennie, so glad for the mug and to see her friend again, take careless and start to hug Trevor, only to hear Walter bellow out her name and ask from the doorway where him was watching, if she never have anything better to do than to sit there and carouse with her man friends in his house. And if she couldn't wait till him leave the house before she do it, him can just imagine what go on when him not there.

Trevor never stay long after that, and shameface, Gwennie just sit down outside on the verandah a long time after him leave. She did have the little mug in her hand and she run her fingers over the rim in deep thought. It wasn't the first time Walter shame her like that, but it was going to be the last. It was that evening too, that she decide that she have to get way from Walter, for him wasn't any good. The loan application still in the bottom of her bureau. Maybe she should go ahead and fill it out afterall. For in a way it was her only salvation. Without the certificate them don't pay her much. And is really lack of money why she stay. The children too. But as the days pass and Walter get from bad to worst, things just seem almost too unbearable. One evening she come home only to find the little 'I Love Miami' mug crack-crack up in the garbage.

So because she never have many friends, or at least any close ones, she never have a return address where Aunty Cora could send the letter before Walter open it. One whole week pass. Not a word from Aunty Cora. She did mail the letter the Monday morning and here, today Tuesday, eight days, and still not a word. Wednesday come, gone, not a word. The following morning Gwennie pick up herself and go over to New Green.

Through the entire bus ride, whole heap of things go through her head. She couldn't figure out if Aunty Cora never get the letter. If she get the letter but don't answer yet, even though Gwennie did ask her to hurry up and answer. She wonder if Aunty Cora already answer, and Walter open the letter and read it. But then him wasn't acting funny a tall; him was his sweet self as usual to the baby and to the other three, and was even acting okay to her. If him already read the letter, him would certainly open his mouth about it. If him waiting on her to say something, shit, what she must say. All these things run through Gwennie's head that Thursday morning in the bus. And even though she love window seat and was sitting at one that very Thursday morning, even looking through it, her eyes wouldn't focus on a thing, for they were full to the brim with worry.

VII

Her Aunty Cora's house was bedecked with seven bedrooms, in addition to her thirteen adult-size cats and dogs put together. Aunty Cora was about sixty, and she live in this huge house with the seven bedrooms with her grandson Leslie; one of the eleven children she raise, George; her live-in helper, Miss Irene; and her cousin Miss Gertrude Fines, who still on extended visit, from May Pen. Her Aunty Cora's been married two times, but both husbands already pass on leaving her with fifty acres of fertile land, two acres of rock-stone, one shop, one house, one church, thirty heads of cow, three bulls, two donkeys, fifteen laying hens, six roosters and one young pullet.

Aunty Cora was fanning herself with a piece of cardboard and sipping white rum from a big mug full of ice, when Gwennie climb up the stairs to the verandah. Aunty Cora never have on her thick glasses that usually sit down on her nose, so she couldn't tell who it was coming up the steps, whether or not it was Leslie or George, or her cousin Miss Gertie.

'But is who that walking up the steps and breathing so hard, mad to blow me way? Is you that, Miss Gertie?' Aunty Cora bawl out, stretching out her neck, squinting up her eyes, laying down the fan and feeling round on the chair for the thick glasses. 'But look at me dying trial! Gwennie Agusta Glaspole,' she bawl out, this time with her thick glasses sitting down on her nose. 'Gal, what you doing here already. You mean to tell me you get the letter already? So where the baby? Gwennie, what happen to you, gal? Sit down on the seat beside me and take a sip of this rum. You look ready to tumble over.'

Aunty Cora take a swig of the rum and give the mug to Gwennie. All this time Gwennie wasn't saying a word, she just stand up on the steps, her face pucker up like she ready to start the hollering.

'Come, come, take a sip. I already bury two husbands. I don't plan on burying another soul before I die, so come. Take a sip of this drink, you will feel much better.'

Gwennie walk over to Aunty Cora, sit down next to her and sip the mug full of ice and white rum.

'Then, where the baby? You mean to tell me that you get the letter already? I just send it two days ago, shouldn't reach till this evening or tomorrow the latest, according to how I was figuring. So what Walter say?'

But it seems like that was all Gwennie was waiting to hear. She start up the crying.

'Come, come, man. Drink up some more of this thing and stop this blasted cow bawling. This is serious business. For if you don't bring the baby, and you don't get the letter, no doubt Walter have the letter right now in his hand reading it.'

'You was taking such a long time to write back.' Gwennie pause

16

through her eye water, 'I was thinking that maybe Walter already have the letter. So I come to find out.'

Aunty Cora take the mug from Gwennie and take a long sip. She pick up the piece of cardboard and start to fan. Perspiration was dropping off her nose where the thick glasses sit. 'Gal, that decision never easy. I into me old age now, done bury two husbands, my time next. The eyes not good, doctor say is cataract, and the arthritis in the two legs now. I don't have any more milk in me titty for such a young baby. So you see, it not easy. But as blood thicker than water, I will do anything to help me family. So I will take the baby, but it not going to be easy.'

All this time Gwennie don't say a word. Her head was reeling hard from the heat, the rum and everything. Aunty Cora drain the mug, slap Gwennie on her leg and say, 'Come, gal, is near lunch time, and you look like you going to pass out right here on the verandah. Come, we go see what Miss Irene make for lunch.'

'Alright, I soon come, you go on. I just need to get me bearings together. I going sit here little bit.' And Gwennie sit down on that bench with Aunty Cora's fan and the empty mug next to her, with her head reeling, and she shut up her eyes and give Papa Jesus thanks. She thank Him for the safe bus ride to New Green, and she thank Him for giving her Aunty Cora such a kind heart. Then she ask if Him could please not let Walter do anything too dangerous to her and the baby. Some things she know she deserve, but after all she only human and . . .

'Gwennie, come on, come eat the little lunch before it get cold,' Aunty Cora shout out from the kitchen. So Gwennie cut the prayer short, cry Amen to Papa Jesus, pick up the fan and the empty mug and step through the kitchen door with her head reeling.

VIII

Aunty Cora's dining hall was almost as big as the entire house put together and just as shine. Gwennie look round for the one picture of Jesus, Aunty Cora keep on her wall, and sit down with her back next to it. Gwennie never like the picture a tall. For is one thing when you pray to Jesus everynight, but is another thing when His picture follow you all about and act like it can read your mind.

After them eat, and Aunty Cora talk to her little bit more about the baby and about Walter and give her money wrap up in a piece of cloth, George and Leslie pack her up a small box of food, walk her to the bus stop, and Gwennie catch the evening bus back to Porous.

But that talk with her Aunty Cora, it look like, was a blessing. For on the bus back to Porous that evening, she make up her mind about certain hard things. First thing was that as long as she live, Walter wasn't going to find out about that baby. It was a shameful thing she do with Luther, a big married woman like herself have no place doing such a thing, but is not like the baby not going be there to remind her. So, no need for Walter to help walla-walla in her disgrace. As early as can be, she going to christen it at church in Walter's name.

Next thing she going to do is go back to school and get the certificate – yes, she going to enrol right away. The money them pay her at the school not worth a penny without the little piece of paper. As she shut her eyes and turn round, her paycheck finish. And the thing that hurt the most is that them don't give her any benefits. She on the last of her four months maternity leave now, and them don't pay her one red cent for it. The man she work at Porous Primary School for, Teacher Brown, been working there for over eight years now, and every time she take time off to have her babies, him tell her him can't promise work when she come back, even though each time him rehire her. But nevertheless, she need the reassurance. She just can't live her life like that – neither coming or going.

As these thoughts run through Gwennie's head, she start like more and more the ring to it. And as she think about it, she decide that that was exactly what she going to tell Walter. Yes, it falling into place now, just like jig-saw. Her Aunty Cora say she never write anything in the letter to raise Walter's eyebrow, except that she going to take the baby. So she going to tell Walter she going back to school, for teacher Brown get real strict these days and all, and him laying off people without certificate. So she going to have to send Rudi, Dave and Del to Grandma, and make her Aunty Cora keep Peppy, for Grandma say her hands more than full with the big ones. She and the baby safe, with it staying up at Aunty Cora's.

Her mind made up, Gwennie step off the bus strong and walk straight-back down Porous road, with the box of food on her head.

Porous road was quiet, except for the Richardson's little baby, Angela, crying in the distance. Besides Gwennie, they were the only other people, out of the five of them that live on the street, that have children. Even the school where Walter teach Agriculture quiet-quiet. Seems like the boys already gone down to supper, she couldn't see any lights in the rooms.

When she reach number fifteen, Gwennie hesitate outside the door before she let herself in, but it look like Walter was setting out for her, for the minute she enter the house, not even put down the box of food good, Walter light into her with his head, his fist, his feet, his shoes, knock her down flat; she and the box hitting the ground at the same time. She never fight him back, for normally when them fight, she hit him back with book, chair, bottle, pot, anything she catch her hands on, and then if things look serious, she run and lock up herself in the bathroom till him calm down. But this evening different. Somewhere deep inside, she have a feeling this was her punishment from God because of what she do with Luther, and so she just lie down on the floor, and hide her head and her face from his blows with her hands, and listen to him curse.

'Who the hell you think you is, making arrangements to give away me pickney without even telling me? You think you is God, woman? Well, if you think you bad, you and your blasted Aunty, take that baby and see what happen to the two of you. Think both of you not damn out-of-order. Don't tell me anything, but making plans behind me back with me own pickney. Everyday you pick up youself, jump on bus, gone here so, gone there so. Don't have time for family anymore. Now, you catch as far as want to give them way . . .'

And although she never want to cry, for she feel she well deserve the blows him bestowing on her, her eyes suddenly get misty and tears start trickling out of them. Maybe she should've told Walter beforehand. Maybe she shouldn't've been so hasty after all. Maybe Walter more ignorant than she think. Maybe she should've really approached it a different way. For if anybody see how Walter coo and caw that little girl, there could never be any doubt about his love for her. It was more than him ever show any of the other three children. Maybe it was a damn wrong thing she do, taking it away from him like that, who knows, maybe the little girl would've brought them closer, and things would've started to work out again, like it used to when them just start out. But these thoughts never linger long inside Gwennie's head.

A little while later, after Walter finish quarrel and fight, and him slam the door and leave for the night, Gwennie try to get up and see if the children okay, and to see if them already eat dinner and so forth, but the pain in her body hurt so much, she just drop back down on the carpet. And as she lay down there, she think about retribution, she think about her children, she think about her life, her marriage, and she think and think till she fall asleep.

That night she have nightmares, one right after the other. Plenty times she cry out in her sleep. The last dream take place down Mile Gully. It was Independence. She was at a pig-roasting party with people from high school days, standing round, drinking rum and beers, laughing, talking. And the one girl she used to compete with often and never like much, come up from behind and push Gwennie straight into the pig. Poor Gwennie bawl out so loud that she wake right up only to find her big son, Rudi, in his night-clothes, with a basin of hot water and a rag sopping her bruises. Gwennie's heart so full, all she could do was hold on to him and whimper.

She wake up next morning to a pounding in her head. The house was quiet except for Peppy, she was bawling. Gwennie leap up, but could only see darkness, her head was reeling. She hold her head with her hands, close her eyes tight, and think hard about the pounding until she figure the darkness gone. Then she open them and walk to where she hear the bawling. For a long time, Gwennie never realize how the little boy Rudi, no more than ten, helpful. She never have to tell him to do anything more than once. Evening time when she make dinner, him always set the table and call the others without telling. Morning time, after him wake up, him help Dave and Del get ready. On Saturdays, him help Gwennie shop and even clean house sometimes. But all that time, she never take much notice of how handy him really was.

But after she see how him was holding and swaying the baby to keep her quiet, her heart tremble, for it was the same way she or even Grandma would do it. As far as she could see, the little boy Rudi did wake up early, bathe and feed the baby and then get the other two ready for school. And when Gwennie see all three of them stand up there ready for school, even though hair don't comb, clothes don't see iron, and shoes don't see polish, she just walk over and hug all three and the little baby to her stomach.

Then one morning, not long after, as them get ready for school, she call them together in the kitchen. 'You not going school, today,' she tell them. 'Go pack-up your clothes. You going down to stay with Grandma for a little time.'

And while Rudi pack up his clothes and help the other two pack up theirs, Gwennie sit down at the kitchen table with the little girl, Peppy, in her lap and begin to write three letters.

The first one she address to Walter, since him already leave for work. Still no mention of Luther. Well, she going to leave it that way. She tell him she and the children leaving for Mile Gully and she going to leave all of them down there with Grandma except for the baby. The baby going to live with Aunty Cora, for Grandma can't manage everybody. Rudi is a big help these days, so him can help Grandma with the other two. Gwennie tell him the reason she leaving is because she going back to school to get the little piece of paper, and she don't want to burden him with all the children. She can't very well pick them up and bring them to the boarding school with her, either.

She tell him that the reason she never mention it before now was because she wanted to make sure everything would work out first before she break the news to him. So all that him do to her that night was very much uncalled for, and that was the next reason why she leaving. She really can't put up with the way him manhandle her all the time. The two of them big people, she don't understand why them can't sit down and work things out like decent human beings. In the last paragraph, Gwennie tell him the name of the school and that him mustn't worry, the children all right with Grandma and Peppy with Aunty Cora, and she know that him will understand that these things she doing are for the better. Then she sign the letter, 'Love, Gwennie', fold it up, put it in the envelope, lick it shut and leave it on his bureau.

The next letter was to the baby-sitter, Miss Icy. She used to look after the last boy, Dave while Gwennie at work. She tell Miss Icy she going to get the little piece of paper and that Grandma would look after the children. But thanks very much for her services in the past and she will make sure drop her a line to let her know how things going. The last letter Gwennie address to Teacher Bailey, Rudi and Dave's headmaster. She tell Teacher Bailey that she was going to get the little piece of paper for good this time and that she going to enrol Rudi and Dave at Mile Gully All-Age School. Gwennie lick on the two stamps on the envelopes and then send Rudi up the road to drop them off at the post.

Then she pack up her things and the little girl things, call and ask one of the handy-men from about the campus to help her bring the heavy grip to the bus stop, and once more, she, Del, Peppy, Rudi and Dave board the bus with the market women and school children for Grandma's house. As the bus pull out of Porous Square, eye water fill Gwennie's two eyes. She never tell Walter whether or not she coming

21

back. But she don't think so. Don't make sense spend your life with a man who only out to beat you half to death. It don't spell sense a tall.

As for Luther, well that is another matter. All she can say is that she should've been more careful, but she not sorry about what she did that night a tall. No, she not sorry. Maybe after she get the certificate, she will find a teaching job somewhere near the college. Then she could take the children. But it going to be hard for she alone to take care of them. Maybe the little girl could stay with Aunty Cora some more. Rudi could help with Del. Dave growing quickly. But first things first. She going to get the certificate and then time will tell.

Gwennie never stay long at Mile Gully. She did only have time to drop off the children and kiss them goodbye before she board another bus for New Green. She stay over at New Green till the Sunday, and that morning she and Aunty Cora christen the baby in Walter's name. Then Gwennie board the bus one last time to Churchill Teachers College.

PART TWO

I

The six months Gwennie spend up at Churchill was the most fruitful of her life for a long time. The first two months she bury her head in her studies, and not a Luther, not a Walter, not a Peppy stir her nerves the whole time. The room them give her was small, and since Gwennie was a woman used to having plenty space, she never know what to do with herself at first. Many nights she wake up at the edge of the small single bed, the mattress hard and tough like woodroot own self, if breeze blow too hard any a tall, she roll right off.

She also was a woman used to having plenty family pictures sprawl out all over her house. Back up at Porous, she did have family pictures put up in every room, from Rudi right down to Grandma's first cousin on her mother's side, Miss Albertine. But in this little cubicle, that she paint beige with grey trimmings, she did only have room for one photo on the small bureau, after she lay out her underarm deodorant, her sweet-smelling cus-cus, her face cream, and her Jergens hands and body. She put up the picture with Grandma and Grandpa, her two brothers Samuel and Jeffery, and her one sister, Icilda, standing in front the church where Grandpa preach and Grandma play the organ, and where she, Samuel, Jeffery and Icilda used to go to Sunday school every God-send Sunday morning.

Them work her like dog up at the college. Plenty days she never even have time to just sit down talk to herself. She go to classes in the morning, break for lunch and was back in the afternoon. Sometimes the sun so hot outside, it make inside the classroom warm. Many days she long to sit down in the back and doze. But the teacher love to call on her it seems, and since she was so anxious about getting the certificate, she more than careful not to get on his wrong side. After she eat dinner inside the big dining hall that always loud and noisy, she study long into the night until around eleven when company come visit.

From the very first day Gwennie never have any problems find friends. She love to chat and argue and people take to her quick. Further more, she wasn't bad looking a tall: round face with full eyes, lovely features, thick head of hair that she pull to the back and tuck under, and pleasant burn cocoa-butter complexion. The fellows at the college who married and unmarried never take long to latch on to her. And so till all hours of the night, she and them would be up in her room laughing, chatting, drinking and playing dominoes. Sometimes them would get down into deep conversation, lasting until early morning when roosters start crow. And them would touch on every subject possible: science, social studies, politics, geography, philosophy, every little thing, and them come to respect her very much, for Gwennie was sharp and her mind broad.

And she get to thinking, here she was with these fellows, about her age or more – Walter's age the most – who think nothing a tall bout asking her opinion to settle whatever little arguments or disagreements come up. She think about when Julia or Trevor or her family would come visit. Them would be sitting around talking, with Walter sitting around too. And anything she say, him would just kind of fling it aside as if it don't count.

Once at a teachers' party with Walter and a whole group of others talking about Prime Minister Lewis and how his cabinet members mashing up the country, him did shame her. For even when every last one of her family and even Walter never into Lewis, she did still manage to keep her faith in him. So they were all sitting around drinking beers and voicing disapproval of the man.

And after them finish, Gwennie turn to the Spanish teacher beside her and quietly say to him: 'You know, all the talking you talking, I still don't hear mention of one good thing Lewis do. And as much as you don't like him, you still have to give him credit. For you can't say unemployment never go down.

'You can't say the price of things never go down. You can't say him never take all the poor people from off the streets, cut taxes. You can't say gas price not cheaper and that him never give country people electric light, run water pipe through them back yard, and asphalt them road. You can't say him never open training centres for the youth or start up plenty literacy programmes.

'But just because the man believe in democratic socialism and friends with Castro and believe that poor people must have a chance too, even if it be at the expense of the rich, you don't like him because him is communist. What kind of thinking that? Tell me how you figure, intelligent as you call yourself?'

The room so silent you could hear a pin drop. Walter just finish call Lewis a blasted idiot and hope that them kick his ass out of power next election. Now Gwennie taking up for Lewis, her voice loud and strong, commanding plenty attention.

Walter take a long swallow of his beer, push back his chair with a loud scraping on the concrete, stand up, yawn, then open his mouth to speak. 'See what happen when you give a woman two beers. Her mouth start fly and you can't get it to stop. No matter if she talking her mouth full of dry horse manure.' Then him laugh, loud and raucous. And the other men sitting round sort of grin with them lips, not long though, for most of them know Gwennie talking truth. And Gwennie laugh too, not with her eyes but with just the corner of her mouth.

And so when she think about how the fellows here treat her good – fellows, for the women don't talk to her much – have respect for her, and give her attention when she want to talk, she just sort of push Walter to the back of her mind.

II

It never take long before one or two of the young men start stay after at night and help Gwennie clean up, long after everybody else gone. This one fellow, Percy Clock, take a liking to her. Most every night him come by and them would just sit up and talk, long after everybody else gone. And him was a soft-spoken and gentle fellow, very expressive with his hands and eyes. Gwennie never know another man who keep his fingernails cut neat and keep clean like Percy Clock. She take a sudden liking to him. She was afraid at first though, and so when him just start come over to her room late, she used to drop one or two hints about her children and about Walter, but Percy Clock never give one blast.

Pretty soon Gwennie loosen up, and she and Percy Clock start to do things together and confide in one another. She tell him how she never know Walter walk round and talk in his sleep till two days after them marry. And how she was frightened, for him would be looking at her, eyes wide open, yet fast asleep, for when she call, him never answer. Now her second son, Dave, have the same bad habit. Only thing though, him walk with his two hands stretch out infront and his eyes close. Percy Clock tell her his wife funny that way too, for even though she don't walk about, she speak three different languages in her sleep even though is only English alone she know well. And she and Percy did grow so close that when she break down in her period of depression that last one whole month, it was him who was her right hand, and who she come to rely on plenty.

It start out with the letter. Gwennie get a letter from her Aunty Cora, saying how the little baby, Peppy, growing up healthy and strong with every mouthful of Lactogen formula she swallow. How her voice loud and hefty and her bones strong, and every day she getting more and more round. Gwennie so glad to hear of it, she read the letter over and over. But then she start to have bad dreams, night after night, and every morning when she wake up, her feelings just sink lower and lower.

The dreams were all the same. Every time she go over to New Green to look for Peppy and see her Aunty Cora, is always like a transformation come over she, Gwennie. And all of a sudden she get afraid and don't want to spend time, anymore. She want to leave. And so she always tell Walter come, we can't leave the other children home by themselves so long. And poor Walter's face used to just puzzle-up, for after all them just arrive, what kind of hurry-hurry so to leave. And Aunty Cora would just look on, not saying a word, just sipping her Red Stripe beer, one swallow after another. But poor Gwennie, in all her fright and confusion, couldn't tell them that every time the little girl turn to face her is not Peppy she see, but Luther's round face with the dimple in his chin. All of the tenderness and softness gone out the baby's face, and a rugged hardness set in instead.

As Gwennie's feelings drag down lower and lower, just like a bad thing, her mind start to bring up things she well want to forget, depressing her even further. And so laying down there in her bad feelings, Gwennie remember the Saturday morning, about one year ago. It was two and a half months since her last cycle and one week since the morning sickness start. Up to this day, she still don't know what possess her that morning, but she remember that after she throw-up and was finally feeling better, she put on her clothes, tell the children she soon come back, and walk down to Porous Square where she catch the bus to carry her to market.

If it was a tall up to her, she wouldn't attempt what she attempted that morning, but something else was holding her hand. So when the bus let her off at Porous Market, she stop inside the bread shop, put on a pair of dark glasses, tie her head with a red and yellow scarf, and proceed back to the market. She know exactly where them sell the herbs, for she used to go all the time and buy different things. Herbs for when the children teething, when them have fever, headache, toothache, bellyache, when them constipated, when them belly running too much. And she know exactly which one she looking for, the one with the plenty small leaves that have a brownish colour to them.

But she wasn't in any hurry that morning. The market yard was filled with plenty people talking loud to one another. Mangoes and oranges selling over in that corner, fresh fish and shrimps over in that other corner, yam and breadfruit over there, pots and pans over here, clothes somewhere else; plenty activity taking place. Gwennie take her time.

She never get to the higgler selling the herbs until about forty-five minutes later, even though the higgler only three feet from where she stand up looking at baby clothes. She walk up close, focus her eyes on the herb, then turn round and look about her to see if she see anybody she know. The higgler start to make up her face, for she is a woman who like when people come, buy what them want, then leave, so other people can come.

But here was Gwennie standing up, looking about her as if she put down something and can't find it, while people crowding up behind her. The higgler wasn't too please that morning, for things not selling quick enough for her, and already it getting late, night soon come down.

'Lady,' she call out to Gwennie. 'Lady,' she call out again for Gwennie was still looking about her. 'Lady in the lovely red and yellow scarf, can I please be of assistance to you, mam? I have lovely herbs today for every complaint, fresh-fresh, just pick them from me garden this morning. So, please, can I be of assistance? That scarf sure is pretty.'

It was the first time since she pregnant that real fear grip Gwennie. And when it dawn on her what she doing, a heat wave wash through her soul that morning leaving her eyes wide open and her mouth corner dry.

'So which one of the roots you want, lady? Tell me the complaint.' The higgler's voice was rising now with the heat simmering off the pavement next to her goods. 'Lady, plenty people behind you waiting.'

'That one over there.' Gwennie point.

'This one?'

'No, that one.'

'Lady, it don't have name? What the complaint?'

'Oh, never mind.'

'What you say, never mind? But Jesas, look down.' The higgler clap her hands loud and look up to heaven. 'Lady, look how you come and waste me whole entire morning with your simple self. Look how much people waiting behind you and you just stand up there like a blasted idiot with that bad-colour rag tie up your head like you mad. Lady, don't pull me tongue this morning.'

But Gwennie already gone. And by the time the higgler finish curse, Gwennie on her way home, her eyes wide open and her mouth corner dry as chip same way.

All these things run through her mind now as she lay down sick in her little room, Percy Clock holding her hand talking to her, and Gwennie looking out her window, her eyes fix nowhere in particular. The depression last one whole month. Every day Percy Clock come with a cup of cocoa or mint tea or steamed ginger root, and him would try talk to her, try comfort and console her.

Then one morning, the depression pick up itself and leave. That morning when Gwennie get up out her bed, her head did feel light, her heart happy. She start sing and dust down her room, put on fresh covers on her bed, and open-up the windows wide to let in freshness. Since them did move the sitting up late at night to somebody else's room, when Gwennie open the door and the surprise to see her pass over, and them see that her face look sturdy and strong again, that her eyes healthy, and she her old self again, them move the domino playing and sitting up late at night, the arguing and the chatting back into her room. And every Saturday after Gwennie finish teach her sewing class, where she pick-up a little income, Percy Clock pick her up in his blue Austin Cambridge, and together them go movies and then to dance.

III

Gwennie start her practical the final few months of the programme. Since she did already have several years of teaching under her belt, she just zips through the practical, but not without plenty headaches. For some of the children's head hard, them just couldn't learn. Day after day she teach them the same Wordsworth 'Daffodil' poem, and day after day them can't recite any further than the first stanza.

Some of them she could tell come to school hungry, for as bell ring and classes start, heads hit the desk-top and don't stir again till twelve o'clock lunch time and three-thirty dismissal. Others, she know, just there to test her good faith. She miss the children up at Porous Primary, for them much better behaving and bestowed with plenty good principles. But no matter how much headache it give her, Gwennie try and make ends meet with the few exercise books and pencils and reading materials the district office dish out, even though them never enough so each student could get their own. But nevertheless, she bite her tongue and try manage. She catch too far now to take careless and lose the certificate.

But beyond even the certificate, Gwennie did have other things on her mind. Time soon come when she have to start making plans for herself and her children. She have to maybe look new work and probably find a place to live. And so the few evenings she have to herself, she comb the Help Wanted section of the Daily Gleaner back and front. And almost like a charm, it so happen that one night after she and her friends finish argue and chat for the night, and everybody leave, Percy Clock stay behind and help Gwennie clean up as usual. But something about him seem different. Him seem more pensive than usual.

But Gwennie never concern herself with it too much, for she figure maybe him have plenty things on his mind. Maybe Percy Clock thinking about his family. Him did tell her his mother pass on just recently from cancer in the blood, and that his wife leave him with the two children, whom his sister looking after now. But then she notice how Percy Clock starting to look like him never want leave her room that night. Every time them finish one conversation and the room get silent, him sigh long and deep. Then just as she about to say goodnight, him cut in with another. After this go on for several hours, Gwennie finally say to him: 'Percy, it look like you not ready to sleep yet, but I tired, bad.' She yawn.

'Well, Gwennie,' Percy start off, cleaning his throat. 'I been thinking lots about you and me, and about how empty me life will be after I leave here.'

Gwennie open her eyes wide and look at Percy Clock. She could see her children in one room cover up safe under warm blankets that smell strong of camphor balls, but she never like what she see in the other room a tall. And as him continue talk about all the feelings that's been

29

building up over the last five months, Gwennie start to frame in her mind news she don't think him particularly want to hear.

For even though him was a fine looking and fine talking man, she never have romance inside her belly for Percy Clock. Only plenty friendship and lots of love. No different from what she did have with her brother, Samuel, before him leave go Foreign. But she keep her face straight and her eyes expressive, listening attentively to what him have to say.

'Together with your four and my two, we could have a happy family. After we get the papers clear, you and me could get married and . . . Well, Gwen, what you say?'

And Gwennie feel the sweat trickle down the middle of her back and stop at the waist of her pyjama pants. All through the proposal, him never look at her once. Fingers twitching and twining by his side, as them express how happy she and him will be together, him stare through the window into the blackness. But now him turn round and was walking over to where she sit up on her bed. Him put his face next to hers, and she could feel his breath warm, reeking of Red Stripe beer. Him was waiting for her to answer, his face close to hers, breath short and hot, eyes searching her face. And Gwennie feel more sweat run down the middle of her back and gather up at her pyjama pants' waist.

'I have to think about it, Percy. I have to think hard on it.' She look towards the window. 'Maybe in about two weeks, I can give you a better answer. You take me by surprise, man. Take me by surprise in truth.'

With that, Percy Clock pick up his hat, pick up his bag, tell her goodnight, and close her door gently behind him. Gwennie could hear his Hush Puppy pitter-patter, pitter-patter down the stairs until she couldn't hear anything else. Then she get up, open her window little bit, kneel down, say her prayers and crawl back underneath her cover.

But as time go by, and the days draw to a close, Gwennie set to thinking again. Here it was now, little more than a week left before the teaching programme finish, and she don't have husband, she don't have place to live, and she don't know where she going to put her four children. And so Gwennie start to think hard and serious about Percy Clock and his offer.

She did still have few more days before she answer. She glad she never tell him what was on her mind that night, but maybe some kind of arrangement could work out between them. Maybe she could rent out part of his house, that him say so big and lovely, and she and her children could stay there till she find work and find a place for them. She can just imagine what people going to say behind her back, a big respectable married woman living common-law life with this man who just as married. It would be such a disgrace if Percy Clock's wife come back and order Gwennie and her children out of the house and fling her pots and pans outside as well.

And all these thoughts linger round and round inside Gwennie's head early that Friday morning, as she stretch out on the little single bed, her floral spread draw up to her neck, listening to the roosters outside.

Then all of a sudden, a little voice come on over the loudspeaker near her room, and Gwennie hear them call out her name. Gwennie fling off the cover. She wonder if is she, in truth. She cock her ears and listen. 'Gwendolyn Agusta Glaspole?' Yes, is she, but who could be calling her up this early hours of the morning. Her mind fly back to the letter she get from Grandma just last week. Grandma say Dave come down with whooping cough again and that Grandpa did have to take him to the doctor. Gwennie start to wonder if something happen to Dave again. 'Lord have mercy,' she moan in her belly, as her breath start to come out loud and fast.

'Gwendolyn Agusta Glaspole?' Them call her again.

'Yes,' Gwennie answer out, 'yes, what is it?'

'Somebody down in the lobby to see you.'

Gwennie fling off the spread and jump out the bed. She hold on to the bureau, her fingers gripping hard onto the brown mahogany. She wonder if is Grandma, if something happen to she or Grandpa. Something happen to Delores. Rudi get in trouble. Gwennie haul on her duster over the pink nylon nightie, and draw the string tight around her waist. She haul on her push-toe slippers, then she open the door. Her hands fly to her hair, it need combing. But Gwennie never bother comb her hair that morning. She pull out her old hat and tuck her hair under it. Then she bolt out the door, down the hallway, then down the steps – two at a time. She wonder if something happen to Aunty Cora, if Walter find out about Luther. If him take away Peppy and Aunty Cora come to tell her . . .

When Gwennie step into the lobby, she never see a soul at first. Then she see him stand up over in the corner looking at pictures of governors and prime ministers long dead, frame-up on the wall, his back to her. Gwennie's head reel and she long for a mug full of scorching black mint tea. Him lose a little weight it seems, trousers kind of sag on his behind, and his headback was thinning out.

31

Then him turn to look at another picture, and Gwennie's eyes spot the box underneath his arm. She know the box. Him used to bring it every week full of paradise-plum, mint-ball and ginger-log, when them used to courten. The reeling stop. Him turn round. Was walking towards her, hefty-like, the same walk him use infront students at Porous Youth Corp. Him give her the box and her fingers close over it. His eyes weren't saying much in particular, and when him open his mouth, the sun coming in through the glass window twinkle on his one gold tooth. Gwennie blink.

'How you do?' Walter ask her.

'Alright,' Gwennie whisper. She could use that mug of mint tea, in truth.

'The children miss you. Them dying to see you again. You must see Peppy, big and fat, cut-puss own self. Aunty Cora feed her in truth. Gwennie, I miss you and Peppy bad-bad.'

Walter turn way his head, and Gwennie notice how the vein in his neck stick out big. Last time she see it so bad was at his sister's funeral. Gwennie swallow and sigh deep. She wonder what him know, but by the way him acting, maybe nothing. Him face her again.

'Gwennie, I change. I had a long chat with your Aunty Cora and I change round for the better.'

Gwennie hold her breath.

'We can try start over. I will try treat you better. I will really try.'

Gwennie tear the tape off the box and open it. Her fingers fasten to the mint-ball right away. She manage to get one off her finger and she give it to Walter. Then she push one in her mouth using her tongue to roll it over to the far corner of her jaw, leaving it there to melt. People were starting to mill round now. She notice them starting to stare.

'Come upstairs with me,' she tell Walter. 'Come see where me live.' His face and eyes light up, and in one quick flash, him look just like when she did first meet him twenty-five years ago in Miss Ruthie's shop buying tobacco for his father. That time him never more than twelve going on thirteen.

'So you think you and Peppy will come back, Gwennie?' Walter ask as them climb up the stairs.

But Gwennie never hear him, Percy Clock was coming down the stairs in front her, fingers fidgeting, face twitching nervous-like. Walter's eyes follow her own, and the vein in his neck pop out again.

'Percy, good morning.'

'Hi, Gwennie.' Him glance over at Walter. 'Just coming from your

32

room. Was wondering where you gone so early this morning. Did come to talk.'

'I was downstairs in the lobby, but I will come by later. I have things to talk with you about, too.'

Percy's fingers were fidgeting even more when Gwennie and Walter continue on up the stairs.

'Who's that, Gwennie?' Walter ask as Gwennie open the door to her room.

'Friend,' Gwennie answer, closing the door behind her.

PART THREE

I

The little baby, Peppy, grow fast with every mouthful of Lactogen she swallow and the new girl, Gizelle, Aunty Cora get to help look after the shop, learning quick-and-brisk. It give Aunty Cora more time to spend with the little baby. And Aunty Cora grow to love the little girl. Every morning after she get up and tidy herself, and after her grand boy, Leslie and her adopted boy, George, bring in and scald the cow's milk, she pour out a mugful, cool it and then pour it little-little over her nipple so the baby can suck it and lick it like the real thing. And when she suck down the entire mugful, Aunty Cora burp her and then sway and hum to her until the little baby fall asleep.

Sometimes when she sit down on her bed with the baby in her arms, Aunty Cora think about her only son, Buddy, Leslie's father, who live in England with his wife and children. And she think about how she never had a chance to rock and hum to Buddy, for her mother did take him and raise him. Aunty Cora wasn't fit to look after him since she was so sickly herself. When she finally married and doctor say she couldn't have any more, she was sad for a long time, for by this time she and Buddy already grow up like brother and sister. She help her sister, Clara, and her brother, Skip, raise them children, but it wasn't quite the same. Now Peppy feel like her very own; only three months.

Even before Peppy start to walk or even chat, Miss Irene would tidy her and put on her clothes, brush her hair and put her in her pram. Then Aunty Cora would take her down to the shop, set her up in the corner next to the beer and soda bottles, and leave her there the whole day with her suck-suck in her mouth while she and Gizelle tend to customers.

Now Aunty Cora was a very large and round woman. And her voice was high pitched. When she laugh, it sounded like a whoop and you could hear it echoing minutes after she finish. New Green was a small district. Everybody know everybody, and everybody know and talk about everybody's business. One whole month pass, and every time customers come into the shop them see the little baby sit down-up in her pram near the beer and soda bottles with her suck-suck in her mouth. And so them begin to talk.

But talk and talk as them want, them make sure them keep the talking outside the shop and on the piazza where plenty people who don't have anything to do sit down on the long bench. And them sit down out there and wonder and talk and try figure out where this baby come from. But none of them did have the gall to ask. Miss Cora was a big respectable woman and if she want to tell you her business she will tell you. But take care you don't play the fool and ask her. For she bound to shame you. And so them wonder and wonder until Babbo, one of the ones who don't have anything to do, couldn't take it any more.

Him step inside the shop one day and start to play with Peppy from across the counter. Him wave his fingers at her and ask her name. Peppy gurgle back to him and grin. Aunty Cora was leaning on the counter facing Babbo, her two hands holding up her jaw, and her eyes looking through her thick glasses at the cows across the street in the common eating up the dry grass. Over in the corner, two men talk quietly over plenty bottles of beer between them. Babbo order a glass of rum and push seventy-five cents on the counter. Aunty Cora refuse to pay both him and the seventy-five cents any mind.

Babbo clean his throat. 'Miss Cora, give me a glass of rum.'

'Babbo, pick-up your money and don't bother me today. For I don't know how many times I must repeat the same thing. I not selling you rum, for when you drink it, you curse and go on like a bloody fool.'

Babbo don't say anything. Him know the tone of her voice, nothing going to move her. Him pick up the money and put it back in his pocket. 'Miss Cora, the little baby, Peppy . . . ' The two men over in the corner stop talk quiet and listen. 'Boy, that little baby look just like you, Miss Cora, dead stamp. You know, Miss Cora, is the first baby I ever see that look so much like the mother. She look nothing like her father.'

Aunty Cora take her eyes off the cows. 'Which father you talking about, Babbo?'

Now everybody sitting outside on the long bench get up and come inside.

Babbo continue. 'Well, for months now, we been looking. Every night we look to see who is the baby father but we don't see anybody. We never see any car come pick you up and bring you to Lying In. We never see you get any morning sickness or anything. So we can't figure where this young baby come from all of a sudden.'

Aunty Cora look up at the crowd in the shop. She look across the counter at Babbo. And she look at Peppy. Then she open up her mouth and whoop. For fifteen minutes nobody could say anything. And after she finish whoop, Aunty Cora take out the bottle of rum and pour Babbo a drink. 'After you drink this, please go home. Cause you don't know how to control liquor. One drink and you tumble over and chat nonsense. Look how me old. Anderson dead now three years. Look how me old, and the whole New Green still think me have man and him get me pregnant. You not shame, huh, all of you sit down and talk about it behind me back. I hear it. As old and blind as I am, I stand up right here at this counter and hear every word you say about me. You not shame?'

The shop empty out by this time, and after Babbo drain the glass and stumble out, only Aunty Cora, Gizelle and the baby remain inside the shop.

II

As the days go by, Peppy start grow and form teeth. Her baby hair start drop out and new roots of thick hair start to grow. She start to eat crackers and banana and bread and chicken back, and she start to curse too. Every word she hear in her seat next to the beer and soda bottles, she pick up, and pretty soon everybody that come into the shop she have argument with them and call out them name.

In no time Peppy turn regular with everybody, the same way Gizelle and Aunty Cora. And so, whenever Babbo and the other men come inside the shop and order drinks, them order one for Peppy too, even though is only milk or vanilla-flavoured nutriment or aerated water. And as Peppy start to walk and pronounce more words, Aunty Cora slip her a drink of white rum or a sip of beer now and again. Peppy seem to like that very much. After every mouthful, she close her two eyes tight, and swallow it the same way Babbo and the other men do it, then she clean her throat after it go down, stamp her feet two times to make sure it go down all the way, and when she certain, she open-up her eyes, look at Aunty Cora, grin and ask for more.

Back up the house, as soon as cock crow and morning come, and Aunty Cora leave the room to tidy herself, Leslie and George grab up the little girl from off the bed, where she sleep next to her Aunty Cora, dress her up warm, and put her on them shoulder. And them bring her with them go pump water, feed chicken, tie out donkey and goat so them can eat fresh grass, milk cow, and chop wood to cook breakfast.

Now all this time Peppy growing, she never take much notice of the brown lady with the burn cocoa-butter complexion and the tall man that come to visit Aunty Cora every three months. All she know is, she never like the brown lady much. The man okay, for whenever him come, him wouldn't always lift and shake her up the way the brown lady love to do it. Instead him give her presents. Each time bringing something wrap-up inside a paper bag. Sometimes mango, starapple, piece of jack fruit, coconut tart, sugar bun, drops, but mostly lollipops. The lollipops she like most, for Aunty Cora didn't sell them at the shop. And him would tear off the plastic paper and push it in her mouth, allowing her to suck and lick and drool to her heart's content. Sometimes the man stoop down infront her while she lick the lollipop and just look at her, his face long and thin and sad looking.

But it wasn't so much the lift up and shake up that cause Peppy not to like the brown lady, it was more her eyes; them resemble the eyes on the dolly Miss Gertie Fines bring her back from May Pen. First of all, both dolly and the brown lady have the same burn cocoa-butter complexion, then its two eyes, wide and piercing resemble the leaves of orange trees when night coming down, sort of greenish-brownish. And it make Peppy feel afraid. Often times, she try digging out the dolly's eye with a piece of stick, pencil, anything sharp. But Miss Gertie would always catch her. And after she tell Peppy how as long as she live she will never give her anything else for she much too damn destructive and things too dear nowadays, she slap Peppy on her fingers.

Then the brown lady would come, stoop down, pick her up from out the pram, and put her face up close. And when Peppy see the eyes, greenish-brownish, peering at her, she open her mouth wide and holler and squirm until the brown lady have to put her down. Then the tall man would pick her up and give her something to eat, and she like the way him smell of sweet-smelling soap and rum mix up together.

And as she suck the lollipop, the tall man walk her around the shop and point out different-different birds and call out them name, and him point out different-different trees and call out them name, and him tell Peppy his name is Walter, and she must hurry up and grow so she can meet his three sons Rudi and Dave and little baby, Jeff, who just one year younger, and his daughter, Delores. But Peppy didn't really care about his name or about the different-different trees or birds or his sons and daughter, all she want was the gold tooth the sun always twinkle-twinkle on, and the glasses him wear for she couldn't see his two eyes through it.

When she come back from her walk with Walter, him would give her over to the brown lady, and Peppy would holler and scream and squirm until the brown lady have to put her down again. Then Peppy would run over to Aunty Cora and climb up in her lap.

And Aunty Cora would ask her. 'Peppy, why you won't go over to your mama and allow her to lift you up so she can see how you growing?'

But all Peppy catch out of the whole sentence was the word mama. And so she kiss her Aunty Cora face with her sticky lollipop mouth and say: 'Ma-ma, ma-ma, ma-Co-ra.'

III

When Peppy turn four, Aunty Cora send her to the little infant school where her cousin Miss Doris prepare children before them go on to big school. And it seems as if Peppy's brain was quick, for she pick up counting and saying the alphabet fast, and so by the time she turn five, her Aunty Cora have her round the counter selling goods, wrapping and weighing sugar and corn-meal, and making change from one, two and five dollar bills, just like she and Gizelle. And as she continue on at the infant school, Peppy turn good friends with Miss Doris' granddaughter, Vin, who just two years older.

Peppy and Vin start to do everything together. Them play together, them go church together. Them play doctor, them play church, them play dolly-house, and it was a great relief to Aunty Cora. For because of the shop, she never have much time to spend and play with Peppy, and since Leslie and George getting up into them teens now, them don't have much time for Peppy either.

She didn't like the way Miss Gertie handle Peppy a tall. She was much too rough. She remember how one day as she was sitting down in her usual spot, on the barrel near the window with the big glass case over in the corner so she can see everything going on outside without moving or turning her head too much, she see a thing that burn her belly-bottom bad-bad. It was a Saturday evening and Miss Irene did cook and send Aunty Cora's dinner by way of Miss Gertie. So Aunty Cora was eating, right over there on the barrel next to the window and the glass case. Miss Gertie did step outside, for she know Aunty Cora didn't like the way her pipe smell with the tobacco. And outside, Miss Gertie see Peppy and three little boys playing police and thief. Peppy was the police, she did just catch one of the three robbers, and the other two were trying to help him escape. All in all, Peppy was in the dirt wrestling with the three boys. And a scowl cover over Miss Gertie's face and her eyebrows furrow up.

For a long time Miss Gertie been grumbling to herself, and to anybody who would listen, about the way Cousin Cora allowing Peppy to grow up. And after she grumble and grumble and it start to become a bile in her belly, she face Cousin Cora about it.

'Cousin Cora, I know is not me business or anything. But when a person see certain things happening, them can't always just shut up them mouth about it.'

Aunty Cora wasn't really in the mood for Miss Gertie, for she find that Miss Gertie complain a little too much for a big woman. But anyway, just for argument's sake she answer: 'What's the problem now, Miss Gertie?'

'Well is Peppy, ma'am. I think that maybe you spoil her. Allow her to get her own way too much. Look how many things you buy her. She have so many clothes she don't know what to do with them. And all she do is dirty them up and give Miss Irene and meself plenty work to wash and iron them.

'And look how you have her down the shop everyday. You won't even send her up the house so me and Miss Irene can train her how to cook and clean house, maybe even crochet and tack on buttons. She's a little pickney, she don't need to hear some of the big-people's argument that go on in the shop. Then look how you have her running the streets with George and Leslie. And look how she destructive, mash-up and tear-up everything you give her . . .'

Miss Gertie did have plenty more to say, but Aunty Cora tell her: 'Come on, Miss Gertie, man. Is only a little baby, leave her be.'

Nonetheless these things Miss Gertie say bother Aunty Cora deep.

For with all the children that she raise, this one the youngest she ever have, and she don't know sometimes if she teaching her the right things or not.

And so as she sit down there chewing-up the spoonful of ackee she just push in her mouth, she hear Miss Gertie's mouth. Aunty Cora push the food to her jaw corner and make it stay there. She cock her ears.

'Peppy!' Miss Gertie bawl out, 'gal pickney, what's wrong with you? Get up out the dirt, right now.' Miss Gertie run over to where Peppy was and start to search round for a nice whip to tear Peppy's behind. 'Cousin Cora don't train you right. Look at your clothes. Look at your hair. Go up to the house right away. I will teach you how to hem and thread needle. You're a gal pickney, you don't business out here. From all my born days, I never see it so, yet.'

And all the while Miss Gertie cursing and looking around for a whip to tear Peppy's behind, Peppy get up out the dirt, brush off her clothes and run into the shop to her Aunty Cora.

Aunty Cora never say a word. She push the ackee from the corner of her jaw back to the centre and start to chew again. She know Miss Gertie won't come inside the shop and knock Peppy, but she hear her outside grumbling out loud: ' . . . spoil that little gal, bad-bad! Is a shame, damn shame!'

And although Aunty Cora never say a word, these things bother her. She like to see Peppy run and jump about the place, but she know that plenty New Green women don't like it. For when them come to the shop and see Peppy outside running and jumping, she notice how the scowl just cover over them entire face. Sometimes she even hear one and two of them comment about how Peppy walk and run about like any boy pickney.

But it wasn't only Peppy alone Aunty Cora have on her mind these days causing her to worry-up herself and sip her waters more than usual. As she get older, the eyes get more and more foggy and the arthritis in her legs cause them to cramp up more and more. She think about the will and how she have to rewrite it. For according to how she feel some nights when she lay down her head, she not so sure she will wake up to see morning. And since she grow so attach to the little girl, she want to make her comfortable, for she don't know what Gwennie and Walter up to, and she don't know how long before the good Lord call her Home.

She know the letter she sent Gwennie a while back now asking if she could adopt Peppy and change her name, never receive good feelings. For Gwennie write her back and tell her in exact words: if she wanted the baby to be adopted, she would've put up notice long before it born. All she wanted was somebody to look after it until she get back on her two feet. Well it look as if it's taking Gwennie a long time to get back on her two feet, for Peppy's been staying with her now all of five years, and sometimes five and six months pass before Gwennie come visit. And as much as Aunty Cora didn't like to think about it, the letter did upset her long and hard. For she remember the day, fairly well, when Gwennie did come to her, almost half dead, and how she, Aunty Cora, open up her heart and take in both Gwennie and the baby, for blood thicker than water. And this was the thanks she get.

Another thing that hurt her is the thanks she get from her sister Clara down in Mile Gully. All because she help bring Gwennie and Walter back together. Nobody, it seems, remember how she send Gwennie money near every week while she up at the school. Nobody think about how she looking after Peppy. Nobody thank her for it. When Walter drive up his car and park it outside the shop front, she remember how she was so frighten for she figure maybe him come to take Peppy. But it wasn't so a tall. Him come into the shop with his face long and droopy like him neither sleep nor eat for eleven days. And him come inside the shop and walk right over to where she sit down on the barrel, her back to the wall and Peppy, about four months then, sleeping in her lap.

Walter did have a big tin of Lactogen baby's formula in his hand. Him put it on the counter. Then him look at the baby for a long time and sigh long and deep. All this time, him and Aunty Cora still don't exchange a word. She remember holding onto the baby tighter than usual, her heart pumping out loud. But when she see his two eyes fill-up with eye water, she finally say to him: 'Come, hold her little. Mind you wake her, though.' And Walter hold and sway the baby for a good ten minutes. Then him give it back to Aunty Cora and she put it into the crib she have in the back room. Then she pour out a tall glass of white rum for Walter and brandy for herself.

'So, Walter, what happen, man?' She put down the glass infront of him. His eyes were red and puffy.

'I not shame to say it, Miss Cora, but I miss Gwennie bad-bad.'

'Drink up the little rum, man. Make you feel good and strong again.'

'No.' Him push away the glass. 'No more hard liquor. I putting all that behind me now. I want Gwennie to be proud of me.'

Aunty Cora peer at him from over her glasses. 'You prefer beer?'

Walter nod. 'Just a little.'

Aunty Cora get up and open one for him. Then she call Gizelle from outside and tell her to come help out in the shop for she talking. Walter sip the beer.

'Then, Walter, what happen between you and Gwennie, man? I remember that Saturday morning the two of you marry in Mile Gully church. You was so happy, love-bird own self. So, what happen?'

'Gwennie, man, Gwennie.' Him shake his head. 'She have too many man friends for my liking, Miss Cora. Too many. She don't care about me any more – she don't care.'

'Between me and you, Walter, make I tell you something. You see me, is one woman friend me have. One! No more. For is them who carry you business. Is them who chat about you behind you back. Is them who lie down-up with your husband and then come grin with you. Gwennie right if she keep plenty man friends. New Green people watch me like hawk, for is only man friends I keep. One woman.'

'It don't matter, Miss Cora. It make me crazy. When we go out, she chat-up and laugh-up with them too much. Make me crazy.'

'But Walter, when you married a good-looking woman, what you expect?'

Walter sigh.

'So you think you will visit her, Walter?'

'Yes, but not right now. I want to straighten out me life first. Stop this drinking for good. I apply for a new job. Would be good if I could get it. It similar to the Youth Corp, but is more pay. And the house them give me to live in have more rooms. So, if I get it and I move, I plan to pick her up, so she can have a place when she finish school. I proud she gone back to school, Miss Cora. I really proud. Them never used to treat her good up at the school without the certificate a tall. But I miss she and the children. Especially Peppy. Lord, I love to see her face and her smile.'

Walter sip some more of the beer, and Aunty Cora swallow all the brandy in one gulp. She lick up the little bit running down her mouth corner with her tongue.

'Miss Cora, it did really hurt me when I come home that evening and find she and all the children gone. I was mad with you and she and her mother. Especially her mother. Gwennie don't use her head when she see her mother, you know. Her mother do all the thinking and scheming for her.' Him pause, then start up again, eyes steady with Aunty Cora's. 'You think she love me. You think that if I get another work, she will come back?'

'Man, what you talking about. Of course she will come back. Just straighten up yourself.'

42

She remember how Walter did look plenty more cheerful than when him first arrive. When time come to leave, him give Aunty Cora twenty dollars to help look after the baby, but she give it back and tell him, send it to Gwennie. And him smile and leave. Him come back one more time after that with his two hands full of Lactogen and box-milk. This time though, him wouldn't touch either the beer or the rum Aunty Cora offer. Him play with the baby until him leave.

And so when Gwennie move back in with him after she leave school, even though him never get the new job, all the thanks she get was a letter from Clara saying is a shame that the two of them get back together for now Gwennie pregnant again. And if Gwennie did only listen to her father and move down here with them, it wouldn't turn out so, for she, Clara, would see to it. And she wonder what Cora telling Walter, for she know Gwennie don't act sensible all the time, but somebody must be advising Walter, for what other else reason could cause Gwennie to do such a fool-fool thing.

And all these things run through Aunty Cora's mind. And the more she think about them the more it gall her, especially the letter from Clara. For even though them never used to be close, she and Clara lose touch completely over the years. And is not cause them live far, or cause them have arthritis and can't travel about as them wish, but it was about MaDee, Clara and Cora's mother.

IV

MaDee was about ninety years old. She live by herself in Maroon Town, calling distance from her oldest boy, Skip, his wife Miss Elsie, and them six out of thirteen children. Two years ago, MaDee come down with a bad stroke, and it leave her stretch out stiff-stiff on her bed, can't walk, and can barely move round by herself and talk. Skip and Miss Elsie move in MaDee with them and move out two of them oldest in order to provide enough room. MaDee been living there now going on three years, and Skip and Miss Elsie say them tired, them want Cora and Clara to help in the taking care.

Clara say the six months Gwennie's three children stay with her while she was up at the school, tired her out so bad, she can barely walk round now sake of all the hassling she meet with them. And as it stand, she don't know how she could manage looking after MaDee. Aunty Cora don't say anything, she know Clara would get away with it. She can just feel it in her belly-bottom. It was always like that.

Ever since them small. Clara getting away with all sorts of responsibilities just because she the youngest girl and Old Tom's – them father – favourite. Would give his eye teeth for her, him often tell people. When Old Tom lay up in bed sick with arthritis, Cora, Skip and MaDee did have to work, while Clara stay home and do the taking care. Him never want her to work, or hassle herself much. Already him did have his eyes set on who she must marry so her life can be easy.

When Clara write Cora and tell her she don't think she can take care of MaDee, Aunty Cora reply with a long letter, reminding Clara about old times, how Clara always have it easy. How she married first. And instead of taking one of the younger ones and putting him through school, she wipe her hands clean of the entire family. And here it is, over thirty years later, and things the same way still.

Clara never write back for one whole year, and so MaDee stay with Skip and Miss Elsie the fourth year. And so here was Peppy five years going on six, Miss Gertie complaining every day that Peppy spoil-rotten, Gwennie vex and upset for Aunty Cora want to adopt Peppy, Walter, as far as she understand, gone back to drinking, and since Clara don't have any intention of helping out, Aunty Cora decide she might as well make room in her house for MaDee.

V

Peppy start off to big school the same year MaDee move in. Her first morning, she wake up early. And after she tidy herself and eat the little breakfast Aunty Cora wake up and prepare, she put on her uniform. Miss Gertie did spend the entire day Saturday sewing it, and Sunday, Miss Irene starch and iron it. So when Peppy put it on the Monday morning, the white blouse and blue tunic and little red tie did stand up stiff-stiff on her. And when she put on her blue socks and brown shoes and Miss Irene plait her hair, grease it up with castor oil, and put in two pieces of bright red ribbon, Peppy couldn't look any prettier. Then she pick up her school bag and the lunch pan Aunty Cora pack, and head off down the hill to the shop where she wait for her ride.

The whole day Aunty Cora worry-up and fret-up herself over Peppy. She couldn't keep her mind on anything too long, every minute it flip back to Peppy: if she all right; if she eat the little piece of chicken-back and rice she prepare for lunch; if she break the new slate and slate pencil she give her that morning; if she pull up her hair or romp too hard and dirty up her uniform. All these things pass through Aunty Cora's head that Monday. Occasionally people had to tell her – two and three times – that is not sugar them want is rice, and no, not one pound, but three.

When the car let her off in front the shop that evening, Aunty Cora was outside waiting. Peppy run up and hug her round the waist, telling all about her teacher Miss Johnson, and her head teacher Miss Bailey, and how Miss Bailey's stockings always wrinkle-up like she not wearing the right size, and how she walk round with a long cane and her voice just as deep as any man's, and how she even have hair growing on her chin. Then she tell Aunty Cora about the many friends she meet, the plenty new songs and prayers she learn at devotion, and finally she show Aunty Cora the writings on her new slate. Aunty Cora couldn't do anything more than hug the little girl and hope that the eye water behind her two eyes remain there.

Every evening Peppy come home with more and more news about Miss Johnson and Miss Bailey and Miss Bailey's stockings and her plenty new friends. And sometimes when she talk and talk, Miss Gertie run her and tell her: 'Lord, Peppy, you tell me that already. Cho, man, you little bit too talkative.' And Leslie and George tell her to go and play with her dolly, for she talk too much and Miss Irene never really have much time. So only Aunty Cora listen, and she listen to the same story over and over again until Peppy finally get tired and stop.

VI

Right next door Aunty Cora's room was another bedroom. And it was in here she hang up Peppy's church frocks that she wear to Sunday School every Sunday morning, her school uniforms and her regular yard and going-out clothes. It was in here that she put all Peppy's dollies and teddy bears and dolly kitchen sets and story books and drawing books and painting sets and colouring pencils and Mickey Mouse curtains with matching spreads and pillowcases.

But Peppy never would stay in the room. Every night when lamp blow-out and it was time for bed, Peppy find herself curl-up in Aunty Cora's four-poster bed with the two posturepedic mattresses and plenty boards lining the bottom. She sit up and listen to Aunty Cora talk and sing to herself and pray. She watch her rub all kinds of funny-smelling ointments on her legs so the arthritis can go away. So since Peppy decide she wasn't going to sleep in her own bed, it was in there that them put MaDee.

Peppy was afraid to pass through MaDee's room, for she look too much like a dead person with her body stretch-out stiff and her eyes closed all the time. Plenty times when Peppy have to go anywhere, she walk through every other part of the house so as not to pass through MaDee's room. Nevertheless, the old lady fascinate Peppy. Plenty times she would stay in Aunty Cora's room and peep through the hinges, taking note of the face with the plenty lines criss-cross all over, the wrinkle-up wrinkle-up hands that stick out through the white sheet, and the shrinky-shrinky body that lay down under it.

As she peep through the hinges at the old lady, stories Aunty Cora used to tell her about MaDee's grandparents and life during slavery would come to mind. And although she wasn't sure what the word slavery meant exactly, she figure it wasn't anything pleasant for a certain hardness would always overshadow Aunty Cora's two eyes.

She remember Aunty Cora telling her how MaDee's grandparents used to be Maroons, how them used to live way up in the hills, coming out only at night to set fire to the big house, often times burning up everybody inside. And Peppy ask Aunty Cora why them do it, if them never love the people inside the big house, but Aunty Cora only shake her head, no, the people inside the big house too wicked and cruel.

So all these things run through Peppy's head as she stand up behind the door peeping at the old lady who lay up stiff under the white covers, with silver hairs sticking out from under. Then all of a sudden, two eyes flicker open, then close. Open again. Peppy notice the mouth moving, finally it open, and the old lady whisper her name. Peppy jump back frightened, her heart pumping hard. The old lady whisper: 'Peppy, why you looking at me so much? Why you won't come and talk to me? I long to hear somebody talk to me. Come.' Then Peppy never hear anything but silence after that, and about two minutes later, light snoring. Peppy never peep through the hinges again, and she try never to have to pass through the room again, either.

But plenty times Aunty Cora would call and tell her to bring in MaDee's dinner, for she awake now, or bring in a glass of water or a fresh pillow-case for she sweat up this one. When Peppy bring in all these things to Aunty Cora, who would be sitting-up on MaDee's bed, trying to raise her up in a sitting position with plenty pillows behind her back so she can eat, the old lady would pick up Peppy's hand in her own and ask why she never come visit her or talk to her. And Peppy would just look down on her shoes and hope the old lady hurry up and let go her hand, for it getting hot and sweaty.

VII

Peppy love to play dirty-pot, and Sundays were the only days she could walla-walla in it to the fullest. During the week, she only have time to change her clothes, eat her dinner, do her arithmetics and learn her spellings before night come down. Saturday was the only other time, but she usually spend Saturday with Vin, and Vin don't like play dirty-pot, for she say it too pickneyish, and she too big for that.

Sunday evenings then, were the only time. And so after she come home from church, she hurry up and change her clothes, rush down her dinner, and then collect up her empty cans and whatever scraps of ingredients she can find. Then she fill the can with water, pour in the dirt, cut up whatever little pieces of onion, or rice-grain, or flour-dust she find in Miss Irene's kitchen, and mix up everything into her pot.

Then she add salt and pepper before serving it up on her plastic dolly dishes that Miss Gertie give her. Now Peppy have one dolly who she call Rose, and she manage to bore a hole through Rose's mouth so she can swallow.

So here it was one Sunday evening, after the sun gone for the day, and shadows falling in, bringing with it cool breezes, Peppy was outside under the orange tree with Rose in her lap. With one hand she squeeze Rose's jaw so her mouth can open, while holding the other hand ready with a spoonful of food. Then all of a sudden she hear foot-steps, and when she put down Rose and the spoon, and turn round, lo and behold, she see the brown lady, well her mother, Miss Gwennie, and Mass Walter walking towards here with about five children.

Peppy didn't know if she must run up to her Aunty Cora, who was sitting out on the verandah watching Peppy feed Rose, or if she must stay. Is a long time since she last see Miss Gwennie or Mass Walter. The four children coming up behind, she never see, yet. Three big ones and one little boy in short pants trailing behind. By the time she turn around, Miss Gwennie was upon her, so Peppy just stand up, brush the dirt from off her frock and prepare to meet her salvation.

'How are things, Peppy?' Miss Gwennie ask, holding Peppy's stiff hand in her own.

'Hearty,' Peppy answer, her two eyes more interested in her shoes than what the brown lady look like. She see Mass Walter's shiny black shoes and then the shoes of the four children as them pass behind Miss Gwennie and continue up the steps to where Aunty Cora was. One or two of the shoes stop and turn round, but then them turn back round and continue on up.

'What's the dolly's name?'

'Rose.'

'Rose, that sure is a pretty name. I hear you in school, now. You like school?'

Peppy bow her head. She want Miss Gwennie to let go her hand. It getting warm and sticky.

'That's good you like school, Peppy. I like children that like school. You know that I'm a school teacher?'

Peppy shake her head.

'Yes, maybe one day you will come to my school, Porous Primary.'

Peppy don't say anything.

'Well, come with me. Come, we go meet your other brothers and sister.'

48

Peppy catch her breath. Brothers and sister. Her mind ring back to what Aunty Cora did tell her about Miss Gwennie, that she must be nice and polite, for Miss Gwennie is her mother.

'How come me have two mothers?' she did ask Aunty Cora.

'Well, she is your real mother. She give birth to you. Me only raising you.'

'So, you not me mother?'

Aunty Cora shake her head.

'Then how come me call you mama?'

''Cause I raising you.'

'But if you not me mother, then I mustn't call you mama. What I must call you?'

Aunty Cora sigh. This was exactly the reason she want to adopt Peppy, for all this confusion not necessary.

'Mama Cora.'

'Yes, Peppy.'

'You think the Lord will still love me?'

'The Lord will always love you, Peppy. No matter . . .'

'Even if me don't love me real mother?'

Aunty Cora's two eyes open up wide and her voice get stern. 'What you mean by you don't love you real mother, Peppy?'

'Me love you more.'

Aunty Cora couldn't say anything. She try pull up Peppy so she can sit down on her lap, but Peppy getting too weighty now, and her arthritic feet too weak. Peppy realize it. So she pull up a chair next to Aunty Cora's own, climb up in it, and bury her head in Aunty Cora's lap. Aunty Cora stroke her little neck.

So as Peppy follow Miss Gwennie up the steps, she figure maybe what her Aunty Cora did tell her about Miss Gwennie was true. But no matter, she still like her Aunty Cora more.

Throughout the whole Sunday evening, only one out of the four children talk to her, the big boy, Rudi. Him ask her name, how old she is, the name of her school and her favourite teacher, her favourite class and plenty more things. After Peppy answer, she ask him the same questions and him tell her. Out of all of them, Rudi was her favourite. She lead him down the steps and under the orange tree to meet Rose. Him tell her Rose is quite pretty and him like her very much. Then him help Peppy open-up Rose's mouth wider so she can swallow better. When time come for Rudi to leave, Peppy start to get sad. She ask if him

49

could stay. But him say no, him have to go to school tomorrow, but would try and come back again soon.

Every day Peppy look out for Rudi, hoping that him would come back and play dirty-pot with she and Rose. But him never come. And she ask Aunty Cora day after day what happen to Rudi. But she wasn't sure what to tell her. It set her to thinking though, that maybe she coop up Peppy too much, and maybe she should in fact send her to spend time with her brothers and sister. After much thinking, Aunty Cora decide upon it. Peppy would leave the Friday after school and her father would bring her back the Sunday evening.

When Aunty Cora tell her she plan to see Rudi again, Peppy couldn't wait. She pack-up all the things she going to carry and show him, three whole weeks ahead of time. And she was in a state of merriment for days and days before the day finally arrive.

VIII

That same Friday, Gwennie decide to take half the day from school. Teacher Brown almost didn't give it to her. Him mumble something under his breath about how she already take few days off last month. Gwennie never say anything, for she know it wasn't so much the days she take, but more the fact that she start up teachers' union at the school, and the teachers been bringing him up on plenty charges, and him don't like it. Him don't like it that them want better wages and more time off when necessary. And as Gwennie is the ring leader, him grow to not like Gwennie too much. Gwennie pick up her handbag and walk out of his office the afternoon, her head high and her back straight, a little smile playing around her mouth corners.

The clouds did make up to rain when Gwennie leave the school yard. By the time she turn down Porous Road, it was pouring down plenty. Gwennie didn't bother run for shelter. She just kiss her teeth, aggravated that her plans spoil for the evening. She did want to catch home early so she could take a puss-nap, then look over the Immigration papers she get last week, if she finish cook on time. Maybe she could bring them to the meeting later and show Percy, maybe even ask him to safe-keep them before Walter find and tear them up.

Gwennie kiss her teeth again. She shiver from the clothes drenched all the way through to her skin. All the pressing and curling of her hair from the night before hang limp and flat at her ears' corners. She open her mouth and swallow some of the water. It feel cool and taste sweet running down her palate. She spy a cedar tree with its plenty leaves and branches spread out wide. Gwennie run over to it, put down her bag at the root, then sit down, her back leaning against the trunk, a peaceful expression covering over her face as the rain pour down around her and not much wetting her. A little pain grip her belly and then it pass. Gwennie sigh. She press her hand to her stomach gentle-like and run her fingers longside the scar. Through the wet clothes she could feel it plain as day. It getting better though. The doctor say it will always stay there. Not much women get rid of it after them have the operation.

Gwennie grimace to herself as she remember Percy's face after the operation, eyes red, face full of fright, and hands barely steady in his pocket, as if him was the one stretch out there flat on his back, in pain, and not she. Afterwards when him was bringing her home him claim him could never go through all those things women have to put up with, for him don't like pain a tall. Gwennie never say anything. She remember being afraid about having the operation, for she hear how sometimes after them sew you up, instead of getting better, it start to fester. She even hear about this one woman who get pregnant after the operation, and how the baby come out deformed before dying. But regardless, she did still want it. Especially since she get the invitation letter from her brother, Samuel, in Connecticut. She know if she take careless and get in family way again, him wouldn't send another letter, for him funny that way.

Percy went with her the Monday morning. After taking the day off from the all-boys High School where him teach Geography, him pick her up at the bus stop the morning in his Austin Cambridge and drive her. Inside the operating room, the nurses address him as Mr Glaspole and hand him a gown. Him never say anything, face just serious as usual, fingers twitching. Gwennie never mention a word to Walter about the operation either. It was her decision entirely. She didn't want any arguing about it.

Percy make and give her hot cerose tea to drink after bringing her home the Monday afternoon. Then him sit down at her bedside until she sleep, wake and was feeling better. Him leave before Walter reach home.

The rain hold up little, and the sun start to peep out its head again. Gwennie wasn't ready to get up yet, even though her purple pantsuit drench all the way through, and her black shoes wet. She like the peacefulness about her, the way the birds were beginning to fly-fly about now, and the way everything look green and cheerful after the little shower. Even the air smell good and her head feel light and clear. Gwennie's eyes catch the rainbow forming over her head, and a broad smile cover over her face. Her eyes follow the different-different colours, from one end to another, until a small noise in the distance draw her attention.

She turn her neck to where it coming from, and to her left, over in the common, an infant school did just get recess it seems, as the children pile out with balls – newspaper roll up plenty times with a piece of string tie round it tight. A little grin play around Gwennie's mouth corner. She couldn't tell the last day she play dandy-shandy. Not since High School. Gwennie watch the game, her face liven up now, just as if she was playing, and she turn and push her neck every which way, so she could see every movement the ball make until the tall girl batting now, send it hoisting, way-way up. Gwennie and everybody else's head turn with the ball only to see it fasten inside a big breadfruit tree. The silence never last long before quarrel break out. Them start to blame the girl, ask her why her blasted hands so long, how them going to get down the blasted ball.

Gwennie leave before the girl with the long hands answer. She walk briskly the remainder of way. She leave her shoes outside on the verandah next to Jeff's outgrown stroller, and let herself inside the house, humming 'All Things Bright And Beautiful'. She drop off her clothes in the bathroom, haul on her multi-colour duster, then she open-up the windows in the living room, letting in freshness and sunshine.

But the minute the room light up and Gwennie's two eyes focus on the pants and shirts and dirty plates and break-up cups and shoes lying about, the pain start to pulsate from out her forehead, spreading down about her two eyes. She stagger out the living room, her two hands squeezing her head, taking long deep breaths, as Percy tell her – relax, deep breath, relax. Usually Rudi and Delores reach home and tidy-up, but today, since Gwennie leave school so early, she reach home before them.

Gwennie make her way to the verandah and sit down on one of the red and yellow chairs, relaxing and taking deep breaths until the headache ease-up. She glance down on her watch and grunt. Almost three o'clock. The children soon come home. She won't get a chance to look over the visa information carefully without any botheration, fill out and sign what she have to fill out and sign, and send it back. Sake of Walter, she can't even read the letters properly, for she know that just out of sheer spite and grudgeful, him would tear them up, for is she who get invitation to go Foreign not him or the two of them.

It was a good lesson she learn from what happen to Aunty Cora's letter. Now she give out the school address whenever she expect things of importance, even though she can't stand it when the other teachers raise-up them eyebrows when them see the big yellow parcel mark U.S. Department of Immigration and Naturalization in her box. But all that matter right now is the chance to get away from Walter. She just want to go someplace where she can cool her brain. She tired. Tired of the way him pick-pick and quarrel-quarrel about every little thing. Now him jealous more than anything about she and Percy and the meetings they've been going to every Friday night. Sometimes she have to stop and wonder how is it Walter turn into such a nightmare.

Him certainly not the man she marry. The man she marry used to sit up at night until late, telling her childhood stories and his plans for them future together. Him used to buy her a record or a book now and again, bring the children out to amusement parks, picnics, shows. Now him the complete opposite. What happen to Walter, what happen? Him don't want her to have have anykind of spare time a tall to herself. Morning time she wake up, make breakfast, tidy herself and the children and leave for school. Afternoons, she come home, cook, mark papers, if she have time she do a little washing or sewing. Then is time to go to sleep.

The one evening she take off to cool her brain, him curse and quarrel that she keeping man with him. And if him should ever see how she and Percy get on, him would be frightened, for them close just like brother and sister. Every since Luther she lose interest. She too afraid. Furthermore she like the activities and lectures at her meeting, the various speakers who come up with plans to build better literacy programmes, to bring electricity and running water into rural areas, to give better training to students who can't pass the Common Entrance Exam to get into high schools, to teach more Spanish in the classroom and enhance relations with Cuba.

Her favourite activity is letter-writing, offering advice to party members about how them can improve welfare programmes, the standard of medical care in public hospitals in rural areas, the availability of effective birth control methods as well as sex education classes, the prohibition of police brutality. All these things special to her, yet Walter don't like it. Nowadays him claim Percy turning her into communist. Sometimes it don't even spell sense to tell him of the things going on. That helping people because you in better position don't mean communist. Percy didn't wring her hands and drag her to the meetings. It was her own decision.

Sometimes she figure she only have herself to blame though. For it was she who agreed to go back to him. But after she see how him was shedding eye water and apologizing, planning to turn over new leaf, only a hard-hearted old mule wouldn't open up her heart and take him in. But it wasn't so easy coming to that decision, she remember well, back in her little cubicle up at the Teachers College . . .

'Anything, everything. I will do it . . . Just come back,' Walter say to her.

After she think long and hard about the way him usually treat her and the children, and how, now, she leaving school in few weeks and she didn't have place to put her head, she feel like she didn't have much choice. And it look like him was really willing to change.

'We have to do things differently,' she tell him, her voice on edge. 'Me have to get me own way more. We have to do more things together as a family. We have to talk about things better. Can't put up with this man-handling business. I want to bring me friends over. I want them to be comfortable.' She look at Walter when she say this, noticing his face shiny with sweat. 'I want them to be comfortable!' She tell him again. 'I want to go about me business without interference.' Gwennie hold her breath, she wonder if she pushing too hard. 'You know, like doing volunteer work when I have time,' her voice soften, and she let out her breath easy.

'Gwennie, I will try. Everything you say, everything you want, I will try. Life just too miserable, just too hard.'

And after all she must give him credit, for him did try hard, three whole years. Him stop drink rum. Them start go out more. Him never say anything when Percy come visit, mostly him just absent himself plenty Friday evenings before her meeting. Him even pick up with the church going again. But it was when she became pregnant with Rosa, the last girl, that everything started to go downhill. The last boy, Jeff, she have right after she move in back with Walter never stir up any problems. Walter was as understanding and gentle as ever, but this last baby, Rosa, it seems, rile him up to no ends.

And it was the first time in a long time that she start to wonder if Walter suspect anything. If somebody tell him. For the day after the doctor tell her she pregnant again and she announce it to Walter, him just change completely. Two whole weeks him wouldn't utter a word to her. If him come home a tall, it was late at night, stone-drunk. And she think maybe him just frustrated, for him not really happy at his job and this new baby just mean more expenses.

But the thing that worry Gwennie the most, though, that cause her to think maybe Walter suspect that like Peppy, maybe Rose didn't belong to him, was the day she see the Austin Cambridge park-up in the school yard, motor running. She figure immediately something wrong, for today wasn't Friday and is only Fridays alone she see Percy.

She figure maybe something happen with Percy and the wife. Various lawyers been writing him, for the wife claim she want the house since she looking after the children these days. Gwennie figure maybe a more serious course of action set in now, especially with the way his hands were dancing around.

'What happen?' she ask him, 'You get letter?'

Him never answer right away. Backing the car out the school yard, him manoeuvre it carefully around school children and fire hydrants, all the while barely keeping the steering wheel steady.

'Percy, what happen? You get letter?'

'See it on the dashboard.'

In her haste to read the contents and find out why Percy so upset, Gwennie didn't take much notice that the letter was hand-written instead of typed, that the handwriting on the envelope with its elaborate loops on the g's and y's was Walter's very own and that the letter was about her, until she finally fling it down, the burnt cocoa butter complexion gone from her face, leaving her feeling hot, then cold, then hot again.

Her mind run back to a conversation she have with Walter not too long ago, one evening out in the living room. The seven-thirty news with Brenton Hall was just finished, and Walter get up to turn off the television. Him pick up the Gleaner, settle down in the off-white couch with his headback leaning against the wall, and put on his reading glasses. Gwennie, who was sitting down across from him, start to grade the Algebra test she give out just the day before. Rudi was at choir practice and Delores was in the bedroom helping Dave and Jeff with homework.

So in tune was Gwennie into her grading, she never notice that the page of the Gleaner wasn't turning much and that now and again, Walter would put it down on his lap, take off glasses, rub eyes, stare at Gwennie for a long time, sigh, put on back the glasses and pick up the Gleaner again. She didn't even hear when him call her the first time, it was upon the second calling that she turn her head. Him hesitate before starting.

'Look like we might have to move. Them not paying plenty money around this way a tall. People on the top levels get plenty money. It hardly ever trickle down.'

'That's the purpose of Unions and strikes,' Gwennie say to him, then sorry the moment she open her mouth to say it.

Walter kiss him teeth and turn his head, disgusted. Didn't say another word to her for a good ten minutes. Gwennie bite her lips and continue grading the papers in her hand.

'Gwennie, how come it seem as if you don't care about the little girl up at New Green? I don't hear you talk about her much to the others. I don't hear you make any suggestion to go and visit her. I don't hear you talk much about you Aunty. What happen? I thought she was only staying up there till you finish school. She up there now going on six years.'

Gwennie put down the red ink pen in her hand, for she couldn't hold it steady, sigh long and hard and look at his headtop where it was thinning out.

'Why you don't let her come stay with us?' Walter continue. 'I know we don't have much room, but we can manage. I like to see all the children together.'

'I don't have the time, Walter,' Gwennie say to him. 'I tired all the time.'

'Maybe one Friday evening instead of going to your meeting, we can go up there. You Aunty must think we don't want her.'

Gwennie don't say anything. She still have the letter from Aunty Cora in her bag, the one where she ask about adopting Peppy. Every time she think about it, it make her hot-hot. By the look of things, when she go up to see the baby, it seem as if Aunty Cora already adopt her. It burn her belly bottom to see how the pickney won't even come to her, cry everytime she lift it up. Even Walter get on better with her than she, Gwennie, Peppy's own mother. She been wanting to go up there and take the pickney, but she afraid. She afraid to have her in the same house with Walter. She afraid to face Aunty Cora too, for Peppy been up there quite a long time. Whenever she go up there, she always feel uncomfort-

56

able around Aunty Cora. And she can tell Aunty Cora just as uncomfortable, for she won't allow her eyes to meet Gwennie's. And she can't really talk to her much with Walter and the children there.

'What you say?' Walter ask, breaking into her thinking.

'Alright. We can go this Friday,' Gwennie did say to him, but she live to regret it. For after that conversation, most every Friday him want go visit Peppy, and most times Gwennie just couldn't go, for her meetings just as important.

Sitting down next to Percy in the Austin Cambridge, Gwennie remember the conversation as plain as yesterday. It was the first time since she moved in back with Walter that the two of them ever discuss Peppy like that. That was a while back. Whenever she could skip a meeting, she would go up to New Green, but it wasn't often. Sometimes it would be two months going on three before she reach up there. But the letter now was truly a surprise. She couldn't make head or tail of it. Percy was looking at her, waiting for her to say something, but she don't know what.

Months later, after the arrival of the new baby, Rosa, all of a sudden the words in the letter Walter send Percy would just dance before her eyes. Percy never come back to the house, as Walter warn him in the letter, and Rudi did miss him bad for them used to be good friends. Percy used to bring him different-different stamps for his collection. She couldn't answer when him stop the car and ask her to explain what Walter mean by 'him want to be certain that him is the father to all his children'. She just couldn't get into it again. She just want to forget everything. She tell Percy, Walter just blasted jealous as usual, and leave it at that. Percy never say anything else about it. She never say anything either.

So all these things were running through Gwennie head that Friday afternoon, as she sit down outside on her red and yellow verandah chair, her two hands holding up her jaw, the headache gone completely. Gwennie look at her watch again, sigh, get up and step inside to start the dinner.

As time was upon her, Gwennie didn't bother to prepare anything too fancy. The rice she put on, boil and swell in no time. She cook it up with some of the left-over chicken, and pour in a little onion, little escallion, little thyme, and whatever seasonings she could lay her hands on. She leave a note telling Delores to cut up some tomatoes and have it with the dinner. She had ten minutes left before she meet Percy up at the bus stop. Gwennie fling off the multi-colour duster, haul on some clothes, run the comb through her hair, haul on a scarf over it, and step through the door with her handbag.

Maybe if Gwennie did have time to press and curl her hair that Friday afternoon she would've seen the letter from Aunty Cora telling her that Peppy coming, fluttering under the Holy Bible on her bureau. For since she and Walter not on good speaking terms these days, him already get the letter about one week now and put it down on the bureau so she can read it. But as Delores is the kind of person who can't bother to replace things where she find them, Saturday mornings when she dust and clean bureaus, Gwennie didn't get a chance to see the piece of paper fluttering under the big brown Bible.

Now Porous Road is a long road. And the route that Gwennie take to get to her meeting is the very same route the taxi carrying Peppy was travelling on. Since Percy did have to stop and carry out a few errands before continuing on to the meeting, there is no doubt that Gwennie and Peppy pass one another right there on Porous Road.

IX

Later that night when Gwennie reach home from her meeting, she was feeling cheerful. She didn't go inside the house right away, but sit down outside on the verandah, on the steps. She did spend a little time with Percy before the meeting looking over the Immigration papers. And it seems as if after she fill in and mail what she have now, once them write her back and give her the okay, she well on her way. Percy told her she won't have any problems a tall getting the visa.

'How you figure?' she ask him.

'Well, the problem not so much in the States,' him tell her. 'Is the Immigration people here who will give you problems. For the government don't want anybody to leave the country. Them want everybody to stay and help build it up. But when them see that you married and have plenty children, that you only going for holidays, and that you have letter from Teacher Brown saying your job waiting, them won't give you any problems. For them know you coming back.'

'You think so in truth?' Gwennie ask nervous-like, well wanting to believe everything Percy saying.

Him nod.

'I know it don't sound good, but I can't wait to get away. Just to go relax. I don't want to leave the children, but I have to get away.'

Percy never say anything. Gwennie know him don't like when she sound so excited about leaving. Him going to miss her.

'I don't tell Walter yet. I too fraid. I have a feeling him would stop me. Say something to the Immigration people. Tear up the papers. It probably best to just wait until everything ready, then maybe a month before I leave, tell him. I don't tell the children yet either.' Gwennie pause long and sigh deep. 'Only Rudi. I don't know what I could do without that boy. Him is me right hand.'

'Him helpful in truth,' Percy agree.

'Is a big responsibility to give him alone. But I don't think Walter going let the children stay with Grandma when I gone. Him and Grandma not on good terms these days. So I know everything will fall in Rudi's lap, between him and Delores, since them the oldest. The whole thing don't sit down with me easy a tall, Percy, but I have to get away, else I go crazy. Maybe I can get a little work to . . .'

'Work!' Percy look at her hard, eyes shining. 'What you mean by work? You not tired? You don't want rest? You don't want just to sit down up and don't do anything for days and days?'

'Yeah, Percy, but . . . ' Gwennie start to stutter, his outburst taking her off balance. 'Maybe I could get a part-time work, not plenty hours, just so I could raise a little money to buy things for the children. Me friend, Julia, who used to go abroad often, say plenty work over there. Plenty.'

'What kind of work you think them going to give you, Gwennie?'

Gwennie never answer right away. She started to feel uncomfortable, for Percy was getting hot-hot by the minute. His voice did even raise-up a few notches, and the people inside the room waiting for the meeting to start was beginning to look round at them.

'You know is only cleaning work them going to give you, or maybe them let you look after people's pickney or maybe wash dishes. That's all them going give you. Nothing else.' Percy's voice was angry and loud same way, didn't give one blast about who looking at him.

'I only going for three months, Percy,' Gwennie lower her voice with the hopes that Percy will lower his too. 'Only going for summer. That kind of work okay. I not going Connecticut to live. Furthermore, me

59

brother, Samuel, doing plenty buying me the plane fare and putting me up, I can't expect him to buy things for the children as well. Is plenty to ask. And you know me, I can't sit down idle for three whole months and not do anything.'

'I can't believe me ears,' Percy's hands start to dance round, chopping through the air. 'You, a big-big teacher for over ten years, and you going to pick up youself, and clean house and clean baby shit. When out here, you have somebody clean you own pickney's shit?'

Gwennie decide to leave it at that. His hands were moving about too much. She know him angry. And furthermore, the meeting was starting. But all through the meeting, Gwennie couldn't help but wonder why him so upset about her working, cleaning people's houses. As far as she can see, all work the same as long as it legal. If she was going there to stay longer, of course she would look for a teaching job, for that is her field. But not when she going only for summer.

Percy didn't mention it again when him was dropping her home, but him tell her she sure going to have a nice time.

'If you get there before July fourth, you will love the fireworks that make the sky light-up bright as day, and just as pretty,' him tell her. 'You will love the skyscrapers. Some of them so tall, them mad to touch the sky.'

Gwennie laugh, her stomach relaxing again.

'You will see the subway system where trains go as fast as lightning. When them stop to let you off, you have to get ready at the door to jump off right away, else the doors shut up and them carry you go way to hell.' Him laugh out loud and hard, his bottom lip quivering like it cold. 'Happen to me one evening I was going work.'

Gwennie didn't ask what kind of work, him was so happy talking now.

'Train pack, everybody going home. My stop was the last one before the train turn express and don't stop again till it feel like. That evening, my foot never even touch the ground. Just sort of perch up. And by the time the train stop and the doors open, and I could catch me bearings: find me two feet, put them down on the floor, and push pass everybody, the door shut long time and the train gone. Gone to blast! I wanted to cry, Gwennie, as big as I am. Did want to just sit down and holler.'

Gwennie's eyes were full of eye water when she step out of his car the Friday night, from all the hard laughing. And it wasn't so much the story Percy telling, but the way his face make up with funny looking expressions, the way his hands frisk around on the steering wheel, the way his eyes twinkle. She going to miss him, in truth.

Gwennie get up off the verandah steps where she was sitting, yawn long, turn the key once in the lock, and open the door to her house. She hold herself steady, preparing to stumble over a pair of shoes kick-off careless in the doorway, before she find the light switch. But tonight when she push open the door, the light was on already, and Rudi was up waiting on the off-white couch, his blanket covering him up from neck to toe.

It take Gwennie a good few seconds before her eyes could get used to the light. At first she think it was Walter sitting up, waiting, but when she move in closer, she notice is Rudi.

'But look at me dying trial, Rudi, what you doing up this ungodly hour of the night? Come, go to bed, right now. You not tired?'

'Mama, Peppy inside sleeping on daddy's bed.'

'Peppy? What Peppy doing . . . ' Gwennie say more to herself than to Rudi, as she feel the pulsing coming on behind her eyes.

'The little girl that live up at Aunty Cora's,' Rudi answer anyway. 'I didn't reach home from choir practice until late-late, and when me come, Daddy-man was cursing. It sound like him come home and find Dave and Jeff beating up the little girl. Them trim off her dolly's hair, you know, her dolly, Rose, and pop out one of the arms. Then them pinch-pinch Peppy and pull-pull her hair.' As Rudi was one for details, Gwennie didn't have to interrupt and ask for any. 'Del was over at her friend's house, Ginger. Only Jeff and Dave was here when the taxi let her off. Daddy-man say him can't understand how you could read the letter and still pick up youself and go off to the meeting.'

'Which letter?' Gwennie ask him, her voice hoarse and tired. She drop down herself on the off-white couch next to Rudi. 'Which letter?'

Rudi was at a loss for words. But not for long. 'I don't know. Daddy say it was on the bureau. About two weeks now. It say Peppy coming, I suppose.'

'And Jeff and Dave trouble her?' Gwennie whisper to him.

'Yeah,' Rudi nod his head. 'Them say she not them sister, only two sisters them have, Delores and Rosa. The little girl and them not anything.'

Gwennie never say another word. She press her fingers to her temples, shut up her eyes tight and relax, take deep breath, relax . . . Her head was pounding.

61

And so she didn't even feel when Rudi push off the polka-dot spread that cover him up, climb out the couch and seat himself next to Gwennie's two feet. And even when him loosen the lace on her lace-up brown Oxfords, slowly and gently take off her shoes, one foot after the other, and massage her foot bottom, in and out, between the toes, she still never feel it.

But all of a sudden, her eyes get misty, for him was massaging her feet the same way as Grandma when the arthritis go down into hers. And her heart was so full and heavy, she couldn't even open-up her mouth to tell him thanks, the eye water just run down her cheeks instead. She wanted to run up the street and use the call box, beg Percy to come pick her up. She couldn't bear the thought of listening to Walter's mouth tonight. She just want a little peace and quiet – that's all she ask. But it was too late and too far to walk, and she tired. Tomorrow she going to tear off Jeff and Dave's behind so bad, them won't be able to sit down properly for several days. Bout she not them sister, only two sisters them have . . . well she going to show them a sauce.

By the time Rudi finish the other foot, Gwennie was sleeping long time. Him get up, swing her two legs long-side the couch, push up the cushion under her head and cover her over with his polka-dot sheet. Except for the two cats outside howling in heat, the house was dead-quiet. Now and then, him hear Peppy turn in her sleep and call out her Aunty Cora's name, but then she stop, and the house quiet-down again. Rudi check the door and the windows to make sure them lock, then him look over on his mother one more time, flick off the light switch and pick out his way carefully in the darkness back to the room him share with Jeff and Dave.

Gwennie have a dream that night. It take place at Hartford, Connecticut, at the house she work two and three jobs for, scraping and saving until finally she buy it from the Trinidadian couple. The old couple claim them have to go home for the cold weather killing them. Them can't stomach the bad winters any longer. Gwennie got the house at decent price, for it was in need of plenty fix-up fix-up. But anyway, after she and the children finally move, she start to notice that most every evening Peppy don't reach home until late hours of the night when everybody fast asleep. She come in, mumble evening to Gwennie, if Gwennie still up, and continue on into her room. Next morning she gone.

And it wasn't so much the coming-in and going-out that hurt

Gwennie, as the fact that Peppy would never lift one finger to help with the cleaning or the fixing-up or the straightening-out of the new house. She never lift one finger to help with the moving-in, almost as if she don't give one blast about how or where them live. Gwennie buy paint and brush so everybody can chip in. More hands make work light. But Peppy's can of paint shut tight sameway, untouched. Everybody else come, help, but Peppy's fingers don't lift straw. One night Gwennie decide she couldn't take it any longer. She have to confront Peppy about it. So she set out for Peppy, and the moment the key turn over in the lock, she start.

'Why is it everybody can come home early and help out with the cleaning-up. But not you? From the day we move in here, you still don't lift your finger to help. Every night you come inside the house late. What you have out the street that is so sweet? What keeping you out there so late at night? Every night?'

That night Peppy just brush pass her, not saying a word. It gall Gwennie to no ends. And so when Peppy step into the kitchen in search of her dinner, Gwennie was behind her quarrelling same way. 'Bad upbringing,' Gwennie tell her. 'Bad home training. No sense of goodness. Aunty Cora break you bad. She spoil you . . . ' But Gwennie didn't even finish the remainder of her sentence before Peppy fly down her throat from where she stand-up over by the stove, her frame almost as tall as her mother's.

'You have a nerve,' she grind out through her teeth to Gwennie. 'You have a nerve. At least she did take me in and care for me. You only give me away. Couldn't even wait till me crawl out the womb properly, you hand me over. Now you talking about spoil. At least she did have something to spoil.'

Gwennie look around her quick, eyes in search of a book or belt, anything heavy, something to bless Peppy with, to make her shut up her blasted mouth. Gwennie double-up her fist. 'Damn ungrateful wretch! Damn ungrateful! I going to show you a sauce! Going to show you a blasted sauce!'

And so say – so done. Gwennie lift her hands and take two steps towards Peppy, eyes big and wide, nose flaring around the edges, mouth corner dry as chip. And she let it go so hard on Peppy's face, her big and heavy hand, that Peppy's face swell up same time, turning into different-different colours, sometimes blue, sometimes black, sometimes purple. Back on the couch with the polka-dot cover over her, Gwennie stir. She open her mouth yawn, stretch, and then she go back to sleep until cock crow the following morning.

Rudi was standing over her with a big mug of steaming hot Milo tea when Gwennie blink open her eyes.

'Where you father?' she ask Rudi first thing.

'I don't know.'

'How you mean. Him not here?'

Rudi shake his head. 'When me open-up the windows this morning, his car already gone. Only the little girl alone sleeping in his room.'

'Where Jeff and Dave?'

'Sleeping.'

'Alright.' Gwennie take the mug of Milo from him and sip it down little-little. She try remember her dream last night so she could write it down. Percy been telling her how night-time dreams suppose to reflect what you think about in the daytime. But she couldn't remember. Gwennie kiss her teeth. She was doing so well all week. But maybe it will come to her later.

Peppy was still sleeping when Gwennie step inside the room and inside the closet in search of a dress to wear that morning to market. As she stand-up by the closet door trying to decide which of the two dresses she have hold-up in her hand she must wear, she feel a pair of eyes on her. Absently, Gwennie lift up her head and her eyes connect with Peppy's two full black ones. A sort of gentle feeling crawl down into her belly causing her to sit down at the edge of the bed next to Peppy. But when Peppy only grunt and roll over, her gaze intense on her mother's face, Gwennie couldn't tell if the little girl just didn't want her near or was just making more room on the bed.

But nothing a tall mattered to Gwennie that morning. All she wanted was to hold the little girl to her bosom and squeeze her tight; run her fingers through the thick head of hair that Miss Irene corn-row so nicely; caress her back and stroke her neck. And as Gwennie reach over to pull Peppy next to her, she see the dolly and then she see the break-off hand, where somebody, must be Rudi, use band-aid and bandage it back into the socket and then she see the eye water gather-up in Peppy's eyes and Gwennie wasn't sure if she to try and press Peppy to her bosom or just let her rest. A firm determination set itself on the little girl's face just like Luther's face used to look – thick eyebrows that furrow together when him thinking hard or vex, lips quivering thin.

Gwennie wipe her forehead with the blue frock in her hand. Sweat was forming over her brows. The memory of Luther flood her mind and cold sweat wash over her. She couldn't believe that after so long, after almost seven years, the thought of Luther could bring back such a feeling. These days she don't even feel much for Walter. Sometimes him come to her at night, but not often, and these days him wear protection. She tell him it's not necessary, she tie her tubes, but him say him not taking any chances for him can't afford anymore children. But even then, she just kind of wish him would hurry-up and finish.

Percy say her feelings natural. Same thing used to happen between him and the wife. After three years or so, the feelings just dissipate and you can't really force them back. But Gwennie wasn't sure how to quite grasp hold of what Percy saying for somewhere deep inside, she know him gone the other way. It wasn't judgement she passing, but she can't just close her eyes to the way him always dress neat, or how his hair and face always tidy, how shirts always match pants, ties always large and flamboyant. Not that Walter slacky-tidy or anything, for Walter have the army training behind him, but there was a marked difference between the two. She can't quite put her fingers on it, but she can tell, even by the way him walk, sorta dainty-like, like him stepping on hot bricks.

Him don't talk much about man-friends, and she don't often see him with any, except for the way him and another fellow from the meeting did just kind of take to one another from the very first. Again, she not passing judgement. For the Bible always say, whoever don't have sin can cast the first stone. And you can't exactly say she clean and pure. But it's different. The Bible say the entire city of Sodom was destroyed with fire and brimstone sake of all that funny-funny business going on. All that unnaturalness.

But then again, him was married. Him and the wife not together anymore, but them tie the knot. Them have two lovely children to show for it, two girls, one two-and-a-half, the other one year. Him show her pictures and talk about them all the time. So maybe . . . Further more, him more than kind to her. Did even want to marry her. Maybe her only true friend.

A little whimpering from behind cut into Gwennie's thinking. She refocus her attention on Peppy. The dream last night flash into her head, but it move out just as quick. Gwennie still couldn't recall.

'What's the matter?' Gwennie ask gentle-like. 'Hungry? Want a little tea?' She reach out again towards the little girl, and as fast as lightning, Peppy pull away.

'But look at me dying trial! You don't want me to touch you?'

Peppy turn her back.

Gwennie take a deep breath. She could feel the pulsing coming on again from somewhere behind her eye lids. 'Tell me what you want to eat? You want porridge? I know Aunty Cora must give you nice corn-meal porridge. Look at how stout you are.'

Still Peppy wouldn't budge.

'How about porridge with plenty milk and sugar?' Gwennie ask in her baby-voice, licking her lips. 'That sounds delicious?'

Still not a sound out of Peppy's mouth. Gwennie couldn't help but wonder to herself why Aunty Cora send her? What it mean. Which letter Rudi talking about? Where was Walter. She get up off the bed and step inside the kitchen. She ask Rudi if him could please prepare some porridge for Peppy and to put in plenty milk. Make sure she eat it up, Gwennie tell him, for the last thing she want is for Aunty Cora to complain how Peppy look drawn, the one time she visit her mother.

Gwennie walk back inside the room and open up the windows. She lean her elbows on the ledge and sigh deep to herself. She wonder what Walter think about all this. What Aunty Cora going to say. It wasn't out of hate and hard-heartedness why she send away Peppy to Aunty Cora. It wasn't out of spite and cruelty. She did only what she thought was good at the time. But it seems as if God don't see it that way, for her punishment seem almost ten fold. The pickney turn complete stranger to her. Won't talk. Gwennie can't touch her. Almost like it wasn't she Gwennie who give birth to her. Wasn't she Gwennie who first suckle and care for her.

Gwennie raise up herself and look at the clock on the dresser. It was twenty minutes to nine. Her chest was feeling tight, her heart heavy. But the last bus to market leaves in twenty minutes. Gwennie haul on the blue frock and tie her head with matching scarf. She tell Peppy she going to market and plan to bring back the prettiest dolly them have. 'It mightn't replace Rose,' Gwennie say out loud to the rigid little back, 'but I trying me best.' On her way out the front door, she beg Rudi, in a tone most pleading: 'Don't forget to look after her, please.'

The letter Aunty Cora send was still fluttering under the big brown Bible when Gwennie board the nine o'clock Grahamm's bus to Porous Market that Saturday morning.

X

Aunty Cora is the kind of woman who don't like anybody to outdo her in any way, shape or form. For from the time she did go down to visit Clara, over ten years ago, and see the luscious green garden Clara have out front, Cora decide she must have a big garden too, just as luscious, if not more. So she hire workmen to come and clear out a spot of plenty rock stone right in front the verandah, and build it up into garden.

Then she would go to town, and anywhere she see a petal she don't own, especially one she imagine Clara don't have either, it come back home with her. No matter if is even in other people's gardens she find it. And she keep up the garden well, but never quite as good as Clara's. For whenever Clara come to visit, she always telling Cora about the different-different things she have to do with her azaleas to make them look as lovely as hers. That fertilizer have to go, she tell Cora one time. Look at what it doing to the marigold's leaves, and my goodness, look at the stems on your petulia. Try and get the fowl manure, medear, for it much better and not as strong. My crotons just sprout up on it . . .

Nowadays with the arthritis in her legs, Aunty Cora can't go out into the garden quite as often. Sometimes it take a whole heap of effort to just pick out the weeds growing up around her plants, ready to choke them. Every three weeks, she pay Babbo to weed out the garden, but him just as useless as she when him drink a little rum. And she afraid to put young people in her garden, for them don't know much about flowers.

The Sunday evening Peppy was to return catch Aunty Cora pouring water at the root of her croton and white witch. No rainfall now going two weeks. She was grumbling to herself about the five pounds she pay Babbo, and that worthless wretch still don't transpose the flowers properly. Aunty Cora kiss her teeth long and hard. She know if she bend over in the garden for any length of time, by the time she ready to straighten up herself, it won't be easy for her muscles not as flexible anymore. And before Miss Gertie come and help, she sit down-up in the kitchen with Miss Irene puffing on that blasted tobacco pipe. She wonder if Miss Gertie ever stop to think that if she fling away that blasted pipe, the cough she always complaining about would stop.

Aunty Cora feel the bad feelings coming on that burn her chest, cause her head to spin and fog up her eyes. She wonder if any more rum in the house, if she did finish off the last flask. Doctor Lord say she must ease up off the white rum for it will cut her off earlier than she think, but sometimes the little white rum is all that give her relief, not the several bottles of tablets and jars of medicine him give her.

So engrossed was she into her gardening that Aunty Cora never even hear when Miss Gertie set down herself on the verandah steps close to her.

'But look at me dying trial! Cousin Cora, what you doing in the garden this hot-hot Sunday evening? Reverend Longmore must did give a good sermon this morning, fill you up with plenty strength and energy.'

Aunty Cora neither answer nor look at Miss Gertie. She continue scrape up fresh dirt with her fingers, then scoop up the dirt, one handful at a time, and put it into the little pot she have with the ganja plant.

'Near every night you complain about arthritis, and how your legs haul up after plenty movement. Now look at you bending down over flowers.'

'Can't do any better, Miss Gertie,' Aunty Cora say to her, trying not to inhale the tobacco smell Miss Gertie carry on her breath. 'Can't do better.'

'But Cousin Cora,' Miss Gertie bawl out, plenty dismay in her voice, 'what happen to the little tree?' She point to the ganja plant Aunty Cora have in her hand. 'You mean to tell me that Mass Babbo picking the leaves?'

Aunty Cora grunt. 'I don't know whether is Babbo or is somebody else. But I just was thinking to meself that I might have to obeah it. For it is the one thing I have to boil and drink every morning to ease the bad feelings. Especially since Doctor Lord caution me gainst drinking the rum.'

'Jesus look down,' Miss Gertie continue, her voice just as loud, and her forehead knit up. 'Is a damn shame when you can't even grow something in your own garden because of damn robbers and thieves.'

Aunty Cora didn't say anything.

Miss Gertie step way oneside to take a drag off the dried tobacco leaves. 'Cousin Cora,' she call out, after finishing, 'I don't mean to be interfering. But I was just wondering since the place so quiet without Peppy running up and down and making noise, when Miss Gwennie coming to take her back or if she going . . .'

Aunty Cora sigh long and hard, walking towards the verandah steps and as far from Miss Gertie and her tobacco smell as possible. 'I don't know what to tell you, Miss Gertie.' She use the tail of her sleeveless floral dress to wipe her forehead.

'Well the reason I asking,' Miss Gertie continue, 'is because yesterday when I was coming back from market, I run into Cousin Doris. She was carrying Vin to dentist. Abscess in her gum, it seems. Puff out her jaws plenty . . .'

Aunty Cora shut up her eyes tight and slowly grind her teeth. She would do anything to make Miss Gertie get to the blasted point of any story she telling. For Miss Gertie is a woman who love to chat long and plenty.

' . . . Well anyway, Cousin Doris tell me that she hear that Miss Gwennie get invite letter from Foreign, and that she leaving soon. Yes, Cousin Cora. Same way she tell me.'

Aunty Cora could feel the bad feelings coming on again. Sweat pucker up on her top lip. She couldn't remember where she hide the little flask for emergency purposes.

'So that's why I ask, Cousin Cora, for I don't know if Miss Gwennie plan to bring the children with her. Or if Mass Walter going with her. Or if is she alone.'

Aunty Cora didn't know if she to bother answer Miss Gertie or if she must believe her any a tall. For Miss Gertie is a woman love add her own thinkings to things. Often times only Jesus alone know the truth. But nevertheless, it bother Aunty Cora. She couldn't understand why no one bother to write and tell her anything. Not a letter from Clara. Not a letter from Gwennie. Not that she don't have the money to look after Peppy, but it would make her feel good sometimes if Clara or Gwennie would show a little interest in her schooling. There it is now, the bad feelings coming up just about everyday, the eyes getting dimmer and she don't know when the good Lord going to call her home. She don't know what going to become of Peppy.

Miss Gertie did want to talk more about Miss Gwennie and her plans for Foreign, but Aunty Cora wasn't in the mood. She cry excuse to Miss Gertie and tell her the bad feelings coming on. She have to go and lay down little.

Up in her room in her four-poster-bed, the sweat was pouring off Aunty Cora's face. She couldn't find the flask, and she wonder if she should send Leslie down the shop for a little rum. The news Miss Gertie tell her upsetting. All the children in her house, from Miss Irene down to George, she raise from them little-bit. About ten children in all pass through her hands. For when people don't have food, or when family life mash up, instead of letting the children suffer, parents send them to Aunty Cora to hold until better days.

Sometimes better days don't come. But she take them in nevertheless. For she can't bear to see children batter-bruised and hungry. If she only have one hand of green banana, she rather share it up for ten children than she alone sit down eat it. And if Gwennie did only know how plenty New Green mothers would gladly give up them children to Aunty Cora for adoption, she wouldn't be forming the damn fool. Better caring and loving can't be found. But Gwennie don't know. She don't know a damn tall.

And so when Walter bring home Peppy the Sunday evening, Aunty Cora couldn't wait until Walter bring up the news about Gwennie. But the entire time, not a word about Foreign mention. Right when Walter was to leave, Aunty Cora couldn't take it anymore, she pull him one side. And for one quick second, it flash across her mind that probably Walter don't mention it for him don't know. And the reason him don't know is because Gwennie don't want him to know. But she push it to the back of her head, for she couldn't understand that kind of family life. Such a big change about to take place, yet the husband don't even know about it.

'Then, Walter, how come you don't mention the little trip to me, man? I hear you going to Foreign.'

'Go where, Miss Cora?'

Aunty Cora could feel the bad feelings coming on again. Lord, she should've gone ahead and send Leslie for that blasted rum.

'Well, is not anything really.' She hold on to his hand. His face was changing into all sorts of different-different expressions. 'Just news I hear. But you know how it is with gossip. Impossible to tell what's true.' It was lame. She know it.

Walter kiss his teeth and shake his head. 'So that's what all the secret-secret about. I see the letters inside the bottom drawer inside a brown paper bag underneath plenty clothes, but I don't touch them, Miss Cora, I don't touch them. She say she want privacy, I give it to her. I try my best to make things easy between me and her, I try.' Walter pause as if thinking, then him start again.

'I should've burned them, Miss Cora, for I know she going Foreign with the man. Miss Cora, Gwennie is not a good person. From she go up to the school and meet the man, most every night them go out together. I send him a letter asking him not to come back to the house. Now she meet him every Friday.

'Gwennie not interested in her family life. I watch where the two of them go. I see them. Sometimes when she come out of his car at night, a shinier and happier face than that you can't find nowhere. But the minute she step inside the house, her face always long-down and frighten-looking. And I just get mad. I want to knock her down. But I control meself. I leave the house.

'I'm tired of trying, Miss Cora. If she want to go, she can go. But I going to tear up the blasted papers first. Now she probably want to take the children too. But if she touch one, Miss Cora, I kill her first. Trust me.'

During this time, Aunty Cora did have her two hands wrap around Walter's back trying to calm him. But nothing doing. Seem as if things been bottled up for too long, now them oozing out. If she did know the one little question was going to create so much botheration, she would've shut her blasted mouth.

Walter never stay much longer. After composing himself, him call Peppy over, whisper in her ears, tell Aunty Cora goodbye, and step down the hill, shoulders droopy, head bow down low.

Aunty Cora shake her head. She couldn't understand modern day family life a tall. For the thirteen years she and Anderson married and live together, them never have arguments so complicated. Thank God, Anderson wasn't a drinker. Not much of a talker, either, steer clear of any contention. And even the first husband, Mass Selvin, who pass on in them third year together, she got along well with. Him used to fuss-fuss more though. Fussy about how food must prepare, how his trousers must iron, even how his side of the bed must spread-up. But nothing a tall compared to what Gwennie and Walter have. Family life like that not suppose to exist. Children suffer too much.

That night when Aunty Cora finally say her prayers, anoint her feet with the various treatments from different obeah-men to make her arthritis go away, turn down the wick under the little 'Home Sweet Home' kerosene-oil lampshade, and turn over in her bed, she hear Peppy call her name.

'But look at me dying trial! Pickney, you not asleep yet. You know you have to get up early tomorrow go to school. Shut up your eyes tight and wait till morning.'

'Them beat me up and pop out Rose's hand.'

'Whatsit?' Aunty Cora catch her breath.

'Me not going back up there. Them say me and them not family.'

Aunty Cora raise up on her elbows. 'How you mean them and you not family? So where was Gwennie, what she say all this time?'

'She wasn't there.'

'How you mean? Then where she was?'

'Me never see her until the next day. The man . . . me father was quarrelling about how she love to walk about.'

'Lord have mercy! Then Gwennie never get the letter? How them mean by you and them not . . . Then Gwennie don't explain it to the children. But is what kind of business this though?'

Aunty Cora fling her two feet to the side of the bed and raise up herself. She reach over to the bureau and turn up the lamp wick. She pull out the right-hand drawer of the bureau and take out the 'White Rose' writing pad. Then she search around in the bottom of the drawer with her fingers for a pen. She have to write Gwennie a letter, for she can't understand what is going on. She can't understand all these plans for Foreign when not a word mention about Peppy. The one time she send Peppy up there to visit, them abuse her. She can't understand a tall – a tall.

But Aunty Cora couldn't find a pen. She kiss her teeth and turn to Peppy. 'Gal, what happen to all the pens. Why you damn hands so touch-touch? Every pen I put down inside this house, you take it away.' But Peppy only quiet in her corner near the wall. Aunty Cora kiss her teeth again and turn back down the wick. But she couldn't fall asleep. Everything just rest heavy on her chest.

PART FOUR

I

The year Peppy turn thirteen was the same year drought strike the island. For months and months, all over the country, people turn up the black of them eyes to the sky, looking for rain, but only fluffy white clouds and bright blue sky look back at them. All of June. All of July and August. No rain. All about, people complain how them hungry, how the markets empty, no yam, no banana, children's mouth-lips parch dry. The government offer out relief. School children get free milk powder and rice to carry home. On Sundays, them drop off bags of sugar and flour and dry cod fish at different-different churches, but that never enough.

Up at New Green, everything dry, even the roads. When cars drive pass, the wheels kick-up dust so plenty and thick, everything cover over brown: people's faces, them clothes, food, even animals and houses and trees turn brown from the dust. Down Mile Gully, Grandpa's cows lie still in the common across from the house and moo day-in and day-out. Grandma give up on her hibiscus and morning glory, for with the tank almost dry, she can't afford to pour water at the roots. So them just hang limp and withered from stalks.

September of that same bad season year, Peppy pass the Common Entrance Exam and enter her first year of high school free of cost. Aunty Cora was so proud, she give Peppy twenty dollars so she could open up a savings account at the Nova Scotia, and five dollars every month thereafter to fatten it. Not too long after Peppy start high school, MaDee take down sick. Doctors come from all about to see her. Them diagnose and whisper with Aunty Cora, shake heads and wring hands. But nothing could be done. Two weeks later she pass on.

It was raining the evening. First rain fall in over six months. Grandma and Aunty Cora did sit down-up on the bed with MaDee between them. She was on her last. After Grandma's shoulder get tired, she shift

MaDee over to Aunty Cora's shoulder. Peppy was on the bed too, but over in the corner. The room was warm. Now and again Grandma and Aunty Cora doze off. Plenty time pass. Grandma get up and shift MaDee over to Aunty Cora. Then them doze off again, the rain beating down hard on the zinc roof outside. All of a sudden Aunty Cora raise up. 'Clara,' she call out, voice almost a choke. 'Clara, I don't think MaDee breathing a tall.'

'Don't talk nonsense.' Clara's eyes fly open. Peppy's too, over in her corner.

'I can't hear a drop of breathing.' Aunty Cora put her head to MaDee's chest.

'Mother Dee,' Clara call, shaking her gently.

'Peppy,' Aunty Cora turn her head, 'pass me the glass.'

Peppy give Aunty Cora the glass she keep on the window-sill at the bed corner next to the flask of rum for emergency purposes. Aunty Cora turn the mouth of the glass over MaDee's nose.

'It isn't fogging a tall,' Clara say out loud to no one in particular. Eye water was running down her face.

'Yes,' Aunty Cora sigh deep, 'she gone.' She hand Peppy the glass.

'Imagine that!' Clara shake her head, stroking MaDee's hair. 'She die right here on me right breast. I can still feel the pressure of her body.'

'Which right breast!' Aunty Cora's eyes open up wide.

Peppy raise up from where she lie down over in her corner.

'Didn't you raise up and pass her over to me? How she to die on your shoulder? It must be on mine.'

'No, Cora. When I was moving her, I remember thinking to meself, Lord, she sure feels heavy.'

'Can't be. She did move her head a little after you give her to me. That must be as she going out . . .'

Well, the two of them sit down-up over the dead woman and talk and argue till about an hour-and-a-half later when them finally get up and send somebody to call the ambulance.

Them bury MaDee in the family plot at the back of Aunty Cora's house next to her two husbands. The service them keep in Aunty Cora's church close to the plot. Plenty people attend the service, even Walter. Gwennie send her condolences from Foreign where she been living now going on two years. In the card she express how badly she wanted to come, but every penny she earn have to go towards the down payment on a lovely one-family house she have her eyes on, so the children can

74

have a place when them come. House and land too expensive in America.

Not even one month proper after the funeral, Aunty Cora take down sick. Doctor Lord say she must careful, for her blood pressure so high, it bound to cause stroke. Rest, him tell her, take vacation. Give up the shop. Rent or put somebody else in there. Relax. Death not an easy thing. She need plenty time to deal with Mother Dee's.

But for all her seventy years, Aunty Cora never know what it's like not to work. She don't know what it's like not to get up every morning, Monday through Saturday, and go down to the shop, open the door and windows and wrap and weigh out one, two, and three-pound bags of flour, rice, sugar and cornmeal before customers arrive. She don't know what it's like not to stand up at the counter, her two hands holding up her jaw, and watch the cows in the common grazing. She don't know what it's like not to be ordering goods, or sitting down-up on her barrel close to the glass case where she can see and hear everything going on outside without anybody seeing her, or chopping up cod fish and salt mackerel for customers. She don't understand what it means to lie down-up inside her bed day-in and day-out, just relaxing.

But she didn't forget what her two younger brothers, Martin and Egbert, tell her at the funeral, that she must come and spend a little time with them abroad.

'We will take care of plane fare and pay for the eye operation,' Martin tell her. 'Just get somebody to look after your land, your animals and your business, and come stay with us. At least six months.'

And Aunty Cora never mind the idea. For she have her passport cover-up, brand-new underneath her bed. She and Anderson did plan to go abroad. And even after Anderson pass on, she still go every four years to renew it. But now she feel too old to travel. It's too hard now to pack up and leave everything and everybody. Her roots set down too deep.

'Old somebody like me too old to travel, man,' she tell Martin and Egbert. 'Old somebody like me must just stay here and die. For I know that the minute I set foot in that plane, I bound to fall over, dead. Furthermore, me can't leave the children. Who will look after them?'

'Nonsense!' Egbert say to her. 'In America, people plenty years older than you get married to young gal and boy every day. Them go party. Them drink rum. Them gamble and travel same way. Them don't know what old age means. People in America don't die till them bloody ready.'

'And about the children,' Egbert kiss his teeth, 'leave them and come. You think if them was going Foreign, them would stop and think twice about you? Leave them and come. Everybody can take care till you come back. Is only for a little time. How them ever manage before you.'

And so Aunty Cora reserve her seat on the airplane the following spring. And all the while she was going for different-different kinds of physicals, and signing different-different kinds of Immigration papers, Peppy didn't start to miss her until the day Aunty Cora was packing her suitcase for the last time.

She and Aunty Cora did sit down out on the verandah. She was folding and Aunty Cora was packing the clothes neatly into the big green suitcase with the four wheels at the bottom.

'Peppy,' Aunty Cora call out after a long swallow of the Red Stripe next to her elbow. 'Take care of yourself. Them boys out the street don't know responsibility. Is you, the gal pickney, that have to be careful. Careful! See you pass exam, you in high school now. I proud of you. Don't allow them boys out the street to spoil your figure. Don't allow them to spoil your future. I want to see you get education and turn out decent.' Peppy fold over the same nightie in her hands. She hate when Aunty Cora talk about these things. She bend her head and continue fold, her forehead furrowing.

'You menstruating now, you have little money at bank. You almost a woman now. Don't bring any babies come. I can't raise any more. You the last one. I don't have eye and strength for young babies.'

'But MaCora, why you think I going to have baby? Why you choose to talk about these things?'

'I will talk about it as long as I please.' Aunty Cora raise her voice. 'I see how you love to chat-up and laugh-up with them boys. I see how them look at you. I know you not a child anymore. I don't want you to turn out like some of them other girls around here. I want you to turn out decent.'

Aunty Cora quiet down for a while. Then she turn to Peppy, and almost in a whisper she say: 'I don't want to say it, but I know you young girls nowadays can barely wait to open-up your legs. Nothing can stop you. Not even the word of God. So use things . . . ' She swallow more of her beer. 'Listen to the radio. Every morning them have a nurse lady on the air that talk about the various protections. I don't even want to see you with the boys from around here, for them don't come from good family, them not clean . . . I don't want you to slut-up yourself with them.' Aunty Cora turn the bottle to her head. She stop and ask Peppy if she want a little, but Peppy shake her head, so Aunty Cora finish it.

'I just thinking,' Aunty Cora say to Peppy after she put down the bottle on the floor near her chair. 'You should stay up at your father's.'

'No,' Peppy bawl out, dismay write all over her face. 'Why me can't stay here?' Eye water fill her two eyes. 'You know me and them don't get on. You know . . .'

'Hush your mouth, gal. Is for your own good. Him will protect you.'

'Me not going up there.' Peppy fold up her hands crossway her chest, lips push out.

'You going.' Aunty Cora's voice was soft but firm. She take up some of the clothes and start to fold them. 'I don't want to leave you here with Leslie. You and him don't get along. I don't want him knock you. You know his temper.'

Peppy didn't say anything. She was afraid of Leslie. Him watch her every movements to see who she keep company with so him can report back to Aunty Cora. Often times him hide and follow behind when she walking with any boy, so him can listen in to the conversation. Miss Irene say is jealousy. When new baby come into family, the older ones always get jealous. Usually them outgrow it. But not Leslie it seems.

Peppy try squeeze back the tears burning behind her eyes. Aunty Cora's voice sounded much too final, almost like them won't see one another again. Even the things them talking about now, baby and men, sound a lot more serious than usual. All of a sudden, Peppy feel lonesome, as if all the family she have in the world suddenly leaving her. Usually she is the one to go away for holidays or to spend time, never Aunty Cora. But this time, everything different. Aunty Cora was leaving. She going to miss her plenty.

'Is for the best,' Aunty Cora continue on, breaking into Peppy's thinking. 'Also, you will get to know your family better. And is only for six months. Furthermore, if them knock you, don't just sit down there like jackass and take it. Double-up your fist and show them that I feed you on plenty good food.'

Them never say anything else after that. Aunty Cora lock her suitcase and lean it up against the wall on the verandah. The next morning, bright and early, them pick her up for the airport. Aunty Cora was crying, eyes red and swollen, face old and tired. Peppy tell her not to cry. Everything will be alright. She is a big girl, she can take care of herself. But the car didn't even pull away from the house proper before Peppy start the hollering herself. And she never stop even when Walter come to pick her up two days later.

II

It didn't take long for Rudi and Peppy to become best of friends. But not even that could replace the empty feelings she have inside her belly sometimes since Aunty Cora leave. Him tell Peppy him more than glad she come, for it was lonesome up there with only Jeff and Rosa to talk to. After Gwennie left, him tell her, Dave and Del went down to Mile Gully to live with Grandma and Grandpa. She know Rudi miss his mother, even though him refuse to talk about it. Him say Rosa don't really remember her, but Jeff still cry sometimes.

Sometimes Peppy notice Rudi's face puckering-up. Not often though, only whenever the mother send letter, always via Percy Clock, once a month. And she would always hold his hand in hers, watching as the eye water bubble-up, then drip down slowly. And it cause Peppy to wonder why the mother leave them and gone for such a long time, if she didn't miss them and was just as unhappy. She could understand if the mother was only gone for a little while, but four years seem way too much.

Peppy still have Aunty Cora's first letter fold up neat at the bottom of her suitcase. It come several weeks after her departure, with a crispy ten dollar bill wrap-up inside. Standing outside the gate by the mailbox that afternoon, heart pumping hard inside her chest, face gleeful, she could hardly wait to tear open the letter. She slip the money deep inside her blue school uniform pocket.

First, Aunty Cora announce her safe arrival, thank Jesus. But Lord, the plane ride way too long. Three whole hours. It's not easy to sit down so long in one place a tall, strap down, can barely shift, bend or do anything. And the reason why it so bad, she write, is that unlike the inside of a motor car where you pass trees and people and dog and house at the roadside, all you can see through the little peep hole them call window is more and more clouds. Only the plane alone big, she state in the letter, everything else no bigger than me little finger. Little plate of food, little cup of water, even the shot of rum them serve, little bit.

Further down the page, she write about her close encounter with her Saviour. It was in the bathroom, Aunty Cora say, so small, she pass it near three times before figuring it out. Then inside is another matter altogether, for by the time she open the door and let herself in, there was only room to do her business, nothing else. Then while she in the bathroom, the plane start to drop. And with every drop, her belly start to drop too. Right away, she could tell it was time to go Home. She didn't know it would be in airplane, but the Bible say the Lord works in mysterious ways. And so when the red button in the toilet start to flash and say she must return and strap down in her seat, she didn't know what to do. She start to sweat, everything going round and round, and by the time she come to, she was back in her seat, strap down, with the air hostess, a nice tall child, asking her if she alright.

By the time Peppy finish reading, it was almost as if Aunty Cora hadn't left a tall. She fold it up and put it back inside the envelope and then put it in her pocket next to the money. She could hardly wait till Rudi return from Percy Clock's house the evening to tell him the news.

Him say him feel happier now since Peppy been living with them. 'Things used to be really bad,' him tell her as the two of them sit down under the big mango tree behind the house, 'especially after Mama left. Daddy would always drink, always complain about how we run up the electricity bills, how we nasty-up the walls.

'Then Jeff used to get sick from the asthma all the time. Sometimes two months straight. Can't breathe, can't talk, can't even put on clothes to got to the hospital. Most nights Daddy never come home. Me alone have to hire taxi and pay for medication.

'I used to give Daddy the money Mama send once a month, like damn idiot. But then me stop for him wouldn't buy Jeff shoes for school or give me money for the house. Him probably used to pay off his debts with it. Then him start to spite me. Wouldn't pay any of the big bills. Everything fall down on me shoulders. One whole month them cut off the lights and Daddy wouldn't turn it back on. Another time him wouldn't pay the rent. Three, four times a day the Chinese man curse and quarrel. Finally when him come with the truck to move us out, letter come and I was able to pay the rent.'

When Peppy hear this, all she could do is shake her head. For sometimes even now, if it wasn't for Percy Clock, many a night them would go to bed hungry. Now and again him come by, hands rarely empty. Sometimes him bring bread and milk, othertimes meat. But him don't come often, not since the day Walter threaten to call the police if him ever set foot in his house again. This was about two months after the mother left, Rudi explain to her.

'Percy come by to see me the evening. Him knock. Daddy meet him up at the door. And I don't know,' Rudi look off into the distance, 'maybe him never see Daddy's car park up under the orange tree or maybe him just never care. But all I hear was the commotion outside.

And when I step out there, I hear Daddy shouting at the top of his voice and asking Percy if him come to poison the children's mind against him, if mashing up his marriage wasn't enough.' And almost as if to clarify whatever thinking was going on inside Peppy's head, Rudi tell her, 'You see, him think Percy the reason me mother leave.' Rudi clear his throat.

'And poor Percy only grin as if nothing a tall the matter, but you could see the fright in his face. Him tell Daddy no need to quarrel, him and Mama just friends, almost like brother and sister. But Daddy didn't care, him move towards Percy with fists fold up, and by the time I could bawl out, Percy was running up the street, leaving only dust behind him.'

Rudi say him never see Percy again until about a month later park up outside the school gate. There was have another man in the car, a tall man, tall and slim and good looking, with his hair cut short and a slight moustache growing. Percy call Rudi to the car and introduce him to the man inside, Martel. Then them drive away together. Percy tell Rudi him hear from Gwennie and that from now on she will send money once a month by way of him.

Rudi don't offer out much information about the mother. Sometimes Peppy is the one who have to ask how she doing, if she alright, for him don't usually show her the letters to read. Him keep everything personal. Sometimes him answer that she okay, other times, him just shrug his shoulders and mumble something under his breath.

One time she boldly ask him if his mother didn't plan to come back. 'I thought she was only gone for few months.' The two of them were lying down inside the bed them share, her head up at the top, his down at the bottom. The lights were off and the house was quiet except for Walter's light snores coming from the room at the other end of the passageway. Outside one or two cars toot as them drive pass the house.

Rudi shift his foot. 'Yeah, she was only supposed to go for vacation, but she decide to stay.'

'How come?'

'More work over there. Chance for better schooling.' Him sigh, uncomfortable.

'Then, what your father say about it?'

Rudi kiss his teeth. 'What him must say. All him do is drink white rum and curse every day.'

'She plan to come back?'

'She want all of us to come over. She say she have a lawyer who trying to get her a permanent visa. And that the lawyer looking about papers for us too, but everything take a long time. She say she want the older ones to come over first, like me and Delores and Dave, so we can work and help pay for the house she trying to buy. Then after that, she plan to send for the others so them can finish school.'

Peppy wonder to herself if she included as well. 'When you going to leave?' she ask Rudi.

His feet shift round. 'I think it depends on the lawyer. After him give the okay, she will mail out application forms. She plan to send extra money so we can get physical and passport pictures.'

Plenty time pass before Peppy ask her other question: 'You miss her?'

'Sometimes,' Rudi answer, sighing kind of loud as if frustrated by all this questioning. Peppy could hear the irritation straining through. 'But she write all the time. She send barrel every Christmas with plenty clothes and food and things for the house.

'She send clothes for Daddy. But him refuse to wear them. When his friends come over, him show them the clothes and laugh. I can't bear that man,' Rudi say through his teeth after shifting round his feet again. 'I can't wait to leave from this blasted place.'

Him turn onto his belly afterwards, and not long after, Peppy could hear his breathing deep and even. She couldn't help but feel sorry for him. Each day the same. Him cook and tidy house, wash clothes and take care of Rosa. The remainder of time him walk around the house glum forehead always in a furrow. Since graduation from high school, him wanted to enrol up at the University about a mile from the house. But Rosa only two and can't start school yet, so him stay home since the money Gwennie send not enough to pay baby sitter.

'I hate to do it,' Rudi complain to her all the time. 'It make me feel like a woman too much. Coop up inside the damn house all day with this frigging baby. And is not even mine.'

Peppy never usually know what to say when him get like this, hostile, irritable. Is only for a short while longer, she would tell him, but him only kiss his teeth and kick whatever in reach.

The only thing that seem to liven him up though, is the weekend visits to Percy Clock's house. For him would always come back bubbly-bubbly and full of stories about the various places them dine, Martel's matches box collection, Percy Clock's grandiose house that have a figurine collection on display inside a large glass chest, imported Venezuelan rugs you barely want to walk on, hand-made furniture from some country or other you afraid to sit on. And when is not news about fabulous restaurants and ostentatious dishes is about Martel's dance class where him teach folk, and how when him dance, a more tall and graceful sight you can't behold.

And so one day when Rudi was going on and on about the two men, Peppy couldn't help but ask him: 'What's the position between Martel and Percy?' She didn't mean anything by it really. For she know him don't have many friends. But there was something peculiar about the way them relate. Something funny about the kinds of presents she hear Percy give Martel. Gold ring at Christmas. Bracelets at Easter. Special kinds of underclothes that fit certain ways.

Rudi look at her, face sobering up all of a sudden.

Him look thinner Peppy think, jawbone sink in more. Clothes just hang off. She like the new moustache him start to grow. Look more dignified with it, especially when him laugh and you can see the dimple in his chin. She know him growing it to look like Martel's.

'How you mean?' His eyes, deep set and round like Grandpa's, look from beyond hers to somewhere over her head-top.

'Well, them not family, yet everyday Martel driving up in his car, everyday him over his house, everyday . . .'

'Them good friends,' Rudi shout at her. 'Good friends like you and Jasmine. Or like you and Vin. You understand. Good friends.'

Rudi stomp out the kitchen the day, and Peppy just look on till him disappear inside the room and slam the door.

III

The second letter to Peppy from Aunty Cora come two months after the first. She did have plenty to say about her eye operation and the two weeks stay in the hospital. She still can't see properly yet, even though them take out the eyes and scrape off the cataract, everyday she have to wear a bandage, rest whole heap, and only for few hours wear the special glasses them give her. Aunty Cora say the special glasses so thick and heavy, that to make sure it don't constantly fall down on her nose and cut off her air supply, she have to tie it up firm around her head with a strong piece of English cord.

Aunty Cora say she hope things going well and that Peppy getting along with Walter. Peppy pause after she read this. For if Aunty Cora did only know what took place in the house this pass week, she would jump on the next plane and come take her away. Rudi still shaken-up about the incident. Him walk round the house like duppy, not a sound, not a smile, nothing.

It happen the evening Martel come over. Him don't visit often. But whenever him come, is grand occasion, for Rudi like his company and him always have interesting tales to tell. All three of them were in the room, Peppy, Rudi and Martel, sitting down on the bed, talking, the room door half-way open. Not much was in the room: only Gwennie's old Singer machine that Rudi use to sew Jeff's khaki school uniform and dresses for Rosa; a small table housing Charlie and Brut spray colognes, a bottle of underarm deodorant, a few mystery and romance paperbacks, and the book of poetry Rudi borrow from the Branch Library.

And as them go on talk, them never hear when Walter push his key into the lock, turn it and slide open the glass door to the house. It seems as if him never drive the car that evening, for the muffler have a tendency to rattle and roar with such ferocity, frightening any hard-of-hearing person out of the way.

Walter did have to pass Rudi and Peppy's room on route to his own. And it was the sound of the strange man's voice coming through the door that stop him, it seems. For without even a knock or a hesitation, him kick open the door so hard with his shoes, the door handle slam-up into the wall, chipping off a little bit. Three pairs of eyes open-up-wide turn to him as him walk over and stand up in front of Martel. Silence deafen the room.

'Who are you, sir?' Walter's voice was slurred from the plenty rum drinking.

Martel stand up same time and extend his hand. But Walter only turn away his head in scorn.

'You,' him point to Rudi's face, 'you think you own this blasted place? Inviting your friends in here as if your damn name on the lease. Or is your sister you bring him here to?' Walter turn to Peppy who was standing with her back to the door.

Peppy roll her eyes and kiss her teeth, disgust write all over her face. Walter slap after her face with his hand, but Peppy was too alert, she duck his hand, and slide out the door, out the room.

'Blasted little shit!' Walter call out, staggering off balance.

Now all of this happen so quick, Rudi and Martel still never have a chance to do anything. Them just continue sitting on the bed edge looking on.

'You,' Walter walk over to Martel, after regaining some kind of composure.

'Leave him alone,' Rudi pipe in, stepping between Martel and his father. 'Is me friend.'

'Friend,' scorn fill Walter's voice. 'You think is your blasted house. Bringing in people like you have a mind. You better hurry up and go to you mother, that worthless thing. That old whore.'

'Leave me mother out of this.' Thunder rattle out of Rudi's voice. 'Leave her out of this.' Peppy could hear it filling the house. Jeff and Rosa huddle behind her.

'That no-good wretch. That fucking old whore.' Walter's face was close up to Rudi's, eyes barely open. 'Pick up her tail. Leave me alone with the whole bunch of you, ungrateful wretches. Is which man she over there with, huh, which man? She leave the other fool here and gone.'

Martel try to pull away Rudi, but him wouldn't budge. Rudi and his father were about the same height, except Rudi was a little bit more broad in the shoulders, Walter's body was running down. 'You think you is man, now,' Walter taunt him, 'you think you big now . . .'

Peppy was outside when she hear the noise and then the grunt, and when she run back into the room, with Jeff and Rosa behind, Walter was holding Rudi by the throat, back ram-up into the wall. Martel did have his bag in hand. Not long after, him slip out.

Rudi's eyes bulge out. Him try opening his mouth, gasping loud as him struggle for air. But Walter hang on, cursing all the while. Him curse Rudi. Him curse Gwennie. Him curse Grandma. Hand refusing to ease off from around Rudi's throat.

Peppy wasn't sure where the force came from all of a sudden, but in a flash she find herself on Walter's back, tugging him one way, pushing him another, till him lose balance and stumble to one side, his grip onto Rudi's throat finally loosening. But him start on Peppy.

'You little shit,' him bawl out, pulling her clothes from off hangers inside the closet, flinging them on the floor, trampling on them. 'Don't let morning catch you in here. Take you shit and go. Go back to New Green. You not me pickney, me not you father. Out of the kindness of me heart I take you in. But you not good, you just like you mother, damn ungrateful same way. Take you shit and leave me house tonight. And you,' him turn to Rudi who was back to normal by this time, armed with the only thing in reach, the broom him use to sweep out the room earlier before Martel's arrival, 'you and she pack your shit and leave. Don't make I see you in here tomorrow.'

And as him go on quarrel and fling out more clothes and shoes and books, Peppy get to thinking. She was sitting down outside on the carport by this time, but she could still hear him inside cursing, quarrelling, pacing round and round. And she wonder what Walter mean exactly when him say she not his pickney. Him not her father. She wonder how much it have to do with the story Vin did accidentally tell her one evening.

It happen while she was still living at New Green. Vin was fifteen years old then, Peppy eleven. Vin was in the kitchen cooking dinner. Peppy did have on her new watch with the round face and thin black band that Walter give her on her last birthday. Aunty Cora caution her against wearing it unless is big occasion, but she was too eager to show it off. Peppy was sitting on top the mortar them use to parch coffee and pound corn. Vin was close by, on the hearth near the fireside, making flour dumplings to put in the pot. Flour dust was in her hair and sprinkled over her shiny face.

'You like it,' Peppy ask her, limping her wrist so Vin could have a better look.

Vin shrug. 'It alright.'

'Me father give it to me. Also the gold chain, the one with the cross on it. Him buy me bag for school too, and shoes. Him always buying me things. You know the red and purple . . .'

'You know him is not your father,' Vin lift off the pot cover and drop in the seven dumplings she just made. The steam was hot, and so she scowl up her face.

Peppy look at Vin as she cover the pot and start to peel green bananas. Vin's frock was dirty, speckled white from the flour dust. It had a tear by the underarm. She never have on any shoes. Peppy's frock was dirty too. Them been playing dandy-shandy all afternoon.

'But is where you get this nonsense from though, Vin?' Peppy laugh out loud. 'Of course him is me father. Who else could it be.'

'Somebody else.' A glint shine-on up in Vin's eye, but then her face cloud over and a furrow appear on her forehead. 'Maybe, me shouldn't tell you.'

'No. Tell me. Tell me.' Scorn was in Peppy's voice, disbelief on her face. 'What you know about me father?'

'You have to promise not to tell.'

'Lightning strike me down, dead.' Peppy make the sign of the cross over her chest.

'Alright.' Vin swallow saliva. 'Aunt Doris . . . well, me overhear her telling somebody that Mass Walter isn't your father. That your father is another man.' She lift up the pot again, scowl up her face, drop in the peeled green bananas one by one, and cover back the pot. Then she start to season up the chicken she and Peppy did kill and pick earlier. 'Them never mention his name. Only that him used to work on bridge. Contractor man.'

'Lie.' Peppy jump up from off her seat on the mortar. 'Pure lie. All because you jealous. All because you don't have father.'

Vin kiss her teeth. 'Go way, me have father. Him live abroad.'

'Yeah. Then show me what him give you.' Peppy did have two feet plant apart, arms akimbo, eyes flashing. 'Show me what him give you. Him give you clothes? Him send you watch? Him post you money now and again.'

'No, but is me father, nevertheless. Me know it and everybody else too.'

Peppy look at Vin long and hard. Eye water was in her eyes, but she wasn't going to let Vin see it. But Vin wasn't even looking the whole time. She sorry she did ever open her mouth and say anything. Peppy grab up her paper ball, and tell Vin she gone home. 'Don't tell anybody,' Vin call after her, but Peppy never answer.

And even after Aunty Cora confirm and tell her yes is true, Walter not her father, she continued to wrap and weigh sugar, as if nothing a tall unusual about the question, even though the glass of rum she was drinking afterwards did have plenty more rum than water in it. But not another word mention about it. Aunty Cora and Grandma and everybody continue on calling Walter her father, and she just continue on to think the same thing, except for now. Now, Walter own self was saying it.

And Peppy start to fret, from where she sit down outside, her face long and sad-looking, her chin lean-up on her knee and her body bend over. For she didn't have any place to go. She too afraid of Leslie to go back to New Green by herself. Even Miss Gertie never stay long after Aunty Cora leave, she hear, for she and Leslie couldn't get on. The only other place she could go and stay is with Grandma, but then again it so far from her school.

And as Peppy go on fret and worry about where she going to live till Aunty Cora come back, Rudi came out and sat down next to her in the darkness. All she could see was the white of his eyes and his teeth. There wasn't a moon or a star up in the sky the night.

'Don't let him bother you,' Rudi's voice was shaky. 'Him just drunk and crazy as usual.'

'But you hear him,' Peppy bawl out, 'you hear him say me must leave for me not his pickney, him not me father.'

Rudi kiss him teeth. 'Him don't mean it. Before you come, him used to say the same thing about all of us. Jeff, Dave, me, Delores and Rosa, him say all of us don't belong to him.' Rudi pause. 'Him just crazy and crack-crack when him drink. Don't worry, tomorrow him back to normal. We can't leave. For who will look after Jeff and Rosa? Him just running his mouth as usual.'

And Peppy did stop the fretting for the time being. It didn't quite sit easy with her, what Rudi tell her, it didn't quite clear up all of the questions forming themselves in her mind, but Rudi must know. Him live with the man longer than she. Him must know. She was afraid to tell Rudi what Vin tell her, for she don't want him feel bad for his mother. But she still have plenty questions.

And so as Peppy turn back to Aunty Cora's letter in her hand, she couldn't help but think about the distance that grow between she and Walter ever since she come. Things were okay the first few months. Them used to get on. Evening time when him come home, him used to call her to come and watch television with him. After the news, him used to talk to her about school or what she plan to be when she turn woman. Sometimes on Saturdays, him bring her to visit his friends. Him used to brag to them about how she smart, how her head quick, how she pass exam and get into high school, and how she get the braininess from his side of family.

During this time, too, him used to take her into his confidence about Rudi. 'The boy not good,' him tell her. 'Imagine, the mother send money and the boy don't hand me a penny. Me alone have to pay everything. The boy take the money and carouse with his friends.' Then Walter would grab her hand and squeeze it. 'I don't want you to mix up yourself with him and his friends. The whole lot of them no blasted good.' And then him would ask if she understand what him saying, and she wasn't quite sure if she should answer 'Yes, Daddy,' for it don't sound good to her, or call him 'Walter' like Aunty Cora. So she always end up saying just 'Yes' and nothing else.

But after listening to Walter and then spending time with Rudi, she couldn't help but take Rudi's side, for is him she see cook and clean and wash and sew, is him she see help the other ones with them homework, is him she see look after Jeff when him sick, is him she see go down to Grandma when food not in the house and carry back plenty baskets full. And yes, Walter carry home things sometimes, him chat up with Jeff and him love Rosa gone to bed, and him pay some of the big bills, but when him drunk, him stay bad, and him curse Rudi and the mother a whole heap. Now him curse Peppy too, for him say she join forces against him.

And is not like she didn't have pity for him when she first saw him drunk. She was sad. But after she see the complete change that come over, the constant cursing, the constant bickering about everything, pretty soon, it wasn't pity anymore but scorn. And the picture she did have of him just start to shatter. And it make her think about how she used to brag about him, how she used to love show her friends at New Green the things him buy her or the places him bring her to. And even at school, she used to brag to her friends, tell them not only she have father, for plenty of them grow with them granny, but her father teach agricultural skills down at the Youth Centre at Porous, him not farmer like most of her friends' father. She used to love add on too, that her mother live abroad and she send out barrel with plenty things two and three times a year. Now she don't mention him a tall if she can help it.

And so these days if she in the living room watching television or listening to the radio, or just reading, the minute his car pull up in the driveway, she bolt to her room and shut the door behind her, for she can't bear to see him anymore. And Rudi do the same thing. The only person to go out and talk to him is Jeff when him not sick with the asthma. And even when him curse Jeff, Jeff still continue to bring him his dinner, that Rudi leave cover-up in the kitchen.

But anyway, Peppy decide she not going to think about these things anymore, for Aunty Cora soon come back and she will make things alright again. She turn back to the letter in hand. Aunty Cora say she went up to Connecticut and spend one whole week up there with Gwennie. She say the house Gwennie buy nice in truth, it have plenty big rooms, and a place outside to plant flowers and vegetables. But she say the house empty, not a bit of furniture to sit down on, only a small table in the kitchen and her bed. Aunty Cora say she get a chance to clear up plenty things she been wanting to talk to Gwennie about for years.

But Gwennie not happy a tall, her jawbone sink-in bad, same way her eyes, the way she work hard and fret about her children. Gwennie was on break when me go up there, but usually she work as live-in helper during the week, and on the weekends, she clean house for another family. Gwennie say sometimes when she handling the baby belonging to the people she work for, eye water fill her eyes when she think about her own Rosa who don't have mother or father. She say sometimes when she come home, the house just empty and dead. No shoes sprawl careless in the doorway to kick out the way, no sound of the children's voice as them chat and argue. She say she miss you children bad-bad, Rudi especially, who probably want to live his own life by now, Jeff and the bad asthma, and you, Peppy, she want to know how you taking to your lessons. She say her belly grieve her when she hear from Clara how Walter treating the children bad, for Rudi don't mention it when him write her, and all she can do is pray to God things will work out with the lawyer.

Aunty Cora say most every weekends, Egbert and Martin have party, and she drink and dance plenty and meet whole heap of people and family she don't see in years. The Foreign rum really weak, she complain, and was glad that she bring plenty of the real thing from back home, for if is Foreign rum to save life and ease up bad feelings, she stone dead as bird. She tell Peppy she hear from Buddy, Leslie's father, him call early one Sunday morning from England and him coming out soon to see everybody. So she will have to paint and clean up the house when she come back home so it can look good for him. In closing, Aunty Cora say her six months almost up, and she can't wait to see Peppy. She hope she behaving herself nicely and doing well in school. The letter did sign off: Love MaCora.

PART FIVE

I

Two weeks before Aunty Cora come back, Peppy pick up herself and go over to New Green. She ask Jeff if him interested in accompanying her, but him say no, so she go by herself. She wasn't sure what got into her the evening as she jump on the bus, but she guess she was just longing to see Leslie and George and Miss Irene and Vin, for after all, them more like family to her.

Most everybody on the bus know her and was glad to see her. Some of them school children, some market women, others of them contractor men coming from work. Them tell her how hers and Aunty Cora's face miss plenty-plenty in New Green, especially down the shop and on Sundays at Communion. And Peppy was happy to see them, for New Green people always warm and loving to her. Them wanted to know how she doing at school, if she enjoy living with her father, when Miss Cora coming back, if she plan to bring things for them little boy, Junior, who don't have shoes to wear to school September coming, or them little girl, Stephanie, whose only church frock on the last. But Peppy only smile and nod her head, yes, Aunty Cora soon come back, but she don't know what she plan to bring.

The bus let her off in front the shop, and Peppy's breath pull in same time. The walls needed a decent coat of painting, not to mention the fence Aunty Cora white-wash every Easter with the limestone mix. That lay tumble-over on the grass, with plenty idlers sitting on top, swinging feet, looking on. Peppy suck her teeth under her breath. If Aunty Cora was still running it, it wouldn't look so disgraceful.

Several bad words reach her ears as she move slowly inside the shop. Aunty Cora never used to allow people to curse in her presence, not to mention gambling inside the shop. Three men sit down around a small square table gambling with cards. Them call out 'howdy do' as she step inside, and Peppy grudgingly force out 'howdy do' in return.

Mass Ernest's picture replace Aunty Cora's on the wall. Other family members paste-up elsewhere. Peppy put down thirty-five cents on the counter and order a bottle of aerated water, champagne flavour. It feel strange buying from her own shop. Mass Ernest pull off the stopper, and she turn the bottle to her head sucking down nearly half. Mass Ernest watch her from the corners of his eyes, so she couldn't really scrutinize the shop as she have a mind. It was dark though, like him don't open all the windows, and the glass case and barrel weren't there anymore. A big table was there instead, and men play dominoes on it. Not much canned goods on the dust and cob-web laden shelves either, mostly liquor.

'Miss Cora soon come back?' Mass Ernest jerk out, eyes following Peppy's.

She suck down more of her soda. 'Two more weeks.' The men gambling look up as she answer and turn back round when she finish. She put down the empty bottle on the counter. 'Anybody see Leslie or George?'

One of the gamblers raise his head, 'Leslie was down here earlier, but him gone up. No sign of George, though.'

Peppy tell him thanks and step through the door, the scent of stale cigarette and day-old beer clinging to her nostrils. Turning the corner at the cedar tree, she call out hello to Miss Beatrice, and her spoil daughter, Angie, to Mr Rob and his new live-in woman. Up ahead she could see MaDee's tomb, the old out-house, white clothes billowing on the line, but no sign of Leslie or George. Peppy walk on up.

The grass in front the house grow up tall. She wonder if Leslie or George plan to cut it before Aunty Cora's return. Making her way up to the verandah overlooking the garden fill up with weeds now, she listen for a familiar voice, or hoop. But everything dead-quiet. She run into Leslie.

'Oh, is you!' Him sound glad to see her. 'I heard the person coming up the steps. How things?'

Peppy shrug, 'Just come to see everybody.'

'Well, is about time. From you leave, you don't even drop a line. Let me know if you still living.' Leslie was short and meager-body, have plenty spaces between all his teeth, and little strands of beard popping out on his chin. Him always pull them while speaking. 'I get me first letter from MaCora just the other day.'

Peppy nod, following him inside the house. She careful not to mention that is four letters she get from Aunty Cora so far. 'Your father coming out.'

Leslie stroke his chin. 'I hope him can take me back to England with him this time.'

Peppy wonder if Leslie wasn't tired of waiting. Him been singing the same Sankey ever since she can remember.

'Where George and Miss Irene?'

'Walk about as usual.'

'I hear that Miss Gertie gone.'

Leslie kiss his teeth. 'What a way news can travel. Couldn't bear her any more, man.'

'MaCora know?'

'MaCora don't matter right now. Me in charge. You hungry?'

'Little bit.'

Leslie leave the room and Peppy look about her. She wonder why him rearrange the furniture. If him plan for Aunty Cora to see it like this.

'You notice how the shop nasty and dirty?' Leslie walk silently into the room with a bowl of soup. Him place it in front Peppy. 'It would never look like that if MaCora did give it to me. Allow me to run it till she come back.'

'I thought she just wanted to rent it out. Get rid of it. Let somebody else take care of it.'

'Yes, but me and George could've run it. Me and George could've taken care of it. We was only in there for few months before she take away the key and complain how we can't do business. She didn't give me a proper chance.'

Peppy didn't say anything else to him, for she know Aunty Cora would rather have family in the shop than renting it out. The few months she allow Leslie to run it, things just start to go bad. For according to Aunty Cora, Leslie not only trust out plenty of the goods to friends, but him wouldn't get up out of bed early enough in the mornings and open the shop, so early-morning-people can get bread or crackers before them go on to work or school.

Other thing was Leslie's lack of respect towards Aunty Cora's older friends causing them to crawl up the hill to the house, no matter how sick and arthritic them was feeling, and to complain how them miss her bad-bad in the shop, for her grandboy, Leslie, don't treat nor talk to them decent. Leslie and Aunty Cora did have it out the Sunday evening.

'Give me the shop keys,' she tell him. 'For if you can't act decent to the customers, it don't spell sense you run business. Business not just buy and sell,' she warn him, 'it take me and Anderson plenty years to turn friends with New Green people. I can't allow you to mash up everything I spend years build.'

Leslie kiss his teeth and fling down the set of keys. 'I can't bear to live with you,' him tell her. 'I can't wait for the day when me father come and take me away. You not interested in me. You not interested in giving me a chance. Peppy alone get chance.'

Aunty Cora grab up her stick to lick him, but Leslie didn't move, him stand up in front her same way waiting till she strike so him could unfurl all his frustration and fury on her.

Aunty Cora let the stick drop back on the floor. Her face seem older than usual to Peppy who was watching from the corner of the doorway. Aunty Cora brush her two hands and shake her head. Eye water was in her voice. 'I finish with you, Mass Leslie, for I see that you ready to lift your hand and strike me. And when a child who me raise, whose shit I been cleaning from birth, who me work hard to feed, done grow big and ready to strike me when I talk to them, I done with you.

'Boy who I spend so much money on. I send you go to trade school, for your head so hard you couldn't pass exam to high school. But you curse the man you apprentice with and leave trade school. I give you a piece of land and few heads of cow, and say go farm, well, the cows almost drop down dead for water, for you wouldn't feed them. The one time you plant anything, grass grow over it and kill it, for you wasn't interested in taking care of it. You say you want motorbike to get around, I buy you a motorbike. Well, the motorbike park up around the house corner. I finish with you, boy.' And with that song, Aunty Cora get up, bend over pick up the set of keys off her bedroom floor, and hobble away on her stick.

'You notice how the place just dark and dirty,' Leslie say to her, breaking into her thinking. 'But that's the way she prefer it. My own granny. Shit, boy,' him say after a while, 'when you have a granny like that, you don't need enemy.'

'Me might go to Foreign,' Peppy tell him, changing the subject.

His forehead furrow-up all of a sudden. 'Miss Gwennie sending for you?'

She sorry she tell him, for first of all she wasn't sure, and secondly she didn't like the sudden edge that attach itself to his voice.

'Well, she sending for all the children.'

'Huh,' Leslie sigh. 'You lucky. If it wasn't for MaCora, I would be in England now.'

Peppy concentrate on her soup, sipping each spoonful carefully. Him was sitting across from her fixing a small transistor, the contents of its belly sprawl out on the table. These days him into technical work, before that it was carpentry, and before that tailoring.

'I going up to Vin's house after I finish eating,' Peppy tell him.

Leslie didn't answer right away. Him fling down a set of keys on the table. 'Don't bring in any of your boyfriends to come carouse now that MaCora not here. I know you.'

Peppy didn't even bother to look at him. She finish off her soup, pick up the keys, wash, rinse, turn down her plate and then make her way up to Brocton, where Vin live.

II

Aunty Cora came two weeks after that. Walking home from school the evening, Peppy spy the white Peugeot park up infront her father's house. She know right away it wasn't Walter's or Percy's car, so it have to be one other person. Water fill her eyes same time and she was afraid to go inside. Aunty Cora look younger and stronger. Seems as if Foreign agree with her in truth. She did have on the same thick and heavy glasses and was wearing the very same piece of English cord tie-up around her head to keep them off her nose.

'But look at me dying trial! Gal, you meagre!' Aunty Cora bawl out as Peppy walk towards her, eyes not paying mind to anybody else in the room. And when Aunty Cora get up from out the off-white sofa and stretch out her two hands, Peppy allow the tears to run down and wet up Aunty Cora's Foreign frock.

'But look at me dying trial!' Aunty Cora say again. 'What kinda cow bawling this?' She hand Peppy her white handkerchief with red and purple embroidery around the edges. 'Gal,' Aunty Cora say to her, after hugging, and settling herself back in the couch, 'how things?'

Peppy never answer right away. She wish Rudi and Jeff and Rosa and Aunty Cora's two friends weren't there. She wish the two of them were alone, so them could talk freely. 'Me alright.'

'How Walter treating you?'

Peppy's eyes reach Rudi's and both sets turn away at the same time. 'Alright.'

'Just alright?'

Peppy nod, shifting her weight from one foot to the other.

'Well, gal,' Aunty Cora say to her when she see she couldn't get much out of Peppy with so many people about, 'as long as you can stand up on your two feet, that must mean you alright in truth.'

Peppy wanted to fling herself down inside Aunty Cora's lap and hug her good and plenty, but she pull up a chair instead and sit down next to her.

'Come down Saturday,' Aunty Cora tell her. 'Then we can talk whole heap. I miss you, gal. Plenty, plenty.'

Well, the Saturday morning could barely break before Peppy tidy herself and hop onto the bus eager to spend time with Aunty Cora again. But as she comb her hair that morning, paying special attention to her appearance in the mirror, she couldn't ignore the gloominess lodged inside her heart corner. And it didn't just start up since Aunty Cora's return, it's been growing steadily for a while now.

She know Aunty Cora will want her to come back and live in New Green especially since Miss Gertie gone. But she wasn't sure she wanted to go back. She and Rudi grow close over the months. She like to spend time and talk with him plenty. Neither George nor Leslie or even Vin hold her interest much anymore, even though them feel more like family to her in some ways. But it was more special with Rudi. These days she feel even closer to him, since him tell her his story.

Sometimes she feel so happy for him, she want to share it with friends at school, but she know she have to keep it confident. It's amazing how well she can read him. Know exactly when to give him a walk, when to spend time, and when some topics make him more bashful than usual. She could tell from several weeks beforehand that something important was on his mind. Every time the two of them alone and the moment seem perfect, him would suddenly get up and turn on the radio, wipe off the counter, or dust down windows. Night time, when the two off them lie still inside the bed, him make sure silence don't linger between them, sometimes talking till long after she drop asleep.

Finally one afternoon him turn to her: 'Remember when you ask me what was the position between Percy and Martel?'

Peppy feel the grin spreading over her face. She know exactly what was coming next. She nod her head and look pass Rudi.

'Well,' him take a deep breath, clearing his throat, 'them together.' Him say it slow, as if uncertain about the timing, then him raise his head and look at Peppy.

Peppy continue to look pass him. Then in a voice trying its best to remain calm and nonchalant, she say to him: 'I know about those things. MaCora tell me about those things all the time.'

Him look at Peppy close, surprise in his eyes. 'Really!'

'Well, you know if you spend plenty time inside a shop, you hear people talk about things. And one time them was talking about this man. Them call him batty-man and was laughing about it.

'So that night when shop lock and me and MaCora was walking home, I mention it to her. And she start to whoop, lasting about four whole minutes. Then she tell me that's what them call men who love other men. And she say nothing wrong with it, but plenty people don't like hear about it. But as far as she concern, people can do whatever them damn well please with whichever part of them body them damn well want. For them not paying taxes for it.'

Rudi grin, relaxing more.

'And you know what else?' Peppy's face was starting to glow. 'She tell me about this woman she used to study cooking and baking and decorating with. Miss Clementine. Rumour had it that Miss Clementine was sodomite. She used to do it with some of the other girls that study there.'

Rudi never say anything when Peppy finish talk. She try to remember other things Aunty Cora did say, but nothing come to mind.

'Well, I'm that way too,' Rudi say to her after a while, letting out a long sigh. 'I mean . . .'

'Nothing wrong with that,' Peppy blurt out. She wasn't sure what else to say. According to Pastor Longmore those things wrong. One Sunday in church, him mention how all those men who go to one another for love and affection had better change them ways, for God just going to shut the doors of heaven in them face. And from where she was sitting down inside the front pew with the rest of children her age, she did turn round to the back of the room to look at Aunty Cora, to see if she listening. For it was just several weeks before, that them discuss Miss Clementine. But Aunty Cora's head was bent forward as usual, as if praying. Beads of sweat gather-up crossway her forehead and she was fanning with her hymn book.

She could barely wait till the sermon to ask Aunty Cora about it.

'Lord, Peppy, man. The sermon was almost three hours long. How me to remember every thing, so?'

'Well, I mean the part about . . .' Peppy pause. She was sure Aunty Cora well know what she talking about. 'I mean when him was talking about those people who not going heaven . . . people like Miss Clementine, I mean.'

'But look at me dying trial! How you and Pastor Longmore know Miss Clementine not going to heaven.' Aunty Cora let out one of her long whoops.

Peppy was certain Miss Gertie going to put down her pipe and run come to find out what Aunty Cora laughing about, for Miss Gertie is a woman who love sweet joke. Peppy wish Aunty Cora would keep quiet and get back to the subject at hand.

Aunty Cora never say anything for a while. The two of them was sitting on the verandah steps, sun gone down for the day, moon lurking somewhere in the distance. 'What a way you interested in these things,' she finally let out. 'Other times, all you do is chat-up chat-up with your friends while Pastor Longmore preaching. Anyway,' she breath in deep, 'you growing. You will understand better as you grow. But not everybody interpret things the same as I tell you. Bible say one thing, John Brown say another. Bible big and open wide. It say plenty things, it mean plenty more other things.'

Aunty Cora wasn't making herself clear, but Peppy think she understand.

'Then how you must know what to believe? How one must know right from wrong?' she ask her.

'Gal, pickney, life is mystery own self. You growing, you will see. Sometimes is you alone, you have to make choices. Sometimes you find out right and wrong only through trial and error. Other times is only by what feel good deep down inside your belly bottom. Nothing else.' Aunty Cora left it at that. She say she was feeling tired and needed to lay down a little. Peppy remain outside on the verandah even after Aunty Cora leave, fanning away mosquitoes. She could smell Miss Gertie's tobacco close by.

Peppy's mind turn back to the situation at hand with Rudi. The silence in the room was overbearing. She wonder where Jeff and Rosa, if them outside playing, or if them listening. She look across on Rudi, perch-up uncomfortable on the hassock, twirling the thin line of moustache that resemble Martel's.

'You have a fellow?' Peppy stutter little bit. 'I mean, you have somebody who . . .'

'I know what you mean.' Rudi stretch out his legs. 'I have one friend.'

Peppy didn't like the way the conversation was taking shape. She wanted him to talk to her with the same kind of confidence, the same kind of enthusiasm, that him use when talking about Martel and Percy, or about the people him dance with down at the Cultural Centre where him start to take lessons. Now him just say one thing and pause, waiting till she say the other bit, before starting again. She want him to talk, like the way Aunty Cora talk, so everything can sound alright.

'So tell me,' she press him, 'tell me his name, what him look like, where you meet. Tell me everything. I want know.'

And Rudi was shy at first, for him was afraid. But then it start to pour out plenty, almost like water through pipe that have wear-out washer, little bit at first, then as the washer get worse, more and more. And him tell Peppy about the boy, Terence, jet black with white-white teeth. And how Terence used to go to the Youth Camp where Walter teach and how them just used to only say howdy-do at first and never quite talk. Then one night, Rudi see him at party and them start to talk.

And Peppy just sit down and listen, for the way Rudi was talking now, confident-like, she could tell that whatever him say was alright, for it sound like it was feeling good to him deep down in his belly bottom. And even when Rudi reach to the part about where them kiss, her hand-middle was still dry, and her breathing never change pace, she only grin instead, and him grin back in return, fingers playing with the thin-line moustache, same way.

So when Rudi tell her these personal things, Peppy feel almost like she and him is one, like them is true brother and sister. And she tell him about her friend at school, Jasmine, and how Jasmine's mother was that way too. For according to Jasmine, that was what cause the final split between her parents, but she already suspected it, because her mother and the lady was much too close. Jasmine say she don't really mind, for the lady nice and treat she, Jasmine, and her two brothers good. And since her father was only part-time anyway, it don't really matter, for she didn't know him well.

During the story about Jasmine's mother she notice him relaxing more and more. And it make her feel even closer to him, like she would do anything to protect him, to make sure him feel comfortable all the time. And as these things run through Peppy's mind as she make her way up to Aunty Cora's house the Saturday morning, she come to a decision about what she going to tell Aunty Cora.

Aunty Cora was stretched out on her big, four-poster bed, when Peppy push open the door and step inside her room. It smelt of arthritis rubbings and ointments as usual, with little Foreign scent mix-up with it. The barrel she bring back was resting near her bed. Plenty of the things from inside sprawl around on the floor.

'I dead tired, gal,' Aunty Cora say in greeting to Peppy.

Peppy walk over to her bed, and sit down at the foot. 'You must be really tired. Near twelve o'clock, and you still in bed.' Concern stain her voice.

Aunty Cora fix the pillows behind her head. 'Ever since I come back, I tired more than usual. I don't know is what. And then, I feel this lump moving around plenty inside me belly, too. Lord, gal, when is not one thing, is another. I have to go and see Doctor Lord.'

Peppy sigh. There now, Aunty Cora sick. Who will look after her?

'You hear anything about Miss Gertie?'

Aunty Cora shake her head. 'I send telegram to her son, so I waiting. Man, I don't know how me and Leslie going to make out. Everything that damn boy do raise me blood pressure.'

Peppy didn't say anything. She never usually know what to say when Aunty Cora complain about Leslie.

'Me talk with Gwennie,' Aunty Cora say after a long pause. 'She want you to come over with the other children.'

'Then, what about you?' Peppy ask first thing.

'What about me?' Aunty Cora fix the pillows behind her head again.

'Who going to look after you when you get sick? Who going to stay with you?' Peppy kick off her shoes and hop up inside the bed beside Aunty Cora, the two heads pressing into the pillows Aunty Cora just finish fluff-up.

'Lord, gal. You chat too much nonsense.' Aunty Cora fix the sheet around Peppy's feet.

'But me serious, MaCora.' Peppy's voice raise-up.

But Aunty Cora only murmur. After a long time, she say: 'Gal, I turn into old somebody now. I soon die and leave you. I want you to go to Foreign and get good schooling. I want you to get a good education, so you can turn out decent. Don't bother to think about me. Is your life now.'

Eye water gather up in Peppy's eyes. She try to hold them back. She

99

didn't want Aunty Cora to see her crying. She big now. Peppy shift round in the bed. Aunty Cora didn't move much. Just lie down still.

'I don't want to go Foreign. I don't even know me mother.' Peppy stop. The word sound strange to her. 'I don't even know her good, how me and she going to get on?'

Peppy did have plenty more questions, but Aunty Cora hush her up. 'Stop your damn foolishness. How you mean you don't want to go! You have big-big opportunity right in front your eyes and you mad want to fling it away. How you mean you don't want to go!' Aunty Cora was facing Peppy now. 'Gal, don't chat nonsense.' Her voice was firm. Peppy know the conversation near finish.

'But I don't know her, MaCora. How we going to get on?' Peppy's voice was firm too.

Aunty Cora sigh long and plenty. 'Don't bother about those things. Just think about going abroad. Think about education and to turn decent. Think about your future. New Green don't have future to give you, only baby and marriage, hungry-belly and poverty. I want you to have more.

'I want you to turn lawyer, or teacher or doctor, even business-woman. I don't want to see you with New Green boys, all them can give you is hungry-belly and plenty children. Things will work out with you and Gwennie. I know it. It won't be rosy at first. For you don't know one another well. But you have to try, and she too. But things will work out good.' And with that song, Aunty Cora put an end to the conversation. And after enough silence pass over them, she start up again.

'You will like the place, Hartford. Nice big shady trees. Gwennie's house right at the foot of a place them call Blue Hills or Fields, I can't quite remember. The Sunday evening I was staying there, her gentle-man friend drive us up there. Gal, you know big house!' Aunty Cora stop and look at Peppy, her eyes wide with wonder. 'Houses big and pretty with big lawn and big car and even swimming pool around back. Gwennie say it costly to live up there though, cheaper houses down at the bottom.

'And even then, if it wasn't for your uncle Samuel who bargain with the man, it would still cost more. But she say it better there than down on Milk Street.' Aunty Cora shake her head. 'Milk Street bad as yaws she say. Plenty gunmen and drugs and informer, just like them bad parts out here. Not safe. But you will just have to care yourself. Don't walk about at night, have company at all times. Believe in you Maker, go to church and pray.'

100

And when Aunty Cora finish about Hartford, she get up and show Peppy the things she carry back from Foreign. She show Peppy the pictures she take, the places she go, church, entertainment parks, zoo, Aunty Cora tell her how the snakes in America as wide as her bathtub, and as long as the entire rope of tobacco down the shop. She show Peppy the things she carry back for herself, curtains and bedspreads and lamps and lampshades and the weak rum, and she give Peppy the bag Gwennie send with food and clothes for the children. Peppy tell her Aunty Cora about school, about the new friends she meet, about Rudi's two friends Martel and Percy, about Rudi's school where him learn folk dance, and how the two of them do plenty things together. And throughout the whole time, not a word about coming back to New Green mention.

Peppy spend the Saturday with Aunty Cora and part of the Sunday. Sunday evening, she pick up herself and jump on the evening bus heading back to Porous. Aunty Cora never ask Peppy when she coming back, she only stand up at the verandah gate and watch Peppy as she turn down the hill, the glass of rum she have, swirling round and round in her hand. She never even move when she couldn't see Peppy anymore. She just turn the glass to her head and suck down the rum. Little bit run down her chin, Aunty Cora pick up her frock tail and wipe her mouth-corner, clean.

III

It usually take Peppy about thirty minutes to walk home from school each evening. And as she never have plenty friends living around her way, she walk by herself, cars and buses and trucks passing her by the roadside, school children in front and behind her, her mind occupied with the upcoming trip.

Rudi just get another letter from the mother, and she send with it plenty forms, some affidavits of support, others just plain application and medical forms. She send money too, for passport pictures and physical examinations. Last week, Rudi ask her to bring Jeff and Rosa to

101

the photography studio. Time soon come to leave, him tell her, while handing out the money.

And she remember feeling kind of glad about it, but also kind of cautious. She mention it to friends at school, but never with any extra eagerness, for things have a way to not always turn out quite the way one would want them. Peppy talk about in length to Jasmine though, for Jasmine travel plenty since her mother is a higgler woman, travelling to Miami and New York two and three times a month, so she can buy sneakers and jeans and sweat-shirt and pants and blender and pressure-cooker and sell them in the market at more bargainable prices. Since she the oldest, sometimes Jasmine travel with her.

And Jasmine tell her, 'Yes, man, Peppy, you going to have a nice time,' in her twang voice, for even though she only been to America three times, staying no more than five days the longest, Jasmine have a permanent Foreign accent. 'And the best thing,' Jasmine tell her, 'is you don't wear uniforms to school. You wear any Jesus Christ thing you feel. Even high heels and tube top.' Jasmine eyes were twinkling when she say it. 'You can burn your green tunic and white blouses before you leave.'

'So I couldn't even wear me uniform even if I wanted to?' Peppy ask her friend out the corner of her mouth, for is not that her closet empty, but she don't change shoes once a week like Jasmine. Furthermore that would mean her mother will have to buy her school clothes for is only yard clothes and church clothes she have plenty, not much going out clothes.

Jasmine laugh out loud. 'Gal, you mad! Then you know what,' Jasmine say to her after a pause in her sing-song Foreign twang, 'you can eat bubble gum and sweetie in the classes.'

'You lie!' Horror form on Peppy's face, her eyes roll over.

Jasmine kiss her teeth. The two of them were outside on the grass behind the classroom one mid-afternoon break time. Jasmine nod her head. 'Yup! I went with my cousin up to her school. The children even rude to the teacher sometimes. You know how we have to stand up and say good morning every time a teacher come inside our class? Well, is not so over there, the children sit down on them tail same way and continue talking to one another.' Jasmine shake her head slow from side to side now. Scorn cause her mouth to turn up.

'Them don't even have devotion or chapel. Even in elementary school, them don't have lunch or evening time prayers. That's why me mother say,' Jasmine turn to Peppy, her face round and pixieish, 'that she'd want me finish high school out here, for some of the public schools over there no damn good.'

Peppy sigh plenty. All of a sudden the schools in America don't sound pretty to her a tall. She wonder if her mother know about these things or even Rudi, if Aunty Cora know the children over there don't even pray before them eat. And these things cause Peppy plenty thinking, for is not only her mother she going to have to learn to live with, or even her brother and sisters, but the children at school over there who if them don't even fear teachers, how them going to fear God?

And as Peppy continue on walking, she think about how even during her classes, she find herself gazing through the window near her seat, thinking about winter clothes. For she see it in magazines and plenty books, and Aunty Cora did mention how the people have to dress up in big hats and warm, long coats and even tall boots so as to walk through ice and snow. Even fingers and throat and sometime ears have to cover-up, Aunty Cora did say. And especially with how she can barely keep on her whole slip and girdle for them feel too damn uncomfortable, she don't know how she would manage wearing so many clothes day-in and day-out during winter.

And so Peppy's mind and concentration would often spend so much time on Foreign that even when her teacher, Mrs Haywood, call out her name, and tell her to answer the question she just ask, the other students would start-up laughing for them know Peppy wasn't paying attention. And when Mrs Haywood see that she can't answer the question, she tell Peppy to go and stand up at the back of the class and turn her face to the wall corner.

The only time she started thinking seriously about living with the mother though was when she was down at Grandma spending time. Grandma send word to Rudi that she long to see the rest of her grandchildren, especially the baby, Rosa. And so Rudi send Peppy with Rosa the Friday evening.

And the first thing that reach her ears all the way out the gate when she jump off the bus with Rosa was Grandma's mouth. She wasn't sure whether or not she should go in or wait outside till Grandma finish, for Grandma's temper don't easily change when she cursing. But she go on in nevertheless, dragging Rosa behind her. She did have to take away the two purple roses Rosa have squeezed up in her hand, slap her on her fingers and then throw away the roses behind the house, over the fence where cows eat the wild grass, for Grandma is a woman don't like people, especially pickney, touch-touch and pick-pick her flowers. She love to cut them and put them on her centre table, next to the old pump organ and the blue velvety-looking settee that still have the plastic on it and that she don't allow any of her grandchildren to sit down on, unless them tidy for the evening, and the black-and-white television her son Samuel send her from Connecticut, that she dust every day and don't turn on for longer than one hour each evening, and two on Sundays for Billy Graham's special broadcast.

Grandma didn't even turn the white of her eyes to look at either she or Rosa as them walk through the verandah, through the living room and into the kitchen, where she stand up over the oil stove, cooking dinner and cursing Dave who was sitting down on the floor in the doorway, not paying her any mind. Nothing hurt Grandma more than when she cursing you and you not paying her any mind.

'I know you break me nice-nice dishes out of damn bad mind,' Grandma was telling Dave, as Peppy and Rosa take a seat around the kitchen table already set for dinner. 'I know is because I tell you not to leave the house, why you break me nice dishes. I notice too,' Grandma push up her cat-like spectacles that was foggy with the steam from her pot, up on her nose, 'that whenever your Grandpa talk to you, you act like you don't hear him, and you don't do as him tell you. The other day him ask you to tie out the cow with the calf, and after the poor man come home tired, him still have to get up and go tie out the cow. And all you do after school finish is sit down on your tail and don't lift straw.'

Grandma stop, catch her breath and turn around to look at Peppy and Rosa. 'How you do me babies. Look how you turn into big woman, Rosa!' Then she turn right back around to Dave and continue to curse, her voice changing only slightly. 'But I know what I going to do. That day when all of you must go to the airport, I allow you to go on. But when everybody else ready to board the plane, you can't put your blasted foot nowhere for I done tear up all your papers.'

And after she say so, Grandma get response, for Dave look up at her for the first time, face tight, eyes shifting round. And when Grandma see him look up, she stop the cursing for she know she get him right where she want him.

Grandma turn back to Peppy and call the baby over to her, then she pull up a chair and sit down, asking Peppy to help serve the dinner for her feet starting to hurt. Dave get up from where him was sitting and grunt out 'howdy' to Peppy, then him pinch Rosa's two round cheeks, and walk through the kitchen on his way out to the verandah. Him was almost six feet tall. Grandma say him is the dead stamp of Grandpa's side of family, long and narrow with big knee caps.

Peppy never like Dave much, at least not anymore than she like Jeff. Them talk, but them don't really talk. As long as she live she not going forget how them beat her up and tear up her dolly, Rose.

As Peppy was serving out the dinner, Grandma say to her, voice sharp, 'Take care of the papers and the passports. As a matter of fact, tell Rudi to bring them down here. For if Walter see them, you can kiss Foreign ta-ta. That man!' Grandma pause and shake her head, looking off into the distance. 'All I can say is I hope Gwennie don't take damn careless and send for him, for that would be trouble on top of trouble and the Lord knows she have enough. That poor child meet it in truth.

'I know you and Gwennie will get on,' Grandma continue on, 'for you quiet just like she, and you industrious, you easy to get on with. But she going to have trouble with Dave and even Del.' Grandma hand Peppy a plate of food, and Peppy put it on the table. 'Del quiet too, but is a different quiet. Quiet enough to deafen you. She and Dave give me and your Grandpa a damn tough time, but is me grandchildren. If them want a place to sleep, I have to give them place. But you and Rudi will be big help to your Mama.'

Peppy try to picture her mother's face, but she couldn't remember more than her eyes, brownish-greenish, the colour of leaves when night coming down. She was light skinned, brown like Grandpa's side of family. Jeff and Dave too. Only thing them have light-brown eyes, same colour as them hair. Del and Rudi dark like Grandma's side of family, Rosa and Peppy in between. She wonder if she and her mother going to really get on as Grandma say, or if it going to be more like what Aunty Cora predict, that the two have to get to know one another first. She wonder if Rudi going to be different around the mother. Right now him don't talk about her much, but she wonder if that would change. If him would take the mother in confidence, tell her some of the things him used to only tell she, Peppy. She wonder if she and Rudi would always remain close too. But as Peppy think about it more and more, that evening as she was walking home, a funny feeling in her belly tell her things going to be different. And so she try push away the feeling, for she never want to think about it.

As for Walter, well, Peppy sigh. She don't really know. Him alright, she suppose. Most times she just feel sorry for him though. For when him don't quarrel and curse, him just quiet and sad-looking. When him come home, just him alone sit down and watch the seven-thirty news

105

with Brenton Hall. Sometimes him eat the little dinner Rudi leave cover-up for him in the kitchen. Sometimes him don't eat a tall. Other times him just take one or two mouthfuls, then call Jeff to come and finish the rest.

Nowadays she hear him pacing around in his room, sighing plenty, two and three o' clock in the morning. She know Rudi hear it too, for his breathing not as deep and even. Sometime she ask him, 'Rudi, what is wrong with him, think him going crazy?'

But Rudi only kiss his teeth and grunt out, 'Cho, don't pay him any mind, just his sins pinching him.'

And although a chuckle form itself around Peppy's mouth corner, she know Rudi not serious. She know him wonder the same thing as she. She know Jeff wonder it too, even if Rosa too young to understand. She imagine Walter must miss them mother and must be going through a damn rough time. She can't imagine it being easy when the woman you love pick up herself and leave you alone a tall, a tall.

PART SIX

I

Gwennie push open the gate and walk up to the door, the big blue woollen sweater she have on over her frock pull up close to her neck. It was only September, but already the evenings starting to blow cold. She never even glance at the letters she pull out of the mailbox, the hurry she in to get inside the house, put down the bag of groceries and sit down rest herself a little before Clive come over.

The house was dark and cold the Friday evening. Gwennie switch on the passageway light and lock the door behind her. She made her way into the kitchen, dropping off the bills and bags on the small enamel table with the four matching chairs. Her brother, Samuel, used to keep it in his basement. Gwennie never stop to turn on the kitchen light or to put the two packages of chicken inside the refrigerator, she made her way into her bedroom instead, kick off her flat shoes, fling off her sweater and crawl underneath the heavy comforter.

The house was quiet except for the clock hang up on the wall in the living room going tick-tock, loud and plenty. She buy it from the department store not too far from where she live. Outside, two cars pass, but except for that, the street was quiet. Not a baby's mouth hollering for it hungry and want feeding. No sound of children making plenty noises as them jump around playing hopscotch or dandy-shandy, or even skipping. No man or woman laughing and chatting and bawling out 'howdy-do' for them glad to see one another. Nothing. The houses on the street just big and far-in-between and cold, especially with the winter coming on.

Gwennie's ears and nose start to thaw out. She could feel the tension that cause her neck and shoulder to ache and throb plenty, easing. She take long, deep breath as Percy used to tell her: in, out, and in again. She miss Percy in truth. Him did plan her going-away party, inviting almost everyone from the meeting. Them was sorry she leaving, for she used to care whole heap about country people who don't get good representation in government. Them hope she would be able to bring her good work elsewhere.

The week before leaving, she ask Percy if him think she would find meetings like these abroad. Him never answer for a long time, face cross as usual, plenty lines on his forehead. She wasn't sure if him hear her. 'Percy, you think . . .'

'I hear you, Gwennie,' him sigh long, shaking his head from side to side. 'The situation abroad different. Them have meetings like these, but the government don't like it. It ten times worse than when Jackson was in power out here. You remember how him wouldn't put money towards social programmes, wouldn't even turn the black of his eyes look at poor and illiterate people; people who don't have work. Everything go into tourism and further build-up of what done build-up already. Over there them have meetings, but them underground.'

Gwennie look over at him, her eyes searching around his face: long and thin and smooth, almost like baby's. Him have a scar over his left eyebrow.

'I have a friend over there,' Percy continue on. 'Now and again him attend the meetings, maybe hand out the newsletter them used to publish, now and then do a little fundraising. Him wasn't involved in any kinda government overthrowing or anything. And shit!' Percy's fingers start to dance round the steering wheel, 'him say all hours of day and night him would notice people watching his apartment.

'Sometimes when him come in at night, him buck-up into strange-looking people just lurking around. Sometimes after him arrange his apartment a certain way, when him come home, everything arrange differently. Him say him was afraid, for the very same thing was happening to plenty people in his group.'

'So what him do?' Gwennie ask, wide-eye.

Percy shrug, hands calming down. 'Nothing. You can't really hide from the government over there. I suppose them either kill you or lock you up on various bogus charges. If them see that you not too dangerous, them probably leave you alone. I really don't know. I don't think me friend go to the meetings as much, anymore though.'

Gwennie never say anything when him finish talk. She face the road ahead, forehead puzzle-up. 'It don't spell sense a tall,' she say to Percy long after. 'After him wasn't doing anything bad, all him want . . .'

'It doesn't matter,' Percy cut in. 'Same way you hear people out here bad-talk communism, same way over there. When them hear the word, first thing come to mind is Cuba and Russia. Them hear the word and them think how people can't own anything for themself. Them can't have three cows when everybody else have only two. Them can't own a shop or supermarket and so on. The government in America not any different. Them want to own the whole damn world. Communism is a big threat to them.'

Gwennie understand. She still hope she'd be able to find a meeting to attend nevertheless, for she like things of that nature. It was of surprise to her when she arrive and ask Samuel and his wife, Dorothy, if them know about any, and all them could suggest was the Caribbean Club that have party every weekend, no community involvement whatsoever.

But apart from the meetings, she still miss Percy. Him was so keen when it comes to how things should be arranged, or how a room must decorate. The children soon come, she need beds, dinette set so everybody can sit down while eating, winter clothes and boots, she need curtains, rugs for the various rooms. She want somebody she can browse around with from store to store, like she and Percy used to do. She don't make plenty friends, yet. And yes, Clive was nice, but she and him have completely different taste in furniture, furthermore him lacking that little quality that was special about Percy.

And is not that Samuel or Dorothy wasn't interested in helping her, for them used to drive her places, and show her where she can buy furniture and such, but she never have the money then. Every paycheck either go to the damn thief lawyer man, or to the bank for the down payment on the house or to the children, back home. Now that she have a little bit more spare money, for things clear up with the lawyer, it look like them not willing to help her as before. And she know it wasn't out of grudgeful and bad feelings, for kinder than Samuel and Dorothy you can't find, but Clive say probably them want her to fend for herself now, and she think maybe is true.

'Them want you to stand up on your own two feet,' Clive tell her the evening down at the Caribbean Club.

Gwennie didn't say anything. She sip her drinks.

'Them find you the house, them find you work, them find you lawyer. Them carry you around, show you things, introduce you to people. Now them want you to do things for yourself. Them want you to be independent and have your own place.'

She remember that after buying the bedroom set and finally moving in, Dorothy and Samuel used to come over often. Sometimes them bring dinner, sometimes a set of dishes, candle and candle holder, calendar, things to make the house smell good. Sometimes them just used to come over and keep her company, the days she wasn't living in at her house-keeping job. And then them just stop. Them still call sometimes. But all-in-all, she barely see them. It used to bother her at first, for she wonder if it was something she say or do, but it spell plenty sense to her as Clive explain it. She also get more time to herself now, too.

Working just about every day, she glad to get the few hours to herself, for nothing please her more than to just chat to herself as loud as she want, cooking whenever she feel, without a worry about children and the plenty energy them take up, about husbands and them sometimish nature, about family and them whole heap of problems. During those times she like inviting Clive over, for whenever him in a good mood, it's a pleasure to be around him.

Sometimes them drive to the top of the Blue Hills, park the car and watch the sunset, for Clive romantic that way. But other times when him come over, him can't get her to budge. She don't have any energy whatsoever, she just want to sleep all the time. And Clive would always say to her: 'Gwennie, since you miss the children so much that you unbearable to spend time around, it spell sense you just send for them.'

But it wasn't that easy. She just can't bring her children to Foreign without first providing beds for them to sleep on. It already take her four good years and plenty money to get permanent citizenship, now she have to wait another two years before it okay for the children to come.

'Times and times again, I wouldn't mind letting them come for vacation,' she say to him one evening while at his house, her forehead knit-up plenty and her face pucker-up like she ready to holler, 'but it too expensive. Might as well use the money to buy one more chair so them can sit down comfortable when them come.'

And as Clive would never quite know what to say to her during these times when her feelings low, him always just clasp her two hands in his and press them to his jaw, his own face puzzle over.

Them keep her more than busy at the place where she work though, and she prefer it that way. Plenty time on her hand just cause her to worry and fret herself over her children back home. Her evenings off, she make sure she keep busy. She watch the little black-and-white television in her room, other times she listen to the radio and read plenty. The man she work for, is a professor at one of the universities in the area, so him have plenty books about the house, plenty leather-bound, nice smelling, interesting books. Every week she read a new one, when is not Dickens or Austen is Thackeray or Edgar Poe. Them remind her of high school back home in Miss Mullins' class.

Sometimes she write one or two letters to people back home, but it always leave her so cut up inside and tired, she don't look forward to it especially whenever she have to write Rudi. Even after so many years, she still can't write Rudi a letter and don't holler and depress for the remainder of week. And every time she get depress, a certain letter Percy did write her a long while back always flash crossway her mind.

It was towards the end of her two months' vacation. Time soon come to return home to her family. But Gwennie was having second thoughts. The little money she earn under the table from day's work was giving her a certain independence. The thought of going home to Walter never bring her comfort and joy. She like the splendour Dorothy and Samuel have. Maybe if she stay and work, she could have it too.

Not that things weren't dangerous sometimes, especially on Main Street with all the shootings and killings going on. Everyday she listen to the radio, and when is not news about somebody's pickney getting kidnapped, is news about accidents caused by rum-drinking. Just last week them set fire to a supermarket close to her street, to get insurance money she hear. Winter was another story. Sometimes the air so cold, if you not careful, you freeze right there at the bus-stop waiting on the bus to come.

But even with them things, she know if she work plenty she can have something for herself, something she can call Gwennie's. Dorothy have her own car separate from Samuel's jeep. When she ready to go about her business, Samuel can't say anything to her cause is her name on the registration. Well, is so she want to have something for herself, something that don't belong to husband, but to she and her children. And so Gwennie did write Percy and tell him, she think she going to stay. Better opportunities, over here, she tell him in the letter, children can go on to college, them can find work easy, and for she, Gwennie, change of direction in her life.

Him write her back, the letter running almost five pages. And after him talk about the two little girls whom Gwennie still never meet, and about the wife and divorce papers, about school and the meetings, him express how proud him was of her, and how much respect him have for her decision, even though her life will be sheer hell.

'For everytime you see a child that resemble yours, you going to start the bawling,' him tell her. 'And especially since you know how crazy Walter is, that alone will cause you to worry more and more. Sometimes you will want to jump on that plane so bad and come back, only ambition, plenty strength of heart, good friends and memory of Walter's nasty ways will hold you back. Sometimes, Gwennie, you going to wonder if it's really worth it, if maybe you mustn't stop and try work out things with Walter and go back home to the children.

'But Gwennie, if I know you like I think I know you, you are stubborn and strong, mule ownself. And if you suffer and go through what you go through with Walter, because of your plenty children, you can go through any damn thing.'

And when Gwennie think about it, Percy wasn't too far off from the truth. Every time the young boys come to the house to visit the professor, she think about Rudi back home who can't even start college sake of the responsibilities she hand him. She think about Jeff who want to turn doctor, Dave pilot and Del school teacher like herself. She isn't even there to encourage them. And she can't count on Walter. The evening them deliver the encyclopedia set she save up and buy so the children could have decent things to read, Walter was so mad with her, curse and quarrel the whole night about how she just wasting her money for him could use it on other things. But she never care. Every other evening she used to drill Del with spelling words so she could enter Spelling Bee. Now she don't even think Walter talk to them much, probably only curse as usual whenever them come home with bad report cards.

The ringing of the telephone interrupted Gwennie's thoughts.

'Hello,' Gwennie say into it.

Clive was on the line. On his way over.

'Alright,' Gwennie tell him. 'But I don't have anything readily prepared. Bring something if you hungry.'

The house was quiet again, except for the clock. Gwennie sigh long and hard and crawl back under the cover. She wasn't in the mood for Clive or anybody, she was tired. She just want to lie down and rest and keep to herself, so her thinkings can flow.

She stay inside the bed about five more minutes, then she get up and turn on the light for the room was in complete darkness. She fold back the cover on the bed, neaten it up, change her clothes, haul on back her thick sweater for the house was chilly, and push her feet inside the house slippers with the fake fur around it. She brush up her hair and run little lipstick crossway her mouth, then she make her way back into the kitchen, flip on the light and start to put away the groceries.

Gwennie turn on the fire under the kettle. She might as well sip little Plantation Mint tea before Clive come over. It wasn't as good as the mint Grandma grow in her garden, but it will pass. She turn on the thermostat too, for as big as Clive was, when it come to cold weather, him worse than baby. It was always summer over his house all year round. She remember the first time she meet him down at the Caribbean Club. Going on year and a half now. She remember liking him right away, for him could joke around plenty one minute, yet serious, sensible-talking, caring, interested in her children back home the next.

At first she used to laugh to herself every time him open his mouth. Him come from Trinidad and his accent was worse sing-song than hers. But she get used to it. She like the way him carry himself, too, always tidy, trousers always tuck in, shirts always clean and without stains. She like his big shoulders and wide chest, his round belly and deep voice that boom plenty. Him wasn't bad looking either. Face long and narrow with a little tuft of moustache over his top lip resembling Hitler's. Him was several years older, but a more kind and gentler man one couldn't find. Him remind her a little bit of Percy and even Luther, the way him would show her how to do things and expect her to do it on her own after that. The only thing she didn't like much is the way him pressure her sometimes.

Gwennie was still sitting down around the table sipping her tea when Clive ring the door bell. She turn up the thermostat one notch more on her way to open the door.

'Jesus Christ, Gwennie, why the blasted house so damn cold,' Clive boom out, fitting himself through the door. 'You not cold?' Him touch her nose with the back of his hand.

Gwennie draw back. 'How many times I must tell you to stop bawl out the Lord's name in vain?'

'Cho,' him kiss his teeth. 'You too Christian-Christian.'

'I turn on the heat, it soon come up.' She lock the door behind him and follow him into the kitchen.

'I didn't bring any food,' him say, pulling up a chair next to hers. Him wouldn't allow her to take his jacket. 'We can go out and get something. A nice little rest . . .'

'I don't want to go out, Clive.' She hand him a mug-full of tea. 'I just want to stay in and rest. I tired. I can't wait for the children to come so the older ones can help me work. I tired to hassle out meself.'

Clive take a sip of the tea. Then him put down the mug, watching his reflection swirling round and round. 'You wouldn't have to work so hard if you come live with me.' The heat start to come up, the heaters were cling-clanging.

Gwennie take a deep breath. She could feel a little twinge of pain in her back. She try relax. 'Don't bother start with that again, Clive. How many times I must tell you I want something for me children and meself. I live with husband too long. When them own everything in the house, them think them can own you too. Them boss-boss you around as them have a mind. I want a different life. I didn't come all the way to Foreign to put up with the same damn foolishness.'

Clive was still looking at his reflection. 'You mean that after how long you know me, you think me and you husband cut out of the same piece of cloth?' Clive's voice was losing the boom. Now it was just deep and low. 'You must know that I'm different.'

'Of course I know you different.' Gwennie pour more water in her cup. 'But I want to live as I please. I want to come and go as I have a mind. I working hard for good reason. So me and me children can live in peace and quiet. When I was doing community work, I used to see baby's belly push out from lack of food, for the worthless father done lose his paycheck to gambling. I see plenty women with faces hang down almost to the ground, for family life giving them hell. I go through it, I don't want it any more.'

Clive never say anything. Only the clock and the heater making noise. Gwennie sip her tea. She like Clive plenty. But him don't understand. Him can't understand where she coming from. Him don't talk much about his wife, but sometimes she wonder if him is another Walter, and that's why the wife leave him. No, him don't go on like Walter. Him don't even drink. But him not a God-fearing a tall, and that bother her plenty. Nevertheless, him is a good man and she like him. But as Grandma used to say, to know dog is one, but to live at home with him is different business.

'Come we go to the restaurant.' Gwennie cover his hand with hers. 'Maybe we can even see a picture after. Some good ones advertise in here.' She push the newspaper towards him. 'Look for a good one. I going to get me jacket and put on me shoes.'

Gwennie put the two cups inside the sink. Clive's cup did still have plenty tea inside. She turn on the tap and rinse them out. Then she step inside her room for the house key and rest of things. She know him vex now. It happen every time them talk about living together. It going to take a whole heap of coaxing before she get him to start talk and liven-up again.

'You ready?' she call out, putting on her coat, switching off the bedroom light.

'Yes.' His voice almost faint now.

'Come on, then. Leave on the kitchen light. I don't want damn thief to break in and take out what I don't have.'

Them step outside into the chilly night air, the heater and the clock making plenty noises behind them.

II

Daybreak Saturday morning catch Gwennie at the bus stop waiting with four other women, for the bus that would take them to do day's work in Simsbury. Gwennie recognize one or two of the women, for she see them every Saturday morning. She nod her head in greetings, ready to start up a conversation, but them only nod in return, face stoney, the duffle bag that contain the extra pair of flat shoes and old frock that best to do house work in, hang off firm from them shoulder.

The one woman she talk to plenty, from Montserrat, Miss Daphne, wasn't there that morning. Usually while waiting for the bus, Miss Daphne would always write down names of West Indian stores where Gwennie can get food to buy. Miss Daphne is a woman who like her Caribbean food gone-to-bed. She say she can't stand American food a tall, it's too bland.

'Me dear, I have to boil-up plenty green bananas and yam and eat it with mackerel mix-up with onion and baby red tomatoes before I can step outside the house each morning,' Miss Daphne tell Gwennie one morning while waiting. 'I too used to the big strong breakfast to turn around and eat cereal and dry bread. I would drop down dead from hungry belly.'

Gwennie only laugh when Miss Daphne say it, for she wonder if after living in America for twenty years like Miss Daphne, she going to still love the food from back home. Hardly a day pass when Samuel and Dorothy don't cook Caribbean food. Only Clive alone not too fussy. Him eat anything when him hungry, pasta, lasagne, turkey pot pie . . . Gwennie's mind run on last night. She wonder how much longer she and Clive will make out. Seems as if them quarrelling more than usual these days. Gwennie kiss her teeth under her breath.

115

It was only after plenty coaxing inside the car, that him finally turn back around to his old talkative self again. Them never bother with the movies, since dinner ran late. Clive drive her home, instead. And all through the driving back him was lively, and she was feeling more and more happy and comfortable with him. But then the silence start again when him turn off the main road and onto her little street at the foot of the hill, with the sad-looking houses on each side. Him cut off the engine when him reach her gate. The car was silent, except for the fan inside the hood humming. The street was dead.

'Thanks for the dinner.' Gwennie fasten the buttons on her coat. 'I glad we decided to go out after all. The food tasted good in truth.' Gwennie pull up the lock on the door of the big, silver-grey Buick.

Clive never say anything.

'You busy tommorrow?' Gwennie look towards him, but she couldn't make out his features inside the darkness of the car.

Clive sigh. It was a long time before him answer. 'You want me to come inside with you, Gwennie?' His voice sounded gruff, as if preparing for some major disappointment.

Gwennie bend over and start to feel for her pocket book. It couldn't be too far away, she just take out her house key. She wasn't quite sure how to answer Clive when him get like this, demanding-like even though it don't quite sound that way. For is not that she didn't want him to come in and sleep with her, but sometimes that is all she want, somebody to lay down close to and hug, so that when she turn during the night, or when she wake up in the morning, the bed won't feel so big and wide. But she won't even bother to fool herself and think she will only get closeness. Is long time she in this world. She know which package come with string and which one empty.

And is not that anything was wrong with the string. For as far as she was concerned, except for the ring around her finger and the people gathered inside the church that Saturday afternoon, and the certificate down at the registry, she and Walter finish. As far as she was concerned, she single. And is not that it take her almost four years in Foreign to find out. She did know long time. She did know from the time she set eyes on Luther and lay up with him inside Grandma's house. She did figure it out then that she and Walter didn't have further to go.

But she did still go back to him and start to have more children. Maybe to try and build back something, maybe to just do her duty as wife, maybe to save face, she can't place her two hands on it right now. But in the middle of everything she still wasn't at ease with herself. The meetings used to help, them used to keep her busy, but at nights she did still have to go home to him. And his every touch used to cause her skin to bringle and his presence made her face fold up and his chuckle never cause her belly to shimmer anymore, instead it add one more crease to her forehead and squeeze out one more hiss through her teeth.

With Clive it was different. She know him would be good with Rosa if not the others. But what she can't understand is how her belly bottom always feel funny when Clive inside her house. Sometimes when him inside her bed, she can't sleep good. Plenty times at night, she wake up, twisting and turning, wondering what Dorothy and Samuel think about she and Clive. If Grandpa was to hear about Clive, what him would think. It embarrass her to tell them Clive stay over sometimes. And it don't even make sense, for the house belong to her and she neither have children or husband or friend to report to. But she still feel shame, nonetheless.

Gwennie turn around in the seat and face Clive. She could make out one half of his Hitler-looking moustache.

'Clive.' Gwennie's voice was soft. 'Is not that I don't want you to come inside. I just don't want what come with that. I tired and I have to get up early in the morning. Maybe Saturday night. But I don't know. I want to get up early Sunday morning and watch Billy Graham on the TV, and then catch a early morning service at church.' Gwennie pause. She push her finger under the latch and pull it. The car door creak open. Cold air burn her face.

'I will call you tomorrow from work.' Gwennie put one of her hands over Clive's. It lay rigid on his lap. 'Take care.'

Still, Clive never say a word. His hand never even twitch under her touch.

Gwennie lift up herself out the car and slam the door shut, house key ready in her hand. She didn't want to look back at Clive, she could just imagine the sadness on his face. She let herself inside and lock the door behind her. The house was nice and warm just like inside Clive's car.

Clive's car was still outside when Gwennie finish brush her teeth and turn down the little button on the thermostat. Even after switching off the kitchen light, turning off the lamp in her room, setting the alarm clock on her bureau and climbing underneath her comforter, she still never hear the engine start up. Not even when she doze off. And Gwennie have a dream that night, not a long one, but disturbing enough to leave her restless the remainder of night, and thinking plenty about her relationship with Clive.

117

In the dream, all the children were here, except Peppy. She and Clive was getting on well. She was only working one job now, for Del and Rudi was working. Clive used to come over plenty. But she would never allow him to stay over, for she never want to set bad example. But anyway, it so happen that one Saturday night Clive did have to stay over. But she was careful, she make sure him sleep out on the couch. The house did have plenty more furniture by then.

Rudi went out the same Saturday night and didn't return till early the Sunday morning, day barely dawning. And the first sight that greet him, when him step inside the house, was Gwennie and Clive sitting close around the enamel table and sipping mint tea. Gwennie was still in her night clothes and Clive was only in pants and undershirt, no shoes in sight. The house was quiet. Everybody else was sleeping. Outside birds chirp noisily.

Gwennie take a big mouthful of the tea, for all of a sudden, her stomach was feeling poorly. And Rudi just brush pass them in a gale of coolness, forehead knit-up, face tight, no utterance of a greeting whatsoever. Something about the expression on his face remind Gwennie of Walter.

For the remainder of week, Gwennie and Rudi don't exchange five words total. Him tell her 'howdy' in the morning and evening as usual, but when him say it, them eyes don't meet. Gwennie look up in his face, but Rudi's eyes seem to always lodge themselves somewhere far pass her head-back, the scowl on his face overbearing. Him used to sit down at the kitchen table and eat dinner with her. Used to tell her stories about the people back home, the ones him work with at the import company, and the ones him encounter on the train. But these days not a word between the two.

She decide to tackle him about it, for she couldn't stand the silence any longer. So one evening as him sit down comfortable and was starting to eat, she approach him. She could feel the tension thick in the room. Her own belly was weak from the thought of confronting him. But she carry on nonetheless, for it was better to nip it in the bud now, than to wait till it grow out of proportion. 'Then Rudi,' she start out, her voice poorly, 'why you won't talk to me, man.'

Rudi lodge a spoonful of rice in his jaw corner, forehead wrinkle-over.

'How you expect me to live?' Gwennie continue on. 'You don't expect me to have friends? You expect me to be by meself. You expect me to be lonesome all the time.' Gwennie's voice was starting to rise little by little.

'I notice how you children treat him. Whenever him come over, everybody clear the room. Nobody anxious to see him.

'Del don't talk to him, you don't talk to him, only Rosa talk to him. She alone respect and act decent towards him. The other day him was over here watching TV, and Dave did have the music up loud in his room. Him knock on the door and politely ask Dave to turn it down a little. Dave tell him to go to his own house and watch TV if him want peace and quiet.' Gwennie pause to catch her breath. 'What kind of behaviour is that? I don't know how we going to manage, you know, for all you children will have to get used to me friends. If is Walter you children miss, you all can go back home to him, but him not going to come here and bother me peace . . .'

The alarm clock did go off same time, leaving everything fresh-fresh on her mind.

Gwennie notice the women starting to shuffle around. The bus was coming. She shuffle around her bag too and join the line them form. She hope Bob was driving this morning for she like him. Gwennie wait till the other women get on. Then she climb up. It was Bob own self.

'Gwennie, how are you?'

'Alright, Bob.' She show him her bus pass and sit down at her usual spot, across from him.

'You work too hard, Gwennie. You're going to kill yourself before you know it.' Bob laugh, jaw and chin shaking, same way his belly, for him was a little bit fattish.

'Aw, Bobby. Can't go any better. I have to eat.' Gwennie laugh. She like Bob, for him was a very kind and jovial man. She can't forget that morning, when on route to her very first cleaning job and did ask him for directions, how detailed and generous he was in his instructions, pointing out places of reference so she could remember and then asking her to recite it back to him, patiently smoothing out all errors till she finally get it right.

And she was grateful, for she'd not too long come to Foreign and did just get the weekend work. But him never think twice about helping her. And after offering out the directions, them start to talk, conversation leading first to his family then to hers back home. All during the conversation, she could feel the eyes of the other women on the bus boring deep into her neck-back. But she never pay them any mind.

The next Saturday, she bring him a small basket of fruit, for Grandma used to say people must always repay kindness with kindness. She hand it to him the morning as she was leaving the bus. She never see him the

119

next Saturday, but she see him the one following. And from she set foot inside the bus the morning till she reach her destination, twenty minutes later, him never finish talk about her kindness.

'You make it worth my while to drive this bus, Gwennie. In all the twenty odd years, I've been doing this, no one has ever given me anything. Sometimes people don't even say thanks when I help them.'

Gwennie only grin, for it wasn't any big thing to her. Back home people give and take like every day is Christmas. Here in Foreign, it look as if people make gift-giving into big thing. She tell Bob him welcome and is nothing. But even when him stop to let her off, him was still talking about the little basket of grapes and banana and orange and tangerine and the one big Julie mango she get from the West Indian store Miss Daphne tell her about.

III

Gwennie did have about quarter mile to walk after the bus let her off. The path ahead was long and winding after leaving the main road, and it was up hill. Every time she walk, by the time she reach her destination, she always have sweat running down her neck-back, pass her ears temple and gathering-up underneath her armpit.

Gwennie grab on to her duffle bag. She look crossway the road two times, then cross the street. A man, a woman and them big black dog pass by. The dog was pulling the man, but him hang on tight to the leash. Them turn around and look on Gwennie, face empty. Then them continue on, heads turn back around, the dog pulling the man same way, not a word spoken.

The road leading to the Duncan's house was lined with plenty trees. With the approaching winter, colours were starting to turn, some red, others yellow, purple, orange. Gwennie look up at the trees. In three months' time all the leaves will fold over dead, every thing cover over white. She can't wait till her children come so them can see these wonders, she know Rudi especially would enjoy it, for him sensitive that way about nature. His fingers can make any flowers grow, bring back

120

any seedling to life. Clive promise was to bring her up to New Hampshire, where the colours of trees even more dazzling. That was one year ago. Gwennie shake her head. That was the other thing about Clive she don't like, him love make promises him won't keep.

The dream last night flash crossway Gwennie's mind. She wonder if she should mention it to Clive. But then him so analytical about things, him would probably blame the dream on her nervousness about the relationship. It puzzle her too, why Peppy wasn't in the dream. She wonder if Aunty Cora plan not to send her after all. She remember Aunty Cora's visit several years back and the endless conversations about the lump moving around in her stomach, beating with a ferocity as if it have its own heart; her son in England; Leslie and how him is a royal needle in her backside and Miss Gertie and her stinking tobacco breath. Aunty Cora did put Gwennie's hand on the lump. Gwennie remember thinking how big it felt, about the size of her fist double-up, and just as hard.

Them did spend a long length of time discussing Peppy. Aunty Cora had plenty to ask, especially about the business concerning Peppy and the rest of siblings. And as the two of them lay stretch-out on Gwennie's bed, the only bit of furniture inside the big, empty Foreign house, Aunty Cora tell her: 'Me love, when that pickney come home the night and tell me that her brothers disown her, that them beat-beat her up and mash-up the dolly, I didn't know what to do. I don't know how me and you was going to make out.' Aunty Cora clap her hands and shake her head slow. 'I was ready to cross you off me syllabus as no-good and damn careless.'

And Gwennie never say anything, for she wasn't sure what to say. She take a sip of the Diet Sprite she have lean up on the floor against the bed. 'Guiding Light' was playing on the TV out in the kitchen on the little enamel table. Now and again when she have the time, she watch it, for it always sweet her to see the deceitfulness in people's heart, the way the characters lie and cheat on one another.

'But thank God for that letter you send, explaining everything. For if you never have a good answer about your secret plans to travel abroad, and about this fellow, Percy, I was going to cross you off as damn worthless.'

Gwennie take another sip of the Sprite, her mind far back to the letter she write in response to Aunty Cora's. She write it one evening before her meeting start, sitting down inside Percy's car.

'I plan was to come up there,' Aunty Cora tell her, breaking into her

121

thinking as she shift around on the bed. 'I figure letter-writing wouldn't be enough. Me and you was going to have to sit down and talk woman to woman. But me heart did soften a little,' Aunty Cora say to her. 'For me heart soften for any woman who have plenty pickney, who work, who have family life with husband to look about, and on top of that, find time to do little community work.'

Gwennie breathe free and easy after that, for she did write in her letter about how plenty times she wanted to come up and talk to Aunty Cora but sake of the meetings and the plenty time them take up with everything else, she couldn't find the time.

'For in me young days,' Aunty Cora continue on, her fingers caressing the location of the lump on her belly, her eyes out of focus and far off, 'when Anderson was alive, I was on a whole heap of board meetings meself.' Aunty Cora raise her fingers off the lump and start to count. She still wear her two married rings. 'Me was on coffee board, school board, church council board, road building board, and it never easy. Sometimes for days Anderson alone running the shop for I was so busy.' Aunty Cora shake her head and push out her mouth.

'And him never like it a damn tall. Him wanted to go out and look after the livestock, to farm and plant yam and potato and banana. Him wasn't interested in shop life and to weigh out flour and sugar and measure out oil and cut tobacco. Miss Gertie used to help plenty, and thank God for Miss Irene, she look after all the children so me could go about me business.' Aunty Cora stop to catch her breath and to sip a little of the Foreign rum.

'But I couldn't figure how you manage to allow the children to beat up Peppy and . . .'

Gwennie sigh deep. 'The man was reading me letters. And after him finish, him tear them up. I didn't know she was coming. All the letters from Samuel and from the Immigration office, I don't let them go to the house. I give them me school address, for I can't put down a thing in peace. Plenty evenings me come home and find the place turn upside down. Walter looking for what him don't put down. Him looking for papers. All me clothes take off the hangers and search, all the drawers pull out, boxes that keep assignments for me students at school turn upside down. One suitcase I have underneath the bed that have birth certificates and receipts and insurance forms, him tear off the lock and turn it over.'

Gwennie raise up in the bed and look across at Aunty Cora. She try read the expression on Aunty Cora's face, but it was mask ownself.

Gwennie remember the Sunday, the Sunday evening Walter come back from New Green, the big quarrel them did have, the last quarrel. She know it was Aunty Cora who tell him she leaving for Foreign, but she couldn't figure out how Aunty Cora find out, for she did warn Grandma not to tell anybody. Walter was not to be trusted.

'Good thing I let me friend Percy keep them at his house,' Gwennie continue. 'I not sure how much Walter tell you,' Gwennie pause, choosing her words careful, 'but Percy is the fellow I met up at the school and turn friends with ever since.

'The week before I leave, I call the children oneside to tell them. It wasn't easy.' Gwennie's mind wasn't on Aunty Cora or the letter anymore, it was back inside the house at Porous where she was sitting down inside the off-white couch, her children around her – she looking on them with sadness in her eyes, hoping them will understand, them looking back, eyes shifting round as if wanting to understand but not quite able to grasp what was going on. 'I tell them I going away to get some rest. For if I don't go, I will drop down in front them. I tell them I love them and that them Uncle Samuel and his wife kind enough to invite me to spend time and to get a little rest.

'And I look at them all around me, Aunty Cora – Rudi, Del, Dave, Jeff, the baby was sleeping, and them just look back on me, not saying anything, almost like them dead inside. I tell them it would only be for two months. By the time them open and shut them eyes, the two months will be over, and I would be right there back with them. Well, is two months going on four years.' Gwennie sigh out loud and the eye water start to bubble-up around her eyes. She reach over for the half-empty can of Sprite, and Aunty Cora raise up and change her position. Outside a motorbike roar pass and after the noise die down, Gwennie continue on, her voice hoarse.

'Del don't even write. Since I left she don't pick up pen and paper to write. Almost as if she vex with me. Dave write, but after him complain how him hate living with Grandma, him send a long list with things I must send. Sneakers and sweat pants and so. No little tenderness inside the letters. Only Rudi alone write . . .'

And with that song, the bubbles in her eyes burst forth and run down her face. And even when Aunty Cora reach over to rub Gwennie's hands in her own, the crying never stop. And Aunty Cora rock her and sway her, all the time muttering over and over again, 'Aah gal, life not easy a blasted tall.'

And after what seem like a good ten minutes, Gwennie take a deep breath and start again, her voice little bit more strong and the bubbles under control. 'When Samuel see how me worry-up and fret-up meself over me children, him go and get the lawyer. The fellow come from back home too, but him damn expensive nevertheless. Samuel file for me citizenship, for me couldn't get any more extension on me visa. Me time was up.'

Gwennie turn around inside the bed and face Aunty Cora. It was the first time since Aunty Cora's visit that she feel relax all the way. The feeling she have now remind her of when Mr Anderson was still alive and she and Samuel used to go over to New Green every Christmas and spend time with Buddy, Aunty Cora's son. Aunty Cora's face was stronger then, her hair not as white, jaw not as slack.

'So me file for them after the lawyer clear me.'

'What about Peppy?' Aunty Cora's eyes cease from wandering around and look hard at Gwennie.

Gwennie catch her breath. She wonder if Aunty Cora think she avoiding the little girl. 'Me file for everybody, all me children.' Gwennie pause long. She feel an aching coming on.

Aunty Cora turn the rum-water glass to her head and drain it. 'You must write to write her, Gwennie. She will keep good correspondence.'

Gwennie nod her head. 'She ask about me?'

'But yes.' Aunty Cora's voice harden at the edges. 'After all she don't know you a tall.'

Gwennie sigh again. 'What she ask?' Her fingers were starting to twine around one another.

Aunty Cora scratch her head. It was silver all over. Since her arrival, Gwennie been combing it, parting and plaiting it every day. Usually she don't get to comb it but once a week for she wear the wig all the time. 'You know,' Aunty Cora wrinkle her brow, 'things pickney ask . . . Lord, I can't remember now.'

'Well, things will be better when she come.'

'No,' Aunty Cora grunt. 'Write her now. Make friendship with her, first.'

'You think she alright with Walter?'

Aunty Cora shrug. 'She and Rudi get on. She don't mention much about Walter in her letters.'

'Rudi always mention her in his. Say him glad she there. The two of them get on in truth.'

Aunty Cora shift around in her bed. 'You ever think about him, Gwennie? Peppy's father?'

'Sometimes.' Gwennie let out a long sigh. 'Sometimes I wonder if him know about her. But I don't think about him often. That pass and gone.' Gwennie raise up. 'Come me fix you another drink.'

Aunty Cora never say anything else. And Gwennie wasn't sure what to say herself. No, she don't think about Luther, often. But then she don't have to think about Luther to remember. Things like these don't go any place but deep inside you belly where them sit down and form things hard like the lump inside Aunty Cora's belly.

And even months after Aunty Cora left, Gwennie would still find herself thinking often about Peppy, even looking forward·to her visit. The other children too, but Peppy mostly. She wouldn't arrive till later though, according to how she and Samuel figure, but that alright. Aunty Cora say she playing the organ nicely at church and her brain quick in school, love to chat and argue just like she, Gwennie. Gwennie did smile to herself. Maybe if them hit it off when she come, them can talk. Maybe she might have interest in some of the meetings, she, Gwennie used to be involved in, but don't have time for anymore. Maybe she will turn out ambitious, make something of herself, so that she, Gwennie can feel proud of her.

Gwennie reach the gate, damp with sweat and out of breath as usual. She careful not to take off her sweater outside, as hot as she was. Samuel tell her that is grounds for pneumonia, for Foreign weather and back home not the same. She pick up the little envelope with the housekey from out the mail box and step through the gate. Only one car was in the driveway, the Volkswagen. That means Lucille on call, and it was Bill's weekend off. Gwennie kiss her teeth under her breath. She hope Bill have plans for the day, for as much as she like the two of them, she still don't want them in her way while she working. Them always want to chat. And is not that she don't like to sit down and chat with them, but she have plenty things to do and she would rather just do her work and go home, for she tired.

Gwennie never have to use the key, for the front door was wide open. She step inside the kitchen.

'Good morning, Gwen.' Bill was sitting down around the table drinking coffee from the big 'Good Morning America' mug. Him get up and pull out a chair for Gwennie, handing her an extra mug. Him was bright and cheery. Gwennie wonder what it was. 'Doesn't this coffee smell wonderful?' him say out loud, filling up her mug.

Gwennie puzzle-up her face. Him was too cheerful. She wasn't really a coffee woman, but she sip some anyway. Then a small smile start to gather-up around her mouth corner. It spread crossway her face. She take another big sip of the coffee. 'Oh! So you buy the coffee from back home. Blue Mountain. You like it?'

'It's really wonderful, Gwen. Lu even took some to work.'

Gwennie grin even broader.

'And you know what else, Gwen?' Bill's grin was almost as broad as Gwennie's. 'Last night Lu and I went to that restaurant, the one on Talbot Avenue that your friend, Daphne gave you the address for.'

Gwennie look up at him. Surprise write all over her face.

'The food was so good, Gwennie. I ate like a pig. I had that Escovitch Fish you were talking about.' Bill lick his lips.

Him did have on thick, black frame glasses that morning. They make him look younger than his thirty-four years. Him was still wearing pyjamas and his wavy brown hair with the sprinklings of white look as if him run neither comb nor brush through it since morning.

'Lu had goat, Curried Goat. She drank about a quart of water with that. It was so peppery, but good. We're going back there, Gwen. We're going to take our friends. It was too good.'

Gwennie put her hand to her jaw. She never know what to say. She just look at the grin spread crossway Bill's face. She did hand them the address last week, but she never expected them to go. Something about Bill remind her of Rudi. She can't quite put her fingers on it. Maybe is the way him was always trying to please her, always trying to get on her good side. Sometimes when she arrive at work with her face a little-bit longish, him would always want know what is the problem. When she just started working there, and him find out where she was from, him went out and bought several cassettes of popular singers back home, playing them over and over till him learn the words by heart. Now his collection even bigger.

But then sometimes him and Lu quarrel, and him turn into completely different person. Fling and break things, and a whole heap of cursing. She remember one Saturday morning, after letting in herself as usual, a whole heap of door slamming and bangarang greet her from upstairs. Fear grab her same time, and she couldn't tell whether or not it was damn thief in the house, or if the two of them was up there killing one another.

She grab a heavy dish pan from out the cupboard, and head towards the stairway, only to see Lu running down the stairs, face red and blotchy and tear-stained, while upstairs Bill was cursing 'bitch' and 'damn' and 'shit', brushing off hand-full of things off dressers, slamming

126

doors, breaking bottles against the wall, flinging out books through the window.

And Gwennie just sigh long and hard, wait till her heartbeat settle down back to normal, then head back to the kitchen to put down the heavy dish pan.

Lu was leaning up against the counter, inhaling deep and exhaling slowly one cigarette after another, grey-green eyes glaring at the curling smoke. 'Listen to that asshole up there breaking up all that shit,' she grind out through her teeth between pulls on her cigarette.

Gwennie never say anything, for it wasn't her business. Not that she don't expect them to quarrel, for them young and married only five years. But Lu is a woman who love to complain at length to Gwennie about Bill. And it wasn't that she didn't want Lu to confide in her, for in a way Lu remind her of an older version of Delores, but she don't want to get mix-up mix-up in them affairs. She's only a worker; them relationship different. She don't want to make recommendations one way or the other, causing bad feelings to develop, giving them reason to fire her. For them pay well and better to get on with than Professor Stevens and his wife, Mary-Jane, her during-the-week employers.

'All because I don't want to go to his mother's house for Thanksgiving. I hate that woman,' Lu drag hard on the cigarette. 'She hates me, too. And he knows it. So I don't know what the hell he's trying to prove. I told him I was never going back there again, and I'm dead serious.'

Still Gwennie never say anything. Standing crossway from Lucille, her back leaning against the sink, all she could think about was what a damn shame it was, for things so expensive. Her own house was there big and empty, yet this big man upstairs was mashing up the furniture like a blasted child. Furthermore, if the blasted woman didn't want to see his mother, then so let it be. Married don't mean Bill say, Lu do. Gwennie wanted to kiss her teeth the morning, but she try and control herself.

'Gwennie,' Bill break into her thinking. 'You're going to have to cook some of that wonderful food for me and Lu sometime. You could cook it here, or invite us to your home or something.'

'That's not a bad idea a tall. I'll think about it though.' Gwennie get up from around the table. She finish her mug of coffee and pour more into Bill's big mug. 'Right now I have to start the little cleaning.'

'Goody.' Bill return to the Hartford Courant, and Gwennie pick up her duffle bag, making her way briskly upstairs, for the coffee rejuvenate her.

She didn't mind cooking for them a tall, but she don't want them at her house. Maybe when she buy more furniture and a decent set of pots, them can come. But she don't even have nice plates to serve things on, either. Gwennie kiss her teeth. Maybe when the children arrive, and the house look more like somebody living in there, she can invite them. She would have to buy wine, make a cake for dessert, but then she don't even have any dessert forks and spoons, she don't have wine glasses either, and she can't jolly-well give them wine inside the same glass she drink water out of. Gwennie wonder when she will finally feel settled, and America feel like home to her.

Percy write and tell her she won't find happiness and feelings of settlement in housekeeping and child care. It won't happen till she comfortable with her life, till she start taking classes again, start teaching, all her children living comfortable with her and maybe a new love in her life. She know him was correct, for in truth she don't right like housework. She spend too many years in school for this, and especially for the children, it wasn't good example. But them soon come, and housework don't require much skills, and she want them to be comfortable. After that she can think about herself.

Inside the bathroom, Gwennie shove her feet inside the mash-down-back shoes, and put on her old frock. Then she hang up her good dress in the closet, sitting down her pair of shoes, side-by-side on the floor of the closet. Next she take out the vacuum cleaner, and the pail with Windex, Fantastik, Ajax, sponge, brush and mop pile-up inside. And after she have everything ready, Gwennie make her way into the private bathroom, for she was going to start cleaning in there first.

PART SEVEN

I

The evening Gwennie's first batch of children was to come, catch her at her house on Evelyn Street pacing through the rooms. She quit the live-in work with the Professor, since Dorothy fix her up with something temporary at the hospital, and Lu and Tom allow her the weekend off. So, all in all, she did have a whole week to herself and her children. She wish all of them could come at once, but according to how she and Samuel figure, it was best that the older ones come first so they can help her work and get a bigger place, and of course the baby as well, then later on Peppy and Jeff, since them would still need to finish up school. It was about five o' clock the Friday evening and the plane wasn't due in till around eight. Clive was planning to come by around seven to pick her up and then drive her to Bradley International over in Windsor Locks.

Gwennie step inside the room that was going to be Rudi's and Dave's. She know Rudi probably want his own room, but everybody will just have to make do for now. Painted white with a yellowish-brownish rug covering the floor, she hung peach curtains to add a little brightness. Other than that, the room was just big and square and empty. But it couldn't go any better than that, for after buying a similar set of twin beds for Delores' room, she'd only have money left over to take care of the children should any emergencies arise. She couldn't buy the lovely oak and dark mahogany bureau and chest of drawers and nice standing lamps she saw, as nice as them look and as badly as she wanted them.

Gwennie get up off the bed and open up the closet. It was empty except for the few pairs of trousers Samuel figure Dave might be able to fit into, if not Rudi, and some shirts. She run her fingers longside the top shelf checking for dust, and with one last sigh, she shut Rudi's room door behind her, fingers lingering on the shiny door knob. She make her way down the passage into Delores' room, but she didn't stay long, just long

129

enough to straighten out the wine-red comforter and shut up the wine red curtains. Then she shut the door behind her and step inside the kitchen. It was only ten past five.

Gwennie serve out a small saucer of food from the pots of rice and Escovitch fish with baby red tomatoes and Spanish onion and steam spinach she had on the stove, and fill up her glass with juice from the white jug in the refrigerator. She make her way into the living room with the plate of food and switch on the colour TV Clive gave her last Christmas. But by the time she settle down into the light brown all-around settee, and the face on the screen start to come into focus, she wasn't in the mood to either eat or watch the five o' clock Headline News.

After about two spoonfuls of rice, she reach over and turn off the television. Everyday the same thing, President Nixon sending more troops to kill off the people down in Vietnam, riots and civil rights activities going on about the place especially in New York and over in Boston, where her friend Daphne's daughter live. Gwennie walk back inside the kitchen and pick up the wall phone. She dial the number on the pad, her fingers folding and unfolding the telephone cord.

'Hi,' she say into the receiver after the operator pick up. 'Please if you could tell me whether or not airplane number 32785 leaving Kennedy International at seven-nineteen and arriving in Hartford at two minutes past eight going to be on time?'

'Thank you,' Gwennie mutter into the phone after the operator tell her yes. Then she hang it up and sigh. It was only five-twenty.

She wonder if the children catch the plane on time, if them tell Walter goodbye, and if him hug them and cry a little. But she should know better, Walter not going to cry, him probably find something to curse about instead. She wonder if him give them any message to give her.

She wonder how him look now after five years. Maybe little bit more meagre, eyes sink in more. Rudi say him don't eat much, drunk mostly. Gwennie shake her head. No, she wasn't sorry she left him. For when a man who used to be so religious turn his back on God, only retribution can follow. For how can he live with himself after turning so many people to Christ. She can't remember whether or not it was the drinking that started first or the back-sliding. But after the problems at the church with the missing collection money and the hiring of the new deacon, him wasn't the same anymore.

She wasn't a regular member of his congregation, for like Grandpa she was Baptist. Walter was Pentecostal, and that jump up-jump up, clapping, singing and loud preaching she wasn't into, but she used to hear about all that go on nevertheless. And although Walter couldn't understand why them needed to hire a new deacon when the congregation was showing him so much love and affection, she'd already suspect them out to frame him.

But even then the drinking wasn't so bad. It escalate around the time when Peppy was on the way. But then him did stop. For when she move back in, after leaving school, him never even used to keep liquor inside the house, but according to Rudi's letters, it seems as if him worse now.

She wonder if Walter wear any of the trousers and the shirts she send down in the last barrel. She made sure to send the colour shirts him like: baby blue, bright yellow, puke green, tan. She send matching man's socks too, and handkerchiefs, spotless white ones, for she know him like to have clean handkerchief each morning, iron neat and fold up into small squares so them can fit neatly in his back pocket with just the tip showing. Him used to look so smart in his khaki pants that she'd starch and iron out stiff the way him like it, shoes shiny as usual.

Him used to conk Dave and Jeff with his knuckles fold up when them wouldn't clean them shoes properly. Not so much Rudi, for Rudi was always neat and tidy. 'You can tell a decent man by the spotlessness of his shoes,' him would say to Dave and Jeff, as them try to dodge the shoe-brush sailing towards them. 'By the looks of the two of you, anyone can tell you won't amount to any damn good.'

She know that all the clean shoes business and conking of head come from the soldier training. That was before them start to courten, before she'd meet him again at Open Bible's church harvest, April 1958. Him was just returning from four years of training at Maybe Soldiers' Camp. She never spot him herself, it was her friend, Lucille Powell, who point him out.

'Gwennie, look. Mass Lindon Glaspole's son! The one who turn soldier.'

Gwennie take her eyes off the minister delivering the harvest service and turn towards Lucille's finger. 'Who?' Gwennie scan the group of young fellows leaning against the wall outside, waiting for the service to end, so them can buy up the harvest food. Walter was standing up out there, with about four other fellows his age, his face turn to hers.

'Mass Lindon's son, Walter. See him in the uniform.'

'Him change in truth,' Gwennie say more to herself than to Lucille, for him was staring at her bold and outright, the fellows behind him

131

grinning, fingers deep inside trousers pocket, hugging crotchs. Him was wearing the gray uniform then, with red stripes spotting the sides of the trousers and shirts, the beret tossed rakish over his eyes.

And Gwennie remember the Tuesday night when him was walking her back from Bible study, for ever since the harvest them been going steady. They were walking slow and holding hands. The night was dark, the air still, everyone else walking up ahead. Now and then one or two cars drive pass or a motorbike roar out loud in the distance. Up ahead girls shriek as boys pinch bottoms and touch bosom on purpose then cry excuse, face cover over in wide grins. Then all of a sudden, she and Walter start to walk more slow. His hands move from her side to settle somewhere near her shoulders, so fingers can easily reach down inside her sleeveless blouse. And him was smelling of Jergens skin lotion, Lux beauty soap, Palmolive hair oil, Mum scentless underarm deodorant and sweat mix up together.

Him ease her onto the trunk of the green skin mango tree without much propelling, lips spread out wide over hers; breath short and hot; hands, hard and sweaty fondling her face, neck, down her bosom, up her skirt. And she wanted to tell him no; she was still a virgin; them should probably wait till marriage; but not a sound would utter out. She wanted to tell him that her mother, not so much her father, would kill the two of them stone-dead if she ever find out, that him was much too big and might hurt her bad, that him was going too fast, too hard, and must slow down, for it was hurting and tearing and feeling like hell but feeling good at the same time. Maybe she could actually grow to like it, for she like him a whole heap, but right now him was going to have to hurry up and stop before the others find out and . . . Something wet and warm and silky was crawling down her leg. Him was breathing even again. His hands relax from around her neck. Him roll off.

Gwennie wasn't sure whether or not it was the phone she hear ringing first or the singing of the kettle she'd put on for tea. She pick up the phone.

'Hello? Oh, is you, Clive. No, I was just sitting here. No. Right out here in the kitchen. I just have plenty things on me mind. No, sir, I not nervous. What to be nervous about?' Gwennie kiss her teeth. 'Yes, them say it on time, eight. Yes, them change over in New York. Alright, I will call again. About seven-thirty. Alright. No, man, I'm alright. Yes, sure. Alright. Ba-bye.'

Gwennie hang up the phone and stare off into a far corner of the room, arms akimbo, face furrow-up, her eyes distant. She know Walter must have women friends. Rudi don't mention any, so maybe him don't bring them to the house, but now that the children gone, or at least the older ones, him will bring them. Him don't know shame. She used to find French letters in his pockets Saturday mornings as she sort through laundry. At the school, people who know them both would tell her about the girls sitting-up on his lap inside bar rooms, sipping beers and blowing him kisses. The funny thing about it all was she never use to feel one iota of jealousy. She would leave the French letters right on top of the bureau so him could see that she know.

For to tell the God truth, half the time she was so tired between school and the plenty children that she never have time to put Walter and his women friends on her syllabus. To tell the truth, she didn't really mind the distraction, for at least if him already satisfied from out the street, him wouldn't have to come to her at nights. Just as long as him don't bring any sickness home.

Gwennie walk over to the settee and sit down. She could feel the emptiness moving around in her stomach. She couldn't figure out any a tall why she have this man on her syllabus, when she must just forget him, take him out of her mind. But it wasn't so easy. She think about him plenty. Especially while at her living-in work, when her bed empty, when she don't have anybody to turn over and talk to. Not that she and Walter talked much. Sometimes weeks going on months before them exchange a word.

The last month before she left, though, was his strangest. And when she mentioned it to Percy, him never seemed a tall perplexed, just that him think maybe Walter suspect that she was leaving.

'But him don't know anything,' Gwennie tell him. 'I warn the children not to say a word whenever him around. Everything I plan to carry abroad with me, I bring to Grandma's and pack my suitcase down there.'

'Yes, Gwennie. But is the sixth sense,' Percy say to her, fingers twining around one another as them sit down in his car waiting for a red light to turn green. 'Sometimes you don't even realize you have it. When I was in boarding school over in England, one morning I woke up and I just knew something was wrong. First of all, I couldn't shut me eyes the whole night. And I didn't want to go classes the morning, I just wanted to stay in bed.

'And even when I was in class or on recess, I was just distracted, couldn't concentrate long on anything. And me is a man love to play cricket and when I wasn't even interested in that, you must know something was really wrong. And right after supper the evening, I got a message in me box saying I must report to the house matron. When I went, she had a telegram from me father saying Grandma Deedy was dead.' Him turn around and look at Gwennie, eyebrows raise. 'Things like that I call sixth sense. And I believe you have to trust and rely on it.'

Well, Gwennie figure that that was probably the case with Walter that last month. More and more evenings, him would come home in the most cheeriest of moods. Sometimes him bring home sugar buns, sometimes greta cakes, board games for the children. Sometimes him play cricket with Dave and Jeff, and with she, although him wouldn't say much, night time when she out in the living room correcting papers him would come and sit down with her. Sometimes him listen to Eric Lisson's talk show on the radio, other times him just read, Westerns his favourite.

And then two weeks before she leave, him ask her out to the movies. She and the children had just finished dinner, and she was sprawled off on the bed in her room. Walter did just come in from work and was taking off his tie. And after him tell her good evening, she know him say something about movies, but she wasn't sure, so she just tell him evening in return and leave it at that.

'Don't bother to tell me you tired,' him say after a while, 'you must want to go and watch a picture?'

Gwennie raise up and rub her eyes. 'Picture show? Who want to go?' She couldn't believe Walter was inviting her out. Since Jeff's birth, them barely go out as a family. Going seven years now. And she wanted to tell him no, she was feeling too tired, she would rather just lie down and rest before she start to make up a quiz for her class tomorrow, but then again, if him want to go to picture show maybe him wanted to talk, maybe him have something to tell her, and if that's the case, she might as well go, for she leaving soon and it could be important. She won't see him again for a long time.

'Well, you want to come or not?' Him was looking at her through the mirror, his eye corners creased up into a grin, half of his gold tooth showing.

And she look back at his reflection through the mirror, then at his back, smooth and broad without the shirt, his voice silky, gentle, almost playful.

'Alright,' she say to him, 'I will go.'

'Sure?' Him turn to look at her, nostrils spread out wide in a grin. 'Don't let me wring your hands, now.'

'No, I'm sure.' She turn away from his gaze, for all of a sudden she never like the sadness in his eyes. She wanted to tell him she was leaving in two weeks.

'Ready in ten minutes, then. I going to eat a little dinner.' Him step through the bedroom door with a white T-shirt in his hand marked: 'Crash Program Week, March 16-22, Keep Your Country Clean'.

During the whole time she was pulling on her jeans and looking around for a blouse to match, she was certain him hear from somebody that she was leaving. And even while him was driving her to the movie house, the car working its way in and out through traffic, she know him was trying to make friends with her, so she wouldn't go, or so she would tell him so him could tear up her papers or prevent her from catching her plane. She remained quiet inside the car, for when him was like this, extra-loving and kind all of a sudden, she wasn't quite sure what to make of him. One minute she want to soften up to him, next, she know she must be careful.

'Two shows playing,' him tell her. 'One Western with John Wayne, and the other is karate with Bruce Lee. Which one you prefer?'

'Bruce Lee,' she tell him, her voice eager. She enjoy watching the various styles of fighting, praying mantis was her favourite, then Shalin. She like it especially when the theatre have plenty people clapping and cheering as the enemy either win or lose, according to how them want it. She and Rudi and Delores and Dave used to attend Saturday afternoon matinees, long while back.

Walter did buy nuts from the vendor at the door. Everytime his fingers knock up against hers, as them reach inside the bag at the same time, she wasn't sure if it was just accident, playfulness or if him was ready to pounce on her any moment. Nevertheless she enjoyed the movie.

'What kind of sudden change is this?' she ask as them make them way back home.

Him face her, forehead puzzled as if him wasn't sure what she was talking about. 'How you mean, change?' Him look in the rear view mirror at his reflection and wrinkle his forehead.

Gwennie smile. 'You well know what I mean.' For in truth she couldn't believe it, just three weeks ago the man was ready to tear down the whole house in his determination to find her papers so him could burn them up. And look at Walter now, face smily-smily like everything peachy.

And as Gwennie stand up in the middle of the living room, eyes fix nowhere in particular, arms akimbo, she was glad she didn't make that evening at the movies fool her, for two days before she leave, him was crazy again. She went to the meeting with Percy as usual, the last one. And after Percy pull up at her gate and she tell him good night and was about to open the car door and step out, Percy pull her back. 'Gwennie, Gwennie look up at the window.'

'Is what?' Gwennie ask, turning her head to follow his fingers. And just as she see it, the curtain draw back same time and the wooden louvre shut up. 'Him watching me,' Gwennie sigh and step out the car. Walter was standing inside the living room when she open up the front door with her key.

'Might as well you just go home with him,' Walter greet her. 'This late time at night, might as well,' him look at his watch. 'Why bother to come home any a tall?' His voice was loud, but it wasn't angry, just tired. Gwennie tried to brush pass him, but him grab her hand. She pry open his fingers, inhaling the rum high on his breath.

'Let me go.' Her voice was low and tired. 'Just don't bother with me, tonight.'

His grip tighten even more, and she sigh out loud. The man in front her now wasn't the Walter of last week, or two weeks ago, or even three weeks. This Walter wasn't the man she go to the movie with, or the one that would come read with her out in the living room. This man was different. His eyes were red and wild-looking and hard. She couldn't read them. But him was sad. The whole room was sad with him. And she was starting to feel sad too. The children were already in bed, but she know them would be up listening. Sometimes she wonder what them think, especially Rudi.

'Walter, come let's go inside the room. Don't bother to wake up the children.'

Him allow her to drag him into the room, and by the time his head hit the pillow, him was fast asleep. Gwennie take-off his slippers and socks and straighten him out on the bed. She pull up the cover over him.

But by morning the cursing start up again. Sunday evening same thing. Him tell her she was no damn good for she was keeping men with him. Monday morning instead of setting off to school, she kiss her children goodbye and Percy, who'd taken the day off from work, help her to pack her last pieces of luggage in his car before driving her to Grandma's. Walter did leave early the Monday morning according to his own plans. Him was going to a convention with people from work.

'But you know, Gwennie, I think that man love you,' Percy say to her the Monday morning. Plenty cars weren't on the road, so the driving was smooth, easy. 'Love you to distraction.'

Gwennie shake her head. 'No, that's not love. That's something else. Something distorted. I don't know what. But that's not love.'

'Then why you think him so jealous? Why you think him watch you so? Why you think him so possessive? Him know you leaving, and even though him nice to you, you still don't trust him to tell him. I think it make him crazy.'

'I don't care what you say, Percy, the man don't have all his faculties together up in his head part. How can one person change like that in the course of two weeks. Change from normal loving human being into wild animal. Explain that to me, Percy Clock.'

Percy couldn't explain it. All him say is that Walter love her but him frustrated, for she Gwennie don't love him back same way. And since Gwennie never agree with him, she try and change the subject. But her heart was heavy. Her children didn't even did get the chance to come and see her off and wave goodbye to her at the airport. Here she was, a big married woman, yet she have to be running and hiding away from her own house, leaving her children behind as if she was doing something wrong. As if she didn't deserve the rights to a little peace of mind and a little rest and . . .

And as the doorbell ring startling Gwennie, for it was Clive ready to drive her to the airport, Gwennie wipe back the eye water that was starting to gather at her eye corners. She didn't know the day would finally come. It take five years and plenty suffering, but here it was. The door bell ring again and she walk towards the door. It was minutes to eight.

'I won't bother to come in and take a seat,' Clive say to her from the doorway. 'It's getting late. Put on your jacket and come. It's a little windy outside.'

'Come in, come sit down little. I have to haul on me shoes.'

'Lord, Gwennie, man. Look from the time I call to tell you I was coming over. What you been doing all this time? Why you not ready?'

'Clive, go and sit down a little bit and stop rushing me,' Gwennie call out from her bedroom.

'Christ, Jesus, why you must take so long to get ready. My goodness!'

'What I tell you about the bawling out of Jesus' name in vain, Cleveland Angels.'

'Lord, Gwennie, just make haste and come. You argue and gripe about Jesus too much.'

137

Gwennie laugh. She was ready, her bag in hand with four warm sweaters inside. She did have on her coat. 'Alright, I ready.' She lock the door behind her, and follow Clive out to the blue Buick. The spring air was a little bit nippy. She was glad she bring the sweaters. It was ten minutes to eight when she buckle up inside Clive's warm car. 'We late, Clive?'

'Gwennie, American planes hardly ever on time, so don't worry yourself.' Clive put the car in drive, turn on the lights, and roll out her driveway.

II

When Clive and Gwennie reach the airport, it was a little after eight-thirty. And all the search them search, not a sign of Gwennie's four children.

'You think we lose them, Clive?'

'Gwennie, don't talk foolishness. How we going to lose them? If them arrive and don't see you, them can sit down and wait. Them is big children. Furthermore them might have to wait long at customs since them from abroad.'

'No,' Gwennie shake her head. 'Them do all of that in New York already. For that is the first port of entrance.'

'Well, them must be around here somewhere, then.' Clive kiss his teeth, eyes squint-up tight as him scan the airport. 'This place is so damn big.'

The two of them were standing up inside the arrival section of Bradley International. It was packed to distraction with people. Every few seconds, a voice over the intercom report which flight ready to depart, which one touching down, which one the people must start boarding and at which gate. Gwennie was standing up next to Clive, the handbag with the four sweaters clutch tight underneath her arm.

'Gwennie, I don't even know who I must look for. What the children wearing, you know?'

Gwennie shake her head slowly. 'Just look for four of them,' she tell

138

him, her voice worried and tight, 'three big ones and one small baby girl.'

But all the look them look, still no sign.

'You stay right here, don't move,' Clive say to her after a while. 'I going to look over in that section, one more time.'

Gwennie's eyes lift up in the direction of his finger. She spot a row of seats where people who just come off the plane, sit down and wait. She wonder if the children change so radically that she was probably looking at them right now and didn't know it. She wonder if Rudi and Dave stout up with beard and moustache, if Del grow turn into big woman and Rosa, big girl. But she don't think so. Time don't fly that much.

'We might as well ask the lady at the counter,' Clive say over her shoulder, walking up silently behind her.

Them push them way through the crowd and up to the counter. Gwennie's back was stiff with worry. She could barely carry herself straight. Another plane had just come in from New York, and Gwennie strain her head to look in the face of every child that pass, to see if she recognize Dave's redness or Rosa's round face in the crowd, but nothing.

'You think maybe them never get on the plane,' Gwennie say more to herself than to Clive. 'Maybe Walter, out of grudgeful and bad mind because I didn't send for him, find out that them leaving and stop them, tear up the papers, bar them from leaving the house.'

'Them have your phone number. I'm sure them would call.' Clive's voice was calm. 'If something wrong, them bound to call.' Clive was a man slow to rise to any kind of emotional stir. 'The way you talk plenty about the big boy, Rudi, all the time, I sure nothing the matter that just won't work itself out.'

'Maybe,' Gwennie say to him, 'maybe.' But to herself she know that it have to be Walter who stop them. She did have her hand on her jaw. Look how she hope and pray for this day to come. Look how she work hard and suffer, with the hopes that one day – one day her children can come and live with her. That them can be one big family again, even if Walter wasn't there. And look, now. All of that for nothing a tall.

'Gwennie, get in line and stop the worrying. I going to call your brother, Samuel, to see if the children phone him.'

Gwennie take the space at the end of the line. Four people were in front. More start to gather up behind. The line was moving quickly. Not as many people were in this section of the airport. Gwennie sigh. Walter no doubt find the letters. That was the only reason she can think of. She

139

don't know why Rudi wasn't more careful with them, why him never just read them, or just tear them up, burn them . . .

'Next!'

Gwennie move up to the counter. Her mind couldn't even focus on the face in front, her eyes were filled to the brim with eye water. Things like these can only cause her to burn candle for Walter and wish that bad things happen to him. She always use to hope that she and Walter would never come to this, that if she ever go back home, them could behave like old friends.

She always used to hear about women back home who tie cloth and soak it in ashes for husbands who ill-treat them, and the husband would all of a sudden come down with sickness: pneumonia, comsumption, bad belly, all kinds of ailments. She used to hear about husbands who lift up hands to strike the wife and when them don't cripple up on the spot, them drop down stone-dead as bird. No, she never thought it would come to this between she and Walter, but now she understand what those women were going through.

She tell the lady at the counter, Patty, according to the pin on her chest, the name of her four children, where them coming from and how they were supposed to get on the flight in New York.

Patty's head float back and forth before Gwennie full-to-the-brim-eye-water eyes, as she shake her brown wavy hair, long, red fingernails knocking impatiently gainst the computer screen. 'No, ma'am. They aren't here. They're registered for the flight, but they never got on. Sorry! Next!'

'How you mean them never . . .' Gwennie say to her, ready to argue. But the man behind was already starting to pull his bags closer to Gwennie's white pumps.

'Next! Ma'am, you're holding up the line. Next!'

'Damn you to blast,' Gwennie mutter under her breath as she cut her eyes pass the man behind her, and the eye water spill over onto her cheeks. Damn you to hell. My four children are lost and what you care, what you business. She walk over to where Clive was standing, nearby the revolving doors, her eyes red, but her forehead knit-up and her jawbone and top lip stiff and determined.

'No luck, either?' Clive sigh as she march over, her footsteps heavy. 'Eh, might as well go home and wait till them call. Samuel say he and the wife been home all evening watching football. Not a word from the children.'

But Gwennie didn't even hear him, she was already through the door on her way over to where him park the car, the nippy March breeze blowing cold around her. If she don't hear from her children by tonight, she would have to send a telegram to find out if Walter was the stumbling block in them path. And if that was the case, she would have to call her friend, Daphne, and ask her about the Montserrat man that have the little one-room, card-reading, candle-burning office not far from her house. She would have to fix Walter once and for all.

During the drive back to Gwennie's house on Evelyn Street, not a word was spoken inside the car. Shadows cover over Clive's features and Gwennie's face was calm, a film of blankness over her eyes. They were focused on the road in front, but them never register the pond near the airport where all the fish have tumour so large, you can't tell the difference between the tumour and the fish own self. Her eyes never register the railway track that follow the highway for miles and miles, or even the billboards that advertise Liberty Mutual Insurance, and Buick, America's No. 1 family car, and Howard Johnson's special weekend rate.

Not even when Clive turn off the highway and move into the Puerto Rican neighbourhood did her eyes register the Spanish-American grocery store, where she sometimes ask the bus driver to let her off so she can buy bulla cake, fifty cents for half dozen, that she like to eat longside with pear and a tall glass of fresh milk. And when Clive slow down to make the right turn on Evelyn Street, her eyes never cut pass the housing project to her right, as usual, that always smell of urine and always have graffitti on the boarded up doors and windows, and where no matter what hour of the day or night, children always outside playing basketball. No, tonight, Gwennie's eyes weren't paying attention to Evelyn Street's big sore.

Instead, it was way back. Back to when she was about eight or nine, trying to figure out what it was she'd done then, why tribulation following her now, thirty years later. She wonder if is because she'd carelessly step on Blossom Pitter's pair of glasses and break them up in two, lens and all, and wouldn't admit to it for fear Blossom would tell her mother, who in turn would go to Grandma for the money and after Grandma and Grandpa finish cipher and give Miss Pitter the money, Grandma would turn around and beat Gwennie same way.

Or maybe is when she and Odette Chambers and Lucille Powell were inside the toilet one recess, panties roll down, fingers probing deep inside one another. But no, she wasn't more than nine or ten. God can't be punishing her for childhood sins. And Gwennie continue to think about the lies she used to tell, the money she used to take out of Grandpa's wallet so she and her friends could have more to spend at Harvest, or the times she used to cheat on exams. Yes, she know God is a good God, but maybe all those times she was testing his wrath without realizing it.

No, is the dog. It have to be the dog, Precious and the time when Grandma send her under the house to pick up the eggs. She'd carelessly fallen down, both she and the basket, breaking all thirteen eggs Grandma was going to sell so she could pay Mass Jasshe for last week's piece of pork. She was so frightened, she stay under the house bottom till Grandma had to call and ask her if she can't find the nest with the eggs. And Gwennie look-up into Grandma's face and tell her no, she couldn't find any, Precious probably eat them, for him was coming out from under the house licking his lips at the same time she was going under.

Grandma did tie up the poor dog to the gutter post and send Gwennie to cut a piece of guava-switch. And after Grandma whip the dog, she give him a poisoned egg, put him to rest. And Gwennie watch as the poor dog sniff the egg, then look at Grandma confused, for it know better than to eat her eggs, or to even go near them. But Precious did open his mouth and nonetheless swallow it down, for after all, a dog is a dog.

But she was young. She used to pray to God several times over asking His forgiveness. She used to hope Precious' soul would go up to heaven. But that was a long time ago. God have to forgive her by now. Maybe it was a sign because of the common life she living with Clive. It have to be. What else could be causing God to punish her like this, to want to keep her children away from her. And so when Gwennie let in herself and Clive inside the house, she sat down opposite him in a high back chair instead of next to him on the brown-all-around settee.

And when Clive say to her, after sitting down lonely for about fifteen minutes, 'Gwennie, how come you sitting so far away. I don't bite, you know.'

Gwennie tell him no, she was comfortable right there in this high-back chair, in a tone chillier than early morning breeze.

Clive never say another word.

Then them doze off, Clive's head rolling from side to side on the settee, mouth slightly ajar, while Gwennie dreamt about fire and brimstone and eternal furnaces. And so when the phone ring, the first thing Gwennie said was, 'Clive, open the door, so that whomever will, can come in.'

But Clive say to her, 'Gwennie, don't chat nonsense, is the telephone, go and answer it.'

Gwennie jump up same time, nearly tripping over herself in her haste to pick up the phone all the way out in the kitchen.

First it was the operator wanting to know if Gwennie will accept the charges, and then it was Rudi, his voice clear like fresh water, and sweet like church hymn when Miss Morgan play it on the pipe organ. And her heart stop same time and start again. Her eyes roll over and brighten, and she shudder, same way she shudder when she turn the shower on her nakedness each morning.

'Rudi, is you this? Look down, dear Father! You mean is you, in truth. Lord, look at me dying trial! You talking to me from Bradley. You come, all four of you. And Walter didn't even prevent you? Thank you, Jesus. I coming right away.' She hang up the phone.

And she didn't need to hear any of Clive's Calypso tunes on the Eight Track cassette in the car. No, her head was playing its own steel band and her heart had its own tune and her fingers and toes found them own rhythm.

When she and Clive push against the revolving door and it let them into the airport, it was the material she recognize first thing. It was a floral print she'd buy in the market that was made in Japan. She remember having to bargain long and plenty with the higgler in order to lower the price. Finally after much going and coming, the higgler suck in her teeth, pull down her mouth corners and give Gwennie the six yards of cloth for twenty-five dollars. Gwennie did make a skirt for herself, one full-length dress for Del and the remainder she send down to Grandma.

And as Gwennie walk over to Del, the steel band moving down into her belly, she notice how Del fill out the dress now. She was no more than stick own self then, her collar bone used to jut out in the wide V-neck and Gwennie had to take in wide darts at the chest, for Del wasn't even busting yet. Now the darts let out, and her curves and weightiness fill out the frock like any big woman. And it was like a dream, everything moving slow, she just a few feet from Del, Clive behind her, and Del just seeing her for the first time. Del's eyes darken then brighten and her mouth round up to form the word Mom, and her hands that were on her lap fold up, reach over to Dave on her left and Rudi over to her right with Rosa on his lap curl up asleep. And then Rudi and Dave's eyes darken and brighten. Then them get up, all of them, and move towards her, Rosa still asleep on Rudi's shoulder.

And Gwennie hug them, Del first. And the smell of Grandma's wood fire smoke in Del's hair cause the eye water to slap Gwennie's two cheeks, but then the Craven A cigarette smoke on Dave's breath as his cheeks rub against hers – Dave who look just the same, same colouring as she Gwennie, but who walk and sound and look just like Walter – slow down the steel band and dry up the eye water for one whole second. But then them start come down again, full force now, like rain in July and August months, as she hug Rudi and Rosa all in one. And in all her bliss, she never even notice the emptiness that cover over her children's face as them eyes brush Clive up and down. But Clive noticed.

And Gwennie's questions couldn't wait till the next day, no, she wanted to hear about the flight, them health, Peppy and Jeff, schooling, Grandma and Grandpa, the people who used to live behind Grandpa's cane field, and little Everton, if him grow into big man now – for when she left, him was not more than a little baby – and if the lady that used to play the pump organ, Miss Imo, still at church or if she dead by now, and the teachers back at Cobbler Primary, if Miss Hatfield marry yet, or Miss Martha have any more children. Gwennie was careful not to ask about Walter and all her furniture that was still in his house; the book case with the set of encyclopedia she save and buy, the set of twin beds in the children's room that she'd borrow money to buy. Them things she just wanted to cover up for the time being.

And Del was quiet from where she sit down in the back seat of Clive's Buick, sandwich between Rudi and Dave. She never have much to say as usual. Yes, she'd fill out her frock with curves and weightiness, but she was quiet same way, not quiet-silent, but according to Grandma, 'a quietness so loud, it could deafen you'. Yes, Gwennie was going have to work on Delores. In truth, Delores was never her right hand, it was more Rudi. Him alone would do everything.

And Grandma used to warn her, 'Gwennie, make them equally your right hand for them close in age, and jealousy's not a good thing. It can breed contempt so sour, it sit down and fester like sore and when it burst open, not even the fact that blood thicker than water going to save you or them.' But Gwennie wasn't thinking about those things back then.

From the back where him sit down, knee caps straining through his trousers and his feet hook up crooked against one another, for there wasn't enough room in the back to allow him to stretch out, Dave did have plenty to say about America with all the observations him make so far tonight since his feet touch New York. Yes, him got a chance to peek inside the New York Times, and was quite glad to see that Mr Nixon was trying his best to restore democracy to the war-ridden people of Vietnam.

And yes, he got a chance to walk about a bit in New York, and it seems as if Connecticut is not as busy and of course as important as New York and if Gwennie think she would move to New York anytime soon, for him understand that the West Indian population in New York is quite large, even though the better schools, according to what him understand, are in Boston. And yes, him been hearing lots and lots about the racial climate in America, and was wondering if Gwennie experience any of it yet, for even though his arrival is quite brief, him already observe that only dark people seem to be doing janitorial services at the airport.

But regardless of all that, him is quite pleased to acknowledge that him won't be tying out Grandpa's cows anymore and as a result become infected with ticks, and yes, it will be the end to that going-under-house business to pick up eggs and to be chased by those damn peely chickens and yes, that church-going business day in and day out that him had to put up with so much down at Grandma's will finally come to a full stop once and for all.

And Rudi, well, him never seem to know quite what to say. Between his mother's plenty questions, and Dave observations and speculations that him hope would hurry up and come to an end, him just relax with Rosa in his lap wide awake now, eye water stains on her face. For from the minute her eyes open and them behold Del and Dave, Rosa start to stiffen up. Yes, them travelled on the plane together, and yes, she recognize them from her frequent trips down to Grandma with Rudi, but that didn't mean she like them, really. But when she see Gwennie and Clive, faces she didn't recognize a tall, for Gwennie left when she was only two, she start to hold on even tighter to Rudi.

And no, Gwennie shouldn't have allowed her feelings to show on her face when she reach out to Rosa and the little girl pull in and cling on to Rudi, whimpering dad-dy, eye water running down her face. Maybe Gwennie should've just shrugged it off and try again with Rosa tomorrow after she get a little rest and was feeling more relaxed. But not so with Gwennie. It was like a splinter to her finger-quick.

And Clive, his back stiff and straight, just silently transport Gwennie and her children through traffic and across town. On the way to Evelyn Street, no one directed neither question nor comment to him. One or two times Gwennie try to include him in the conversation, but him never have much to contribute. When them reach, him take out the baggages and drop them off in the respective rooms. Him didn't tell Gwennie him was leaving, but him never drive off right away. And Gwennie was so busy with her children, trying to make friends with them all over again, trying to make them comfortable, trying to welcome them, she didn't get a chance to tell him thanks or even to listen to whether or not Clive drive off.

III

Stirring didn't start-up in Gwennie's house till early afternoon the following day. After everybody settle in and eat and chat the Friday night and she finally turn off lights, fasten the night latch on the front door and bolt the back one, she never shut her eyes till about five the morning.

It pleased her heart in truth to see the children sitting around together, eating and laughing. No, it wasn't all of them, but that was soon to come. And no, it wasn't around the long, oval, mahogany dining table with the six matching straight-back chairs with candles lit-up all around, but that too was soon to come. They sat down around the small enamel table with barely enough chairs. She'd have to borrow a few stools from Clive. Rosa was asleep on her bed in Delores' room, and Gwennie was using for the first time, the brand new china Samuel and Dorothy gave to her. And even when Delores spill gravy on the new white tablecloth and Dave carelessly drop one of the plates and break it, as him reach across the table for his fifth helping of food, Gwennie was just too content to make things bother her.

Delores remain quiet throughout the entire meal, but Gwennie didn't care, it was enough to just look in Delores' face and brighten with pride to see how she ripen into womanhood. And Dave, Gwennie had to shake her head, for every time him open his mouth to speak, she hear Walter's voice. But not even that was going to interfere with her happiness. When dinner was over and Dave push back his chair and light up a cigarette, with the argument that him understand that children in America can do anything them please, them not as backward and country-like as those

146

back home, Gwennie didn't even quarrel with him and ask him to please put it out.

But after him take the last several puffs, she let him know that as long as him living under her roof, him will please not smoke in her house, for him couldn't damn well smoke inside Grandma's kitchen, so she can't understand why so soon him ready to come and take advantage of her. But even them things didn't bother her, for life was too just too sweet for clouds to come and cover it over.

But after Gwennie lay down in her bed the Saturday, her mind rerunning all that happen the day before, she couldn't help but feel an aching somewhere deep inside. And she know the feeling in her belly didn't have anything to do with Rosa for she'd already patch up things with her. For after she hear Rosa hollering out in her sleep in the early morning hours, she dragged herself out of bed and brought Rosa back with her.

And when Gwennie's hazel eyes meet with Rosa's light brown ones, the hollering ceased. But then it start up again and Gwennie had to pull out the bag of clothes she picked up at J. J. Newbury's and show Rosa the skirts, full-length ones for church and shorter ones for school, short sleeves summer blouses and boxes and boxes of toys. But nothing a tall could pacify Rosa. It wasn't until Gwennie pull out the bag with the shoes, that Rosa's eyes start to pick up interest. In no time she was fast asleep again, but not before she find out from Gwennie if all the frocks and games belong to her in truth.

But the person that cause Gwennie the most grief was Rudi. No, him wasn't the full-face little boy with knock-knees she'd left back home, he'd lengthen out into a big man now. For when she saw him at the airport: face cool and smooth, eyebrows fluff-up and neat, hair cut close to his head with not a strand out of place, and the moustache just like a line on the top of his lip, she just wanted to shield him from Clive. From out the corner of her eyes, she could see the look that shadow Clive's face then pass, but not without little of the hardness still remaining in his eyes.

And it wasn't anything that Rudi said or did, it was just the way him carry himself: clothes neat and close-fitting, colours blending in so well causing both she and Delores to look like butu compared to him. Not to mention Dave, who look just like an old cruff. But she could see the word imprint on Clive's brain as the little knob in his throat bob up and down: batty-man.

'Them is an abomination before God and man,' Clive used to say to her, face cover over with scorn as him point out the young fellows in the mall down town. 'Look, look at that one, Gwennie!' And her eyes would follow his fingers to see a nice looking chap, in tight faded jeans walking briskly towards them, earring in one ear, hips swaying delicately; other times towards a group of them sitting down on the bench in the mall that surround the fountain, legs fold up as them chat and laugh, voices high-pitched, hands laden with jewellery of all sorts as them pose and posture to one another. Sometimes a pair of them walk past, fingers almost touching.

And as Gwennie is a woman who don't love jump to conclusion and pass judgement, for who she to judge, to cast the first stone, she who sin herself, she used to say to Clive, 'But I don't see anything wrong with them? Granted them loud and raucous with faces as pretty as money, but . . .' For in truth, them was regular-looking, even though something about them would always bring to mind visions of Percy, but she couldn't quite put her fingers on it. 'Some of them look a little effeminate,' she would tell Clive, 'but that don't mean anything for I know a few ministers at church back home who used to look and even go on like these fellows. Some even married . . .'

As she continue on telling Clive, her mind run on the men she knew back home who people called batty-men, but she didn't pay much attention to the name calling, for usually they were big and respectable people in the community. She'd even hear that her very own Teacher Brown was that way, that him live in the big white house on the hill with a fellow from Vere. The older gentleman that run the festival each year, Robeson, she hear was that way too, and the young man at the post office . . .

'Them not always effeminate,' Clive break into her thinking, trying to explain, distaste written all over his face, 'sometimes them manly like me, big shoulders and everything, but if you look in them face you can tell . . . it's just soft and tender like a woman's . . .'

So when her eyes bless Rudi for the first time at the airport, and after him put down Rosa and started coming towards her, she wished she'd ask Samuel and Dorothy to accompany her instead, for them more tolerant about these things. She remember the evening when she and Clive were over at Samuel's house watching the documentary on homosexuals, and how Clive had to take it upon himself to let his feelings be known about the matter.

And even when Samuel claimed that him live in America too long and life was way too short to allow anything to bother him except water pollution and nuclear war, Clive was still disgruntled. But Dorothy did shut him up good and proper when she tell him that she used to dabble-dabble in it before she got married and was even still on good terms with the woman.

'But that's different you see,' Clive explain to her. 'For you married now and was only going through phases then.' But Dorothy let him know, after Samuel leave the room, that if she was ever to leave Samuel she would probably go back to Dawn for that was one of the most balanced relationships she'd ever have. Clive never have much else to say after, except that him can't decipher what it is exactly that the women do. And as Gwennie know that Dorothy is a woman who wasn't bashful to explain things in great detail, no matter who the company, she cry excuse from the conversation and left the room.

She couldn't understand why her feelings towards the subject was seeming to lean towards Dorothy and Samuel's argument. But maybe it was because of the hatred and comtempt she hear so much in Clive's voice that cause her to adopt another view of the matter altogether.

Laying down in her bed the Saturday morning, Rosa fast asleep next to her, the remainder of household just beginning to stir, Gwennie decide she will just have to bring Rudi down to the church and make him meet some of the people down there. Them have young people's groups and choir and prayer meetings, she would have to make sure him join them and keep himself busy, for it was too easy to fall into sin and bad ways and the devil always have work for idle hands. That one she would have to nip in the bud right-a-way before it grow and fester. Not that she was any strong church-goer herself, but with all the violence she see and hear about, she realize only the Lord alone can be her protector, not husband, not friend, not gun, not dog.

And as Gwennie prepare lunch the Saturday afternoon, it strike her again, as it strike her times and times again, the way life was funny. For maybe if she'd stay with Walter and look after her children, maybe Dave wouldn't take up smoking and hatred of church, maybe Rosa and Delores wouldn't be so distant, and maybe Rudi wouldn't be so different. No, but she didn't want to think about it, for it wasn't fair. She didn't leave them for selfish reasons. Everything she did was for them betterment, so seeds fall along the wayside, she guess, but she was going to fix that, she along with the covenant of God.

Saturday evening Samuel cook as usual, for Dorothy don't like the fireside much, and invite them over. Sunday morning bright and early, Gwennie parade them off to the little Baptist church not far from her house. After church, she introduce them to all and sundry. The Goodisons that live further down on Evelyn Street and who own the laundry mat chain, the Tomblins whose daughter teach in the same elementary school she plan to send Rosa, the Whiteheads whose son Gerald was in the choir.

She was feeling a little let down when Rudi tell her him not in the choir anymore, but she was going to change that. She bring him up to the director of the church choir, Mr Cruise, to let him know that not only did her son have a lovely singing voice, but him couldn't wait to audition.

And as if Sunday morning wasn't enough, after dinner and a fresh change of clothes, she bring them to Young People's meeting Sunday evening after much grumbling and cursing from Dave, who claim him was almost certain this blasted church-going business was over with. But Gwennie was already determined that no one was going to remain in the house after she lock and bolt the door behind her. At Young People's meeting, she have Rudi, Delores and Dave sign up for Bible Study, Tuesday and Thursday evenings, eight to nine-thirty, and Rudi for the choir and Rosa for Sunday school.

The remainder of week, she register Rosa and Dave in school, bring the other children downtown to show them around, and so by Monday morning when she started off to work at the hospital, Rosa started off at Eliot's elementary, Dave was waiting to hear from the Youth Program up in Springfield, and Rudi and Delores knew where to find the grocery store in order to buy the newspaper and scour it for work.

IV

As the spring months began to get warmer, and the snow wasn't as plentiful, and the trees were starting to look green again, and Rosa started to make friends at school, according to the report from her first grade teacher, and Delores and Rudi found work, and Dave was calling home every weekend complaining about the food and his two room-mates, Rudi and Gwennie were starting to fall out. Delores was well into the church now. She'd been going for four months straight, never yet missing one meeting or late for any. But it was a totally different story with Rudi.

Him went the first two weeks, then never again. Him didn't even turn the black of his eyes to look at Mr Cruise's phone number, who call and leave messages just about every day begging him to come, the new voice is desperately needed. Sunday mornings when everybody else get up and start to fix-up for church, not so with Rudi, him was just ready to pull up the comforter over his head, stretch out his two feet, and settle back into sleep.

One Saturday night about nine-thirty as she hear him starting to get ready to go out, she make her way over to his room and seat herself on his bed. She wasn't quite sure how to begin, for them almost like strangers these days. She'd ask Clive if him could please talk to Rudi, but that only made matters worse. Rudi told Clive plain and simple to please stop interfering and trying to run his life, for Clive not his father. Sunday mornings Gwennie curse and quarrel, but it didn't matter. Rudi refuse to pay her a drop of mind. She didn't quite know exactly what to say to him as she watch him in the doorway of his closet, pondering his attire for tonight's party.

'You hear from Peppy, lately?' She decide to start off with a bit of pleasantry.

Rudi didn't turn around. Him barely grind out a 'no'. Gwennie wasn't sure if him hear or not.

'I get a letter from Aunty Cora,' Gwennie tell him. 'She say the eye operation didn't last long a tall, that the eyes worse than ever now.' Gwennie stop, waiting for a response. She continue on. 'She say Peppy helping her out plenty, though. But she don't like the company Peppy hanging around with these days.' Gwennie pause again and shift round restless on the bed. Rudi pick out a pair of trousers and match them against two shirts.

'She say her son Buddy from England came out and caused quite a stir in her life, rise-up her blood pressure and almost cause her relapse. She say him ask to see the will. And when him see that him only get the church and few heads of cow, while Peppy get the house, Leslie the shop and few acres of land, George and Miss Gertie get land too and a cow each, him started to go on real bad, demanding that she change the will right away. I don't know what she ended up doing, but Mama will soon write.' Gwennie stop to catch her breath.

'So where you going, tonight?' Her voice did have a calm and softness she didn't quite feel inside her belly. She could hear the hangers clinching against the steel railing in the closet, as Rudi pick through the row of clothes hang up, and the tap inside the bathroom dripping. She's been asking him going on two weeks now to pick up a washer at the lumber placé, but it seems as if she might have to do it herself, for Rudi wasn't showing any interest in the running of the house.

'Party,' him sigh out loud.

'Where?'

'Downtown. Friend's house.'

'Which friend?'

Rudi turn around to look at her for the first time, forehead crease-up, eyes narrow. 'What you mean which friend?' His voice was sharp.

'Church friend, work friend, friend friend?' Gwennie's voice rose to the occasion.

'Work friend.' Rudi back off.

'So when you think you will come in? I was hoping all of us could go to church tomorrow and . . .'

'Church, church, church,' Rudi fling down the shirt in his hand and slam the closet door. 'That's all I hear in this damn house, day in and day out. 'Mama, when you plan to stop nag-nag me about church.'

'Please don't raise your voice to me, sir. Me and you not the same size. Tomorrow I want the whole house to go to church. I don't know where you and Dave get this nasty habit from. The man call here every day about the choir. But you're not interested in God, you're interested in party and friends. You don't even invite Delores. You don't tell anybody about your friends, you don't invite them over or anything. You just come to America, you don't know what America gives, but every night you pick up your tail and go to party. Your Bible sitting down in the kitchen catching dust.'

By this time Rudi did have on his clothes and was combing his hair. Him rush inside the bathroom and haul on his trousers. Gwennie was inside the room same way when he came out ready to put on his shoes.

'I won't tell you that you can't go out,' Gwennie tell him as him pick up his keys ready to leave, 'but we leaving here tomorrow morning eight o' clock, sharp.' She brush pass him out the room, her breath coming out light and fast. She didn't know the day would come when she and Rudi would come to this.

152

V

Gwennie heard the phone ringing early the Sunday morning, but she was too tired to reach over and pick it up. Seven o' clock Sunday morning when she wake up and start to prepare breakfast, she still didn't hear any stirring coming from out Rudi's room, but she was determined not to wake him. Twenty minutes to eight, she and Rosa and Delores eat breakfast in silence for she wasn't going to ask any questions, and Delores, who was half asleep when she pick up the phone and wasn't really sure if she'd talk to him or not, didn't remember to tell Gwennie that Rudi called to say him wasn't coming home that night.

Eight-fifteen when them pick up the bus at the foot of Evelyn Street, Gwennie sigh throughout the entire twenty-five minutes bus ride. Several times Rosa have to stop and ask her, 'Mama, what's the matter?' But Gwennie just shake her head, lips clamp shut. The letter she receive from Grandma not too long ago was still dancing around in her head, for Grandma tell her, even though Rudi might not give her much headache, she know Gwennie must be meeting hell with Delores and Dave.

'The children growing up,' Grandma write, 'them don't take telling as easy. When me and your papa talk to Dave, him turn his back and kiss his teeth. Delores, she, just shrug and go on about her business. The only reason I don't tear them behind is cause the arthritis gone up inside the hands, can't grab them and drive that switch crossway them backside like first time. So, you have to watch out. Them children will give you a damn warm time.' So say, so done.

Gwennie couldn't concentrate on one word Reverent Simms utter that Sunday morning, her mind was elsewhere. When time comes to sing hymns, her lips could only form over the words, her heart wasn't there. When service was over, she didn't gather around and chat as usual, she leave Rosa with Delores and she alone catch the twelve o' clock bus for home. She didn't know what she was going to say to Rudi, but someway, somehow those children will have to understand that she is the one running the show. She didn't have husband to do it, therefore when she talk, she mean business.

VI

Gwennie didn't stop the bus at Evelyn Street, she continue on. For to tell the truth, she couldn't face the house, she couldn't face Rudi, and she just needed to air her mind a bit. She not too long send off a letter to Peppy and one to Aunty Cora. She didn't have any problems writing to Aunty Cora, but the one to Peppy wasn't easy.

She start the letter one night as she lay down in bed restless, and by the time she was finished, she'd have several sheets of paper rolled up and crushed on the floor. She finally send off the letter ten days later, but with her heart heavy, for she wasn't at ease. She could imagine Peppy's face, after she get the letter. She wouldn't jump up and down like a normal child when she see the ten dollar bill fold-up, no, she would probably just turn it over in her hand, to make sure it wasn't counterfeit, then put it back inside the envelope longside with the letter she'd probably read three or four times looking for message Gwennie didn't put in there.

Gwennie sigh to herself, maybe she not to think these things, for after all she didn't even know the little girl. When she left back home, Peppy wasn't more than seven going on eight, but ripe nevertheless, face round and her grin spread out just like Luther's. What little news she hear about her, come from either Rudi or Aunty Cora. She know Peppy's the apple of Aunty Cora's two eyes, for when Aunty Cora start to talk about her, Peppy don't hear, don't talk, don't see evil. She get good marks in school and was inquisitive. Even Rudi was taken with her, too. When him just come, the first month or two, every week him dispatch off a new letter to her, and in almost every conversation she and Rudi have, the little round face girl was always mentioned. No doubt, Peppy's the apple of his eyes, too.

Him don't even spend much time with Delores. Him don't talk to Dave a tall. Him even tell Gwennie him and Dave don't have anything in common. Dave was too damn slacky-tidy and nasty. And Delores, she don't even know. Sometime she hear the two of them inside the room talking good-good and then all of a sudden voices start to rise, like heat simmering off hot piazza after a long rainfall. Then she would hear Rudi give out, 'But Delores, it was only a movie, you know. Why you have to include God inside everything, so?' And Delores would raise her voice to

154

meet his and to let him know that God was everywhere, was inside everything, even inside the head of the man who write the script.

And Rudi whose face would be already puckered, and whose lips would be slanted to one side, same way the moustache, would suddenly storm out the room muttering, ' . . . Blasted church brainwash you, you can't even think straight, can't even hold a blasted argument.' And as Delores is a woman who love to hold grudge and malice after any disagreement in opinion or argument, seven going on eight days would pass before she even stretch out her face to grin.

One summer day Gwennie beg Delores to please accompany Rosa to a function at the Youth Camp, since she had to work late the evening. 'Why Rudi can't bring her, ma'am. I have plenty things to do down at the church tonight.' And as Gwennie was starting to notice the blue VW that was always parked up outside the gate half hour going on forty minutes with Delores inside, she was starting to wonder what was really going on down at the church. For Delores just keep on explaining to her how the fellow driving the car was just a church friend, nothing else. And so when it seemed as if Delores didn't have any intention of bringing Rosa to the function, Gwennie had to raise her voice.

And the evening she stood up inside the doorway of Delores' bedroom and tell her, 'Missus, is one bull in this pen, and that is me. I don't care how big you be, I am still the bull. So you please bring Rosa down there and don't let me have to open me mouth about it again.'

And Delores bloat up and sour up herself like any spoiled breadfruit, ready to burst forth any day now, and the evening she brought Rosa to the function, but she didn't say another word to Gwennie going on weeks. So when it wasn't Rudi, Delores have up inside her crop, it was Gwennie. Rudi say him can't bother with her a tall, she's too some-timish. Him just dying for Peppy to come.

The bus was starting to empty as it approach the terminal. Only a handful of people remain. Gwennie get off one stop before the terminal and wait at the bus stop with about five other people for the Hartway bus that would drop her off at Samuel's house. She never have long to wait.

Samuel was just rolling out of bed when Gwennie ring the door bell, and it wasn't till the third ring that Samuel open up the door. Him was still in his robe, with Dorothy's bed slippers to match, heels hanging over the back.

'But look at me dying trial! Gwennie Glaspole, you know I just finished calling your house to invite you and the children to dinner. I pick up some lovely pieces of oxtail yesterday down at the Farmer's Market. And I seasoned it up well last night so we can have it today.'

'Rudi answer the phone?' Gwennie ask him as she step inside the house.

'No. No one was home.'

'Rudi wasn't home?'

Samuel look at her, a grin forming around his mouth corner. 'Him didn't come home last night?'

'Why? Why you ask that?'

'The expression on your face. What's wrong, now? You and the children cutting one another's throats.'

Gwennie follow Samuel into the kitchen. 'Where Dor? Still asleep?'

'No. At work.'

'Today, Sunday!'

'Gwennie, money still has to be made.' Samuel pull out a chair give Gwennie and pour out a tall glass of juice for her and one for himself. 'Hungry?'

Gwennie shake her head.

Samuel pull up on chair next to her own, take a long drink of the juice, set the glass back down on the table, belch long and deep, ask pardon, and turn to Gwennie. 'Rudi never sleep home last night?'

'It seems that way.'

'Him find a young lady.' Samuel's eye corners wrinkle as him try and hide the grin that wanted to cover over his face that look so much like Gwennie's; same cocoa-butter complexion and hazel eyes and light brown hair and round face.

'I don't know what him find out the street. But whatever it is, it must be sweeter than church. For him show no interest a tall in going.' Gwennie stop, she know Samuel wasn't the person to talk to about church, for him only go one or two times a year. 'Every night him out.'

'Gwennie, nothing the problem if the boy find a woman.'

Gwennie kiss her teeth. 'I'm not so sure it is a woman, sir. A fellow keep on calling the house asking for him, so I don't know.'

Samuel take another long drink of the juice and then get up to replenish his glass. Gwennie's own still wasn't touched. Samuel sit back down. 'Gwennie, you can't jump to conclusion.'

'I not jumping to a thing. I just telling you who call and don't call at the house for him.'

Plenty time roll pass. Gwennie sip the drink and Samuel finish off his own. Gwennie sigh and Samuel shift around in his chair. Gwennie's eyes brush over the pictures Dorothy have on the walls from her photography class. Some were close-up shots of things you see every day: chair leg, somebody's head back, the base of a kitchen pipe, but by the looks of them now you could never tell.

'Then the two of you talk about it, Gwennie?' Samuel's face was tired. Black stubbles swarm his cheeks like sugar ants on sweetened condensed milk.

Gwennie shake her head. 'Him there vex, now. Say him tired to hear the word church mention.'

Samuel got up and reach inside the fridge for the pan with the seasoned oxtails. The smell of onion and garlic and black pepper and ginger root and thyme and scallion fill the room. 'Well, Gwennie, I don't know what to tell you,' Samuel say to her, 'you and him will have to work it out, come to some kind of compromise. You going to have to give a little, take a little. But don't forget Rudi is a big man. Him almost twenty-one. Which means him going to want to lead his own life, come and go as him please without much interference. His plans for life may not follow the same route you have mapped out for him, but you going to have to give him room.'

Samuel turn on the fire under the big aluminium Dutch pot and pour in the oil. 'If him don't want Jesus and church, you can't force him, try and try as you might. Mama and Papa wanted me to become a minister, but those weren't my plans. Till this day, me and Mama can't look in one another's eyes straight. Papa not too bad, but Mama still have me up somewhere inside her belly. Don't chase away Rudi.' Samuel pour out the entire dish of oxtails inside the Dutch pot, and the frying was so loud, not a word mention again for a while.

'But them have to listen,' Gwennie tell him after the noise die down.

'Yes, but careful. Don't chase him away.'

Gwennie didn't say anything else. She pick up her handbag with her Bible and hymn book from off the long oval oak table with the six matching straight back chairs and tell Samuel she heading out.

'You need a ride?'

'No, don't bother,' Gwennie tell him. 'It's nice and warm and sunny outside with just the slightest little breeze blowing out hot air. I love to feel it on me face. I just want to get out the house a little and to clear me head. You go on and enjoy your oxtail.'

157

And with that song Gwennie left. Samuel watch as she step through the door, turn left out the gate and make her way down the street. But Gwennie wasn't on her way home. She stop off at the telephone booth not far from Samuel's house, and call Clive to tell him she coming over. And Clive's response was just dead, no little emotion or anything a tall in his voice. After hanging up the phone, Gwennie wasn't sure if she was doing the right thing. She have a feeling Clive wasn't going to be easy to get on with.

Him never kiss her cheeks at the door as usual, nor did his face light up as if glad to see her. His eyes were sombre, they weren't dancing around. Seems as if the candle inside his heart blow-out for her. Clive's apartment was on the second floor of a big three-family house. It was spacious and bright, windows open wide and shades pull up, to let in freshness. The stereo in the living room was blasting Calypso tunes. It's been almost two months now since them last see one another.

Whenever him call to make plans, almost like a bad luck, she always busy. And since the children don't show him much respect, him don't come around as often. Only him and Rosa get on well, sometimes through the mail, him send her colouring books, crayon, dolly or jacks set, children's records and tapes. Plenty times when she want to use the phone, Rosa's on it with her friend Clive, as she call him. Him and Delores polite with one another, but him and Rudi can't bear to be in the same room. Up till now him still don't tell Gwennie why. And she don't ask.

'I'm outside on the patio drinking a cold beer,' him tell Gwennie. 'Want one?'

She nod.

Outside on the patio, she kick off her black shoes and stretch out her toes with the pink nail polish peeling off. It was cooler up this area than over at Samuel's. She sprawl out herself on Clive's open-back chair.

'Didn't think you'd ever want to see me again, since your children arrive,' Clive say to her, as him hand her the glass of beer and sprawl off himself next to her on his own open-back chair. Him wasn't wearing a shirt and Gwennie could see all his scars from childhood that grow with him.

Gwennie kiss her teeth. 'How you mean? You know that's not true a tall-tall. I just busy.'

158

'Only Rosa alone call. Everytime I try to make plans, you cancel. Say you're busy or you're tired. I thought that with all your children around now to help, you would have more free time.'

'Yes, you're right. But here I am now. I come to visit.' She didn't want him to get on the subject of how him think Rudi wasn't helpful enough as a big son should, and how this couldn't be the Rudi she use to talk about so much. She turn sideways to look at Clive. 'I wanted to get away from the children and the house a little and just relax meself.'

'So I am the escape route.' His voice was scornful. 'I guess I should be thankful that at least I still serve a function.'

'Clive,' Gwennie put out her hand to touch him.

Him pull away. 'No, don't stop me, I talking the truth, and you know it. I try with you and your children, I put in plenty hours, Gwennie. But I'm not happy. I'm not satisfied. I don't feel good. You say you're interested, but I don't think so.' Clive turn around to face her. 'I don't think you care about my feelings a whole heap, Gwennie. I don't think so a tall.'

And to tell the truth this wasn't the way Gwennie wanted to spend her Sunday evening. She wasn't sure what brought her over there, but maybe somewhere deep inside she just wanted to put a full stop to things with she and Clive once and for all. And no, it wasn't that she not interested in him, for she like him plenty, but Clive ready to marry and turn father to Rosa, and she didn't have married life on her syllabus. Maybe if she was more in love with him. Love. Gwennie stop and smile to herself. The word sound foreign to her. It's been so long. She was in love with Walter at the very beginning she think, but not since. Maybe for the short while that she knew Luther. But she wasn't sure.

Gwennie reach over and squeeze Clive's hands in her own. They were warm and sweaty. She was afraid to look in his face, something tell her his eye water was just waiting to bubble over. 'Is not that I don't care, Clive,' she tell him, her voice soft and calm. 'But me and you don't want the same things. You ready for marriage, but I don't want another man in my life right now.'

And him start the hollering. Not a sound at first, except for one or two short snorts, but his belly was shaking the whole time. And all of a sudden she started to feel sorry. Sorry for the grief she was causing him, sorry if she'd lead him on, sorry that she couldn't reciprocate the loving. For something tell her him would make a warm and caring husband, an attentive father, a good friend, but she was too afraid to try again. And what's the point of trying if her heart wasn't in it. And as she continue think these things, Gwennie feel her own eye water starting to bubble up behind the lids. She pull Clive to her close and hug him, stiffling her tears on his breast.

And after them cry and talk some more, him ask her to spend the night, but she tell him no, she have to get up early tomorrow. Finally him drive her home in silence, and drive off the minute she let herself in. Rosa was fast asleep on her bed when she turn on the bedroom light and Delores was inside her room reading yet another Mills & Boon. No light was on inside Rudi's room, but his stereo was playing softly. She didn't even bother to put down her bag and change her clothes and shoes, she step right inside his room, pausing just a little bit outside the door.

She could only make out the white pajama pants and the white of his eyes in the darkness. Standing inside the doorway, she switch on the light to her right. She watch as him shield his face from the glare. She clean her throat. 'I don't make many rules inside the house,' she start off, 'but if you plan to sleep out, call. Say something. Because you have me here worrying-up meself half to death. Don't know if something happen to you out the street, if car run you over, people shoot you dead, nothing.'

Rudi never say anything and Gwennie continue on. 'Next thing,' and she sigh long and hard before she say it, then she race it out as if she have plenty more important things to get on to. 'You don't have to go to church every Sunday, but I expect you to show your face now and again. Goodnight.' And she switch off the light, pull the door behind her, say her prayers and roll into her bed. She wasn't sure what brought her to that conclusion, but she wasn't in the mood to fight with him or chase him away.

By Monday morning, she and Rudi were back to normal again. Him wake up early make breakfast and pack her a sandwich and a piece of cake from Delores' Sunday baking. Wednesday and Thursday evening, him come home early and sit down inside the kitchen chat and laugh with her while she cook dinner, and later on, him help to put on buttons on the dress she was making on the little Singer sewing machine she pick up on sale.

Sunday morning, him get up early make breakfast and the whole family attended church together. Him never go the week after that or even the one after that, but him did go the following week. And although she wouldn't allow herself to see too much of Clive, she still miss him, but not as much, for she did have her children back together, all differences cleared up. And since a girl was starting to call the house for Rudi and did even come to pick him up one or two Saturday nights, things were alright now. Well, at least for the time being.

PART EIGHT

I

Two months before Gwennie's second batch of children was to come, she get a letter from Walter. Rudi get one too, and since Delores keep up general correspondence with him, she send even him postcard this past June on his birthday, it never come as surprise to her. But Gwennie wasn't ready to hear from him, yet. For she at a point in her life now where nothing a tall feel settled, and if she don't stand up on her two feet strong, she might carelessly tell Walter what him want to hear and put herself in worst predicament. The break with Clive leave her lonely, for she miss the intimacy, even though now and again him visit, but only to see Rosa, him claim, no one else. Rudi's goings and comings start to worry her again, for him don't tell anybody where him go to at nights and she not so certain him keeping the right company. The pending arrival of the new batch of children causing her additional expenses and confusion.

These days in the newspaper she see it print up often, children growing up in households without fathers can't form good relationships with people. Plenty of them grow up without proper direction and sometimes the boys don't turn out manly enough. And she can't help but look at her own children and shake her head, for her belly hurt every time she see Rosa climb up onto Clive and hug and kiss him all over his face, the few times him visit. But then again when she think about those women back home who have to raise children all by themselves for the husband either dead, or left them for another woman, she don't bother to pay the newspaper any mind.

Miss Lilla back home, for example, did have to pick up herself and her three children and leave the husband, for when him drink the rum him was the devil from hell. More destitute than those children you couldn't find. Shoes use to have holes, school uniforms have patch on top of patch. The little money Miss Lilla make from day's work couldn't stretch far. Day's work back home don't pay as good as abroad. But nevertheless, one turn out lawyer, the other one school teacher and the young one work on the *Daily Gleaner* as news editor.

But then again when she look at Rosa's school report and notice that she not passing, she can't help but start the fretting. When she go up to the school to see the teacher, the lady never have good things to say. Rosa don't show interest a tall, she complain, concentration span light. All she want to do is play. And when Gwennie think about Delores, she just kiss her teeth, for she can't understand how a young person can just spend all her time down at the church so, interested in nothing else, no book club or even political group like what she, Gwennie, used to join back home. Not that anything wrong with the constant church-going, but as time go by, she notice that the people down at the Baptist Church – and she don't have anybody else to blame but herself, for Dorothy did tell her that those people down there not nice – not interested in community service like her own church back home.

When she bring it up one Sunday after church, everybody gather around giving laugh-for-peas-soup, and ask the three ladies standing next to her, if them interested in community service, them turn up them face and comment on how her accent lovely.

And Dave, granted she don't see it in his possession, but she know him mix up in the ganja smoking at the school up in Springfield. She can see it in his eyes when him come home on weekends, blood red. And him eat and sleep and spit all the time like a blinking jackass. Then there is Rudi – Gwennie sigh out loud. Him puzzle her more than ever. Plenty times at night, late late hours, when the house still and the only thing she can hear is the humming of the refrigerator, she hear him on the telephone chatting for a long length of time.

One night she even hear him hollering. And to tell the truth, she didn't know whether or not she should interfere. She pray day in and day out, asking the Lord to guide and show her signs as to how best to run her house, mind her children. But the signs, it seem, taking a damn long time to come. And so with all these things on her mind, she wasn't ready for Walter's letter and his proposal to her. She really hope that that wasn't the sign God showing her.

She remember the evening she see the long red and white airmail envelope in the mail box. She recognize the handwriting sprawl over it same time, and her chest tighten for it bring to mind the letter him did write Percy cautioning him against coming to the house. She pick up the letter and slip it underneath the phone bill and mortage payment plan.

163

As far as she can see, letter from Walter can only mean problems and contention.

She was glad when Rosa come home from school, for since Rosa is a woman love to chat about every little thing that happen at school, it would provide plenty distraction. But as them talk about what Rosa ate at the cafeteria for lunch, and about the girls she play jump rope with, Gwennie couldn't help but to ask her if she miss the father. And Rosa, almost as if she never hear Gwennie's question, continue to talk about her friends Michelle and John and how Michelle's glasses thick, and how she, Rosa, think she want glasses too, and if Gwennie can please buy her some. Gwennie did have to ask her a second time, for in truth, Rosa don't talk much about back home. Now and again when Delores in conversation bring up Jeff's name, her eyes twinkle as if she remember him. Sometimes she even ask Rudi what happen to Peppy or Grandma. Sometimes she ask about her father, but not often.

'Rosa, I talking to you,' Gwennie say to her, for as much as she don't want think about the man, him up front in her mind. 'You don't miss your father?'

Rosa stop and look at Gwennie, annoyance strong in her gaze and in her sigh. Then as if to block out further interruption, she continue on with her conversation about Michelle's new school bag and John's crew-cut hair in a voice way louder than before. Gwennie just let it drop. She never mention the letter to anybody, not even Rudi. But by the time dinner finish eat, plates wash up and turn down for the evening, floor sweep and counter wipe down, she couldn't hold out anymore, she shut her bedroom door and tear open the envelope. And even when days turn into weeks and weeks into months, she did still have the letter fold up same way underneath her mattress. Only she alone and God sharing in the details of the contents. And perhaps it would've stayed under there fold-up neat if not too long after Rudi get a letter as well.

'I wonder what Daddy-man want now,' Rudi give out to no one in particular as him sort through the pile of bills Gwennie divide between him and Delores. Finally him tear it open. Silence fill the room. And after what must be the second reading, Gwennie hear him mutter out under his breath, 'Wretch! Monkey never know one day the well would dry up.' And then after an even longer pause, him sigh again, this time sad and heavy. Then him push open Gwennie's room door and perch himself on her bed.

'Him want to come over.' Disbelief was in his voice. 'Him say that him miss us.' Rudi shake his head. 'Can you imagine? After all me go through at the hands of that man, now him want me to send him invitation letter.' Rudi start to pace around her room. 'What a way the world turn! So you going to send for him, Mama?'

And Gwennie choose her words careful, for she didn't want to sway neither one way or the other in her response. 'It depends on how you children feel,' she start off, voice calm with a serenity she wasn't sure she feel. 'Cause if you children want him to come, I wouldn't prevent you from having that.'

'If him come, I am leaving,' Rudi tell her, determination strong in his voice. 'Me and that man could never live under the same roof again. Not as long as I live.'

'But how you mean?' Her voice not a tall convincing. For to tell the truth, she wasn't sure she wanted Walter to come herself. But after she think about it, it turn bile to her belly, for if Rudi can have that kind of hatred for his father, why not for his mother too, someday. 'Is your father. The Bible say obey . . .'

'I don't care what the Bible have to say, Mama. All I know is if him come, me gone.' And Rudi's voice was calm with a surety Gwennie wasn't sure she like.

'Think about it. Is your father. Your days will be long upon the land. One good deed repay another.'

And even though Delores never have a direct answer – 'if him come, him come, if him don't come, him don't come, it doesn't really matter' – only Rosa alone say yes, her eyes glued to the TV screen same way, voice irritated as if she would rather watch the programme in peace. Gwennie was back where she started. She still never call Dave to ask him, for she have a feeling that him would be the only one to say yes and mean it.

And when she see that the children not coming forth with any uniformity on the matter, and weeks were turning into months, she decide to drag out the matter one last time and work it through. She bring it up to Samuel one evening out on the front porch, thumb playing with the married ring on his finger, brows creased from the contents of Walter's letter. Don't turn the children's mind against him, the letter threaten, for him miss them dearly and really want to come over and fix-up things, even if is for two months – maybe start over brand new.

'It's not because I don't like Walter why I saying this,' Samuel start off, voice frail, 'because there was a time when me and him used to be really close.' Sweat start to gather up on his nose. 'But I not going to lift one straw to bring him here. I don't have any respect for a man who like to manhandle woman. My father never used to do it. It shouldn't

165

happen.' Samuel's voice was gaining in momentum by now. 'If you want him to come, you can bring him. You been here long enough. I washing my hands out of your married life.'

All this time Gwennie just look on. She wasn't sure she wanted him telling her how her life must run. She rather make her own mistakes. Not that she don't make enough already to last the rest of her life, but still she don't want Samuel talking to her as if she no more than fifteen going on. But Samuel endeavour to continue.

'As for the children, them might claim that them want him to come. But is your bed him going to sleep in, and is your life him going to stand up and walk around in. So you must know. I send for you to come and live in America so life can be easier, but if you want to haul down crosses on yourself, that's your business.'

And still, Gwennie couldn't do more than just look on. She never see him so serious and cross about anything before, not even those times when Dorothy deserve it with some of the things that fall out of her mouth. But this was the story of her life. Everybody telling her how her life must run. When is not Grandma is Walter. When is not Walter is Clive. Now is Samuel.

'You think Walter's a fool?' Samuel's eyes look deep into hers. 'Walter's no idiot. Nothing more than him want to come abroad and using you and the children as pass. As far as I can see, that man not up any any frigging good. Excuse me language.' And him step inside the house for his car keys.

Long after him gone, Gwennie was still standing up outside on the front porch, Samuel's last sentences ringing around in her head. Grandma did tell her in the last letter, she never know Walter could be so nice with the children. Everytime him pass the house on his way up to Georges Valley to see family, when him don't stop to give Jeff money and ask how him settling down in Mile Gully All-Age School, him come inside and ask she, Grandma, about her arthritis and Grandpa about his cane crop and the headaches him continue getting, no matter what kind of medication doctor prescribe him.

According to Grandma, it get to the point now where them watch out for Walter every other Sunday. And although she, Grandma don't know exactly what Walter is up to, it can't be any damn good, take it from her. So Gwennie had better be careful, for next thing she know, the children might soon start to tell her that them can't live without the father. And as God see and know, Gwennie don't want that man back inside her life. Best thing she ever did was to get up and leave him. Don't spoil it, now.

II

Gwennie never have much preparation to make before the second batch of children arrive. Delores and Rudi take care of the buying of warm clothes for the winter coming on. Three weeks before the arrival, she take out money from her credit union, and she and Rudi drive over to Glastonbury in the little white four-door Ford Escort him buy.

She didn't like the idea of him buying a car, for with all the accidents and drunk driving on the road these days, she was afraid for his life. But Rudi never pay her any mind. Him come home early the evening, face light-up shine, eyes merry and take her outside to see the car parked by the gate. Then him drive them around the block, she and Delores and Rosa, all the while showing off how the gadgets work: windows that slide down when you push the button; doors that lock simultaneously from another button; and so forth.

Over in Glastonbury, at the furniture warehouse, she pick out the mahogany table and the eight matching straight back chairs. A certain warmness fill her heart as her bottom sink down into the seats, just like the advertisement did say. And the Saturday when them deliver it, she never feel any regret putting Samuel's old enamel table to rest down in the basement.

The whole business with Walter seem settled for the time being. She wasn't sure about her plans exactly, but she write and send away for the proper Immigration papers, nonetheless. For as bad as everybody make Walter out to be, even she in her moments of wrath, can't help but to feel sorry for him. Maybe him well miss the children. Men don't give birth. Them don't carry around babies in them bellies for nine months. But that don't mean them can't feel attached, can't love them, can't miss them just as much. When the papers arrive, Gwennie file them underneath her brown Bible on her bureau. And every Saturday when Delores dust, she wipe her rag longside the papers taking care not to spray Endust on them.

Two weeks before the children arrive, Gwennie get a letter from Aunty Cora and one from Peppy. But as eager as she was to hear news from back home, she was afraid to open them. Walter's letter and the news it bring still rest heavy on her mind. She open Peppy's first. The letter was short and to the point. Her handwriting neat and tidy. All letters form the way, she, Gwennie, used to teach grade one school

167

children. All commas and full stops in them proper place. She thank Gwennie very much for the money she send, and yes, she plan to put it to wise and meaningful use. Peppy continue on to say she's quite happy to come abroad. Aunty Cora mention that the possibilities there are endless, therefore she's looking forward very much to come and especially to see Rudi again. Hope to see them all soon.

And after she read the letter two times over, her mind run on the compositions about 'My Pet' she used to assign her grade two children, even though she know most of them never have any. But them put imagination to good use. 'My pet is a dog by the name of Rover,' them would write, 'I feed her three times a day and take her for long walks in the park.' Gwennie fold up the letter and put it inside the envelope on top of Walter's immigration papers.

But it was Aunty Cora's letter that stir her up, causing her to become more and more apprehensive about Peppy's coming. Aunty Cora start off: 'Don't be surprised if she start to ask plenty questions about this father business. Everyday she bother my tail about who this father is. I write Clara and ask her what to do. But she never have much to say, for it's such a long time, she can't even remember the fellow's name or where him come from. And as Peppy flowering out and turning into big woman, she need to know these things . . .'

Gwennie never read anymore. She fold up the letter and push it back in the envelope. She was sitting down around her new table-and-chair set in the dining room, the Saturday morning, a steaming cup of mint tea in front her. Delores and Rudi were out, and Rosa lay sprawled off on her bed watching Saturday morning cartoons. Gwennie stretch out her two hands on the table and rest her head on them, eyes close. For all of a sudden she was feeling dead tired.

Imagine all this time she thought it was over and done with. But not so. It seems as if she going to be on trial for the rest of her life. As for Luther, it seem so long ago now and far back. If Peppy never resemble him, you could almost swear it never happen. Luther Rowe, she think his name was. She don't even know where him born or even grow up. She think maybe him did mention something about Actingbeddy school, but who to tell.

Never talked much about family. But she think him have a half-brother that run a restaurant at one of the big tourist places, either Negril or Montego Bay, she can't quite remember now. His mother pass on when him was small, in childbirth with his sister. Baby's cord knot up inside, choke her to death. His father bring in a lady to live with them

168

after that. She don't know what she going to tell Peppy if she start to ask questions. Personally, she would rather if things just lay down sleep and not bother her head, for what she can't understand is who put it in Peppy's head first of all. Only Aunty Cora and Grandma know, unless damn inquisitive Mile Gully's people say something to her. That was the very reason she beg and caution Aunty Cora against sending Peppy down there too often. Then if Peppy know, Walter bound to know. But then him don't mention it in the letter.

Maybe him waiting till she send for him, then him bring everything out into the open, shame her in front the rest of children, call her all kinds of names. Sweat trickle down Gwennie's hair root, and as she reach out her hand for the mug of mint tea so she can sip it and settle her stomach, a sharp pain knife through her shoulder causing her to bawl out in alarm. She reach for the mug again, and this time the pain wasn't as piercing, but her shoulder continue to tingle.

The same week Peppy and Jeff was to come, Gwennie find herself lay-up in bed, can't move a tall, all kinds of rubbings and pain relief and hot water bottle prop up around her. Delores and Rudi did have to help with the cooking and cleaning of house. The very Friday evening Peppy's plane land, only Rudi alone could meet her at the airport. Delores stay home with Gwennie, who, although wasn't as bad the day before, take a turn for the worse, Friday.

PART NINE

I

Peppy and Jeff never have the same long line to wait in like Rudi and Delores and Dave. There was only a forty-five minutes wait at Customs, where the men in uniforms search through suitcases and stamp passports five and six different times.

Peppy spot Rudi right away. For although him look different, his knock-knees give him away. For only them alone knock that special, causing his feet to flare out at the edges while the knees gather together, no matter the cut to the trousers. His hair wasn't as tall either. It was close-cut to the scalp and laying down flat with a part to the side, like she see the black guards wear at New York airport. Him never look as stout either, with all the junk food she hear so plentiful in America and bad for the heart, his clothes sit on him neat as always, colours blending in well. But the way him stand up now, back straight, head hold high as it turn from one end of the airport to the other, looking for she and Jeff, him give off a sense of sureness about life, almost as if him comfortable with himself; spirit was at ease. Only Pastor Longmore up at Aunty Cora's church on Communion Sundays give off such an air.

'Watch the bags. And please watch them properly. I going to call him,' Peppy tell Jeff, for Aunty Cora tell her, if you not careful in America, them steal out your very eyes out your head and you don't know it. Then she walk over to where him stand up – Peppy, now fifteen, limbs stretch out tall, lengthening her up to almost the same height as Rudi.

And is only when she reach up close and take a good look at his face that she realize what was so different about him. Him was happy. Not just glad she come, that too, but the happiness she see now that ripple out of his belly, widen out his face and brighten up his eyes is the same kind Pastor Longmore claim him get when the spirit fill his soul. And she know Rudi don't go to church for him write often about the

170

arguments between him and the mother, so it was a happiness coming from source Pastor Longmore don't mention yet.

'Where is everybody?' she ask, after hugging, and Rudi explaining that him have so much to tell her and so many people him want her to meet and so many things to show her, that him don't quite know where to begin.

'Something happen to Mama's shoulder,' him say, as them walk back to where Jeff was guarding the suitcases, 'so Delores stay home with her. Sometimes she's alright and can work, but other times she have to take to her bed. Doctor say is stress-related, she must relax more. She think is arthritis, though.' Him shrug.

And as Rudi hug and kiss Jeff and comment on how Grandma's cooking well agree with him, for him certainly sprout up the short time him was living there and turn handsome from the fine haircut Grandpa give him, Peppy's mind run on Aunty Cora who she left back at home in bed just recovering from a case of bad sickness.

Everything was going okay. Aunty Cora seem more than excited she leaving for Foreign. 'Gal,' she say to Peppy one day, clearing her voice and eyes that seem to be constantly watery these days. (Aunty Cora claim that it's the cataract growing back and the plenty pressure it put on her brain cause her eyes to fog up and turn red often. But Peppy know better). 'Gal, I know you have ambition, so you will go far. I won't live to see or hear about it, but I will rest in peace, for I did me duty.'

Then one week before she leave, almost like a bad luck, Aunty Cora take down sick. Miss Gertie, who'd agreed to come back after some form of compromise between she and Leslie and Aunty Cora, try and nurse Aunty Cora as best she could. And when is not Cerosee tea she boil and give to her, is ginger root. And when is not Bitters, is dry Excelsior crackers or plain rice without salt and butter to calm her stomach. But Aunty Cora couldn't keep down a thing in her belly. And all Peppy could do was sit down beside her and hold her hand. She'd never seen Aunty Cora so afraid, the eye water falling just as plentiful as the vomiting.

When the vomiting start up again the second day, with sprinklings of blood inside it this time, Leslie send for Doctor Lord to come quickly. And after him take temperature and perform tests, stop the vomiting and was inside with Aunty Cora alone for about two hours going on three, taking urine samples, asking her questions and probing her belly with his fingers, him finally step outside to where almost all of New Green was waiting in the yard to hear the final diagnosis.

171

Doctor Lord call Leslie alone, and the two of them walk towards the back of the house, talking together in low tones. Not long after, Doctor Lord gather up his bag and drive away. Leslie didn't even bother to tell Miss Gertie, for him claim her mouth too blasted flighty, but him tell Peppy and a few of Aunty Cora's close friends. Peppy wasn't sure what him tell New Green people to pacify them, but when him tell Aunty Cora's two friends, them just grimace and walk way, face and eyeballs expressionless, back bend slightly forward.

Peppy wasn't quite sure what to do with the news. According to Doctor Lord, Aunty Cora didn't have much time left. The cancer in her belly was spreading fast and that is why she can't keep down her food. She's too old to cut, him tell Leslie, so we just have to wait till she erupt. One day when she get up to go to toilet, the entire belly will just fall out. Him did leave plenty bagfuls of medicine and pain killers on Aunty Cora's bureau, but him caution Leslie don't say a word to her about how serious it is, for no matter how strong she might be, she will never bear up under this kind of news.

The news rest heavy on Peppy's chest, this whole business about eruption and what it means. Leslie didn't know either. Him tell her about the woman who did have it in her breast and how maggots take to the breast and eat it up. But Peppy tell him no, that different. That wasn't going to be the case with Aunty Cora. Aunty Cora was too God fearing, and according to what she hear, that woman used to drink rum and curse plenty. Would never go to church and treat her children decent. Aunty Cora's too good for that kind of suffering to overtake, Peppy explain. She have too much strength of heart. She joke around too much. Too many people love and respect her.

A few days later Aunty Cora was back on her two feet as Peppy expected, chatting and laughing with her friends again who climb all the way up the hill to visit her, and sipping her white rum on the side same way although Doctor Lord caution her against it.

'Peppy, come on,' Rudi bawl out, 'time to go home.'

She never have much to carry. Only the same big green suitcase with the four wheels at the bottom that Aunty Cora travelled with three years ago. And with the heavy coat, Rudi brought, wrap around her body, Peppy run the suitcase through the sliding exit door into the cold January night over to where Rudi parked his car.

II

Gwennie was lying-up in bed when the children come in, four soft fluffy pillows holding up the hot water bottle pressed to her back. With every car that pass, she hold her breath and listen, waiting to see if it was Rudi. Then just as she start to doze off again, the slamming of doors wake her up.

'Come in,' she say to them, motioning with her head as them file in. 'I'm as sick as a dog, but I want to see how me children look.' And them walk around to her bed, Jeff first, then Peppy.

'Jeff, is you this? Oh my goodness! Where you growing to, boy? Dead stamp of your uncle, Samuel. Same pinch face smile. Same flare out nose. How the asthma?'

And as Jeff turn around to explain that him think the asthma is psychologically based, for ever since him relocated down to Mile Gully it wasn't as persistent, Gwennie's line of vision shift from off Jeff to focus on Peppy, whose size and height and looks was unfathomable.

'Peppy, is you that? But look at me dying trial!' And in her haste to raise up and look close at Peppy, the pain rip through Gwennie's shoulder blade, causing her to shut her eyes tight all of a sudden and squeeze out the pain. 'This can't be,' Gwennie think half to herself and half outloud. 'This can't be the same little girl that was up at Aunty Cora.'

For in truth, it was as if a total stranger was standing up in the room with her. The little resemblance to Luther that was there earlier, gone. Every last drop. And it make Gwennie think maybe all those times she thought she'd seen resemblance, it was her own head telling her nonsense. For in front her now was a brand-new person. Face pretty like money, but a hardness around the eyes and mouth corners bringing to mind people who suffer from hard life or preparing to meet it. No resemblance whatsoever to anybody in her family as far back as she can think.

'Rudi say you have arthritis. How're you feeling?'

Gwennie never know what to answer. Her mind was back down at Grandma's listening for the ring in the voice, the joke that was always lurking around door corners, the mischief in his eyes as them used to twinkle up to her, but nothing a tall like Luther. Peppy's tone was dead flat. No sign of life. Almost as if the question come natural, she ask it all

173

the time out of sheer good breeding, but in actuality couldn't care less if Gwennie was really okay or not.

'Not too bad,' Gwennie answer, everybody else in the room blind to her. She never see Jeff hovering around the other side of her bed, eyes and nose wide open with the newness of Foreign. She never see Delores in the doorway blocking it with her tall frame, or Rudi peering in from underneath Del's arm. Only Gwennie and Peppy alone in the room. 'The doctor say is stress, me worry too much. But them don't know what them talking about. And them charge so damn much to look at it and not even know what it is.' Gwennie kiss her teeth. 'Is arthritis. Mama did have the same thing and her mother before that. It knife you more than usual when the weather turn cold. When it get warmer, it won't be as bad.'

'You have ointments for it?' Peppy ask, glancing at the bureau. No signs of the plenty bottles of Arrowroot or Bitterbush or Bayrum and other bad smelling vials of rubbings. Nothing except for the small black-and-white-radio-television at one end; matching comb and brush set, underarm deodorant, dish of face powder, tube of lipstick bunched up together at the other end, and a family photo in the middle.

'No, me dear,' Gwennie answer her. 'Him say I must take vacation. Take time off from work and travel for a while. Lay down sleep and wake late in the mornings. Exercise, jog or walk long distances. Too many things on my mind. But I can't afford vacation now. Too expensive.'

And she and Peppy continue to talk, nothing personal that would make them uncomfortable first thing, but about Miss Gertie and Leslie, Aunty Cora and the shop, school and the quality of education these days and plenty other trivial things. A little later, Peppy cry excuse to Gwennie, say goodnight to Rudi and make her way into Delores' luxurious queen size bed, that she'd bought to replace the twin bed not long after her first paycheck. There, she settle in for the night, twisting and turning over on her belly then her back and sides till finally she drop asleep, body bruise-up and tired from all the hassling.

III

Peppy's first letter to Aunty Cora ran almost five pages back and front. She dispatch it off exactly one month after her arrival. She write Jasmine too, for them did grow closer and closer over the years, and Vin.

It was a Saturday morning when she write the letter. And except for the heater knock-knocking now and again, the house was dead quiet, everybody sleeping. Peppy take her time and crawl out the bed, blanket and pillow dragging behind, careful not to wake Delores, for Delores is a woman who don't like anything to wake her up before one o'clock Saturday afternoons. Sprawl-off on the carpet, head cover-up, windows rattling from the howling wind outside, she start her letter Dear MaCora.

At first she ask after Aunty Cora's arthritis and lump, if any improvement taking place. Then after Marlon, Leslie's little boy him have with the Creole woman, and who Aunty Cora raising now, if him bad as yaws same way and giving plenty trouble? How Babbo and Miss Doris? How poor Miss Gertie and Leslie making out? Then Peppy tell her about the school she and Jeff attend, that's not too far from the house; how the Black Americans in her class laugh at her accent and the other West Indians standoffish. Always acting as if them better, refusing to speak to her. Then Peppy tell her about teacher Biggs who's been advising her about the plenty scholarships she must apply for next year so she can go on to university. And Peppy remember to tell Aunty Cora that yes, it look as if her plenty prayers working, in truth.

Home life. Peppy pause long and hard on this one before she continue. For in truth only she and Rudi really get on. Delores too steep in the church and in her Western and Mills & Boon Romances to give attention to anybody or anything else. And furthermore, her moods too swing-swang. One day, nicer than Delores you can't find. Chat and laugh loud and plenty. Next time, she don't speak whatsoever.

Peppy and Gwennie? Well, them just sort of step outside one another's way. Sometimes she get the feeling that her mother just constantly waiting to hear questions she imagine Peppy plan to ask. The two definitely have to get to know one another. Sometimes when everybody around the dining room table chatting and laughing, she notice the definite familiarity among Jeff, Delores, Rudi and Gwennie.

175

Knowing glances only them alone understand. Old jokes and secrets, them alone privy to.

Whenever Gwennie address her about anything: 'Peppy, how school today?' or 'Peppy, where you and Rudi been all afternoon?' 'How Aunty Cora, when last you hear from her?' It's always like a cloud cover over her brain and she can't remember. Almost like the room suddenly hot and she suffocating. And she can feel sweat trickling down her back bone. And she want to scratch for everywhere itching at once. But somehow, some way, she always manage to answer, her voice barely audible, her answers far from coherent.

And Gwennie have to always ask her over and over what is she saying, voice gaining in irritation each time. For after Peppy finally answer 'Me and Rudi was driving around', depending on the question, she just purse up her lips, sullen-like, for she couldn't think of what else to say to her mother. And during these times she always see the strained expression on Gwennie's face, in her eyes, sometimes even in her voice, almost as if she can barely contain that scream struggling inside her chest.

Her relationship with Jeff and Dave, come and go. So that really only leave she and Rudi, or better yet, she and Rudi and Craig – thirty-three year-old Craig, whom she meet the very next day after she arrive, and who's been sharing the same apartment with his mother for over twenty years. Rudi met him at the same bar Percy Clock used to frequent several years back when him was living in America.

'We just connect with each other really well,' Rudi tell her, not long after her arrival. 'We don't have that much in common. For one, him way older than me. But him really nice. We travel all the time. Him really caring and giving. Father died during the war. Korean, I think. Him write poetry on the side like me . . .'

And as him go on talk, Peppy could see it in his face again, that same surety bout life she saw at the airport. And she get the sudden feeling that when his mother find out about his way of life, for that bound to happen soon with this new attitude she see, is either Gwennie put up with it, or she don't do anything a tall. For it seems as if Rudi reach a stage now where no coaxing or begging can change him. She could just see the constant fighting that would take place if the father ever come. It always please her to hear Rudi say that if is a tall up to him, Walter's two feet never touch Foreign soil.

'Craig say him want to meet Mama and Delores and everybody,' Rudi continue. 'Him even want us to go back home on vacation for a week. But I don't know.'

She could tell too that Rudi was just bottled up with plenty things, that him was just waiting to unload on her what letter can't convey. The first two weeks, them stay up till two o' clock each night, catching up on nine months' worth of news. News about Percy: how Martel leave him for one of Percy's good friends; and that even now, Percy still hurting from the break-up. But according to Martel's letters, Percy was cloaking him too much. Him needed breathing space. Him getting plenty of that with Bill, the new fellow.

Then she ask if him remember her friend, Jasmine, for Jasmine's mother, the higgler lady, was that way too. Jasmine invited her over to her mother's house and she met the lady, Miss Pearl.

'Is almost like them married,' Peppy tell him, 'for them each wear a gold ring. I did expect that maybe one of them would play the father while the other one play the mother. But nothing like that.' Peppy shake her head. 'Miss Pearl was just coming back from work, when me see her, and she did have on high heel shoes and silk frock, looking like Queen of Sheba, ownself. Jasmine say every Sunday morning Miss Pearl get up early, ready Jasmine's two little brothers, and carry them to St Richard's Catholic Church where she sing tenor in the choir. She not manlike a tall,' Peppy assure him, 'she just as feminine as Jasmine's mother.

'And them loving to one another, too.' Peppy continue on. 'Jasmine say them have quarrels, but nothing compared to what used to go on when the father was there.'

'Then, Jasmine tell children at school about her family life?' Rudi ask her. 'She not afraid them laugh?'

'She only tell me, I think, since me and she close.' Peppy's face was pensive. 'To other children, she refer to Miss Pearl as her mother's second cousin from country who just spending time.'

But that was all Peppy could tell Rudi. Somehow she never feel comfortable telling him about New Green people, about Leslie and his little boy, about Aunty Cora and her lump. Him ask after them, and Peppy tell him, them hearty, but she don't get the feeling that him really care, or want extended information. It's almost as if New Green belong to she, same way Del and Dave, Jeff and Gwennie belong to Rudi.

So as Peppy hear Delores raise up in her bed, turn over and continue to snore, she tell Aunty Cora that family life going okay. She and everyone getting along fine. Don't worry herself. For somehow she just couldn't tell Aunty Cora that even though she and Rudi get along fine, every time the two of them talking, no matter how important the subject matter, if the phone ring any a tall and it's Craig on the line, everything else put on hold. For whenever Craig clap, Rudi jump. The foundation of them relationship it seems. Then Peppy tell Aunty Cora about the coldness of weather, how sometimes temperature reach as far as thirty below. Still no signs of snow, although it's suppose to this weekend. She tell Aunty Cora about Gwennie's old boyfriend, Clive, who don't come over as often anymore, and who is only on good terms with Rosa. Then Peppy ask her to please reply soon, she can't wait to hear more news. And when she finish lick the airmail envelope shut, she start on Jasmine's letter and then Vin's.

IV

So as March turn into April and April into May, and the few seeds of tomato, hot pepper and carrot Gwennie sprinkle behind the house started budding, and the pain in her back and shoulders subsided to only spasms now and again, the things that used to clog up Peppy's brain back home, that was on hold now till she finally settle down and was comfortable with Foreign life, started to flood her mind again. The dreams about the man: medium height and dark-skinned; whom Aunty Cora hadn't seen herself, but was quite certain him was a contractor on the bridge that separate Mile Gully from the town Walter's people come from.

And the man would never show his face in any of her dreams. Everytime she'd go up close, him would always turn his back or disappear from her line of vision completely. But she know him wear glasses, thick dark glasses to protect his eyes from splinters. And she know him wear khaki trousers sometimes, or wash-out dungarees other times, but always with the behind and knees tear out and patch several times. And she know him always smell of sweat, sweat that drip from his neck down into the collar of his open-neck dirty shirt, ripped underneath the arms, staining it, a musty yellow.

And she know him wear gloves, heavy brown gloves that protect his fingers that she more than certain resemble hers: long and slender with rounded tips and half moons. And she know him always carry a canvas work bag with the zipper torn out, fill up to the neck with the water bottle, plane, saw, flashlite, box of cigarette, trowel, tape measure, hammer and nail. All different shapes and sizes of nails.

Sometimes the dreams come once a fortnight. Sometimes once a week. Other times every night. And even when she get up in the middle of the night thirsty, or to go to the bathroom, by the time her head hit the pillow again, the smell of sweat was upon her so strong, her nose twitch. And she did get up one Sunday morning determine to ask the mother about the man: the man whose name she wasn't certain about, but whose voice she recognized as him laugh and joke around with the other contractors, the grin – widespread and engaging, covering over his face like hers; the man who Aunty Cora imagine still living, although she don't quite know whom him is herself, Gwennie the best one to ask – but careful how you ask, for things have a way, especially when them hard to talk about, to come out in ways you don't quite expect or even want.

The Sunday morning Peppy put on her robe and proceed inside the kitchen where her mother was frying ripe plantains, eggs and johnny cakes for breakfast. Not quite certain how to begin, she find the dusting rag and start to dust off the mahogany table, Gwennie don't allow anybody to sit down around unless them have to, then she spread the table cloth over it for breakfast.

'Nice to see you out of bed bright and early.' Gwennie remark, as if noticing Peppy for the first time. 'Have things plan for today?'

Peppy open her mouth to begin, but not a sound.

'Whatsit?' Gwennie lift her head, waiting for the response, back turn to Peppy sameway as she watch the johnny cakes turn golden brown in the frying pan.

'Nothing,' Peppy sigh out. 'Just can't sleep, that's all.'

And after she set out the plates and forks, Peppy crawl back into her bed defeated, but planning ways nevertheless to broach the subject.

And out it came, full force and flushy one day while Rudi was out carousing with Craig as usual, Delores was gone with Rosa and Jeff to a programme at the church, and only Peppy and Gwennie were alone at the house. Gwennie was frying fish the Saturday, lovely red-belly porgies she buy at the Grand Union. And as Peppy is not one to start up conversations with her mother, Gwennie did have to call her into the kitchen.

'How school?' Gwennie roll the fish in the bowl with the flour. 'Jeff bring his report card to show me. Where yours?'

'Inside.'

179

'Here, peel this.' Gwennie hand Peppy a big piece of yellow yam she get at the West Indian store. 'What it doing inside? You must bring it and show me. I want to see how you doing at the school.'

'I will bring it when I finish,' Peppy reply, her voice meek and mild, for she always feel tender under Gwennie's gaze.

'If you're bright and work hard, them will give you scholarship. Your Aunt Dorothy did get a scholarship.'

And she and Gwennie continue on in conversation, her tongue and mind loosening with each new sentence. Peppy tell her about Miss Biggs, and how only encouragement and praise fall from her lips. Then Gwennie tell her she'd be more than lucky if she can get a scholarship to attend university, for sometimes she wish she could take classes up at the community college few nights a week, herself. Social Studies and Civics her favourite. But she don't have the time.

And as them go on talk, it roll out of Peppy's mouth with such ease, she never even have time to stop herself. 'Ma'am,' she start off, for she still not used to calling Gwennie Mama like the others, 'Who is me father? What's his name?'

Peppy turn around to look at her mother. But Gwennie's back was still facing her, straight and rigid same way.

'What you mean by that? You don't know your father?'

'No. I mean yes. But them say Walter's not me father. Them say . . .' Peppy couldn't continue anymore. Clouds rolled threateningly cross-way her brain. She rub her fingers against the slices of yam on the plate, waiting for the pot of water on the stove to start boiling.

'Who is them?'

Gwennie's back still faced Peppy.

'Grandma. Aunty Cora.'

'I don't know what you talking about, me dear,' and as if to bring the conversation to a close, Gwennie drop the fish into the hot oil, and the frying was so loud, it cut off all forms of communication.

Peppy turn on the tap and rinse off her hands. Then she dry them off with a sheet of paper towel. And without another word to Gwennie, whose back was just as straight and as rigid, she step inside her room, pick up her jacket and let herself out through the back door.

Outside was warm. Tiny breezes caress her cheeks and blow against the eye water that was running down. She could feel the dreams crowding her head, the sweat even though faint, pinching her nostrils. She try pushing away until night time, but all her efforts seem hopeless. Evelyn Street was empty. She turn onto Watson Avenue and step inside the Convenient Store. She miss the sound of dominoes slapping hard on tables, the triumphant laughter of victors, the haunting face of the loser, back hunched over, hate in hims heart. She nod hello to the man around the counter, and play a game of Miss PacMan before leaving.

She continue on her walk, pass the parlour where Delores and Rosa get them hair straightened every two weeks, and Gwennie get her perm every six weeks. She pass the barber shop where Jeff get his hair cut, and Dave too, when him visit. Rudi cut his at the place Craig recommend. She call to the fat man who always stand up outside the Kentucky Chicken place, no matter what day of the week or what hour, and walk pass the bank where her class mate work as teller. There were no children in the street skipping, no firewood smells or overripe fruits. Nothing. Peppy walk on over to Gutman Park where she sit down and watch ducks waddle in the pond and concentric circles formed by the rippling water.

Monday morning she join the after school programme Miss Biggs suggest, and so when she leave home each morning, she don't reach in again till six o' clock, just time enough to do her homework, eat her dinner and go to her bed.

And when Gwennie stop her, ask her, 'Peppy, why you coming home so late in the evenings? I know school let out from two and I expect that since you're older, you should stay home with Rosa and Jeff.'

Peppy only mumble something about study programme and Miss Biggs, her hooded eyes lodged somewhere over Gwennie's head top.

'That is nice. How come you didn't mention it before? You don't think I want to know how you progressing?'

And Peppy just shrug her shoulders and walk away. She know Gwennie's back started paining her again, but she couldn't find any pity inside her belly for her mother.

Two weeks later, Peppy start the weekend job Dorothy find her at the hospital filling up her days. For she never want to have time to think. Think say maybe her mother telling her lies, her own mother. And it seem like after the incident, nothing ever come as surprise to Peppy anymore. She felt numb inside. And so when Rudi move out, it never shake her any, for the same way distance had grown between her and her mother, it had started to grow between she and the other children as well, Rudi included. For as much as them close, she still don't feel comfortable bringing up things to him about the mother, even though now would be a good time since him and the mother also at odds.

Gwennie came home one evening only to find a copy of one of the magazines Rudi bring home from the bars on his bed where him carelessly leave it. Usually him hide it somewhere under his bed, or throw it way. But this time him leave it out. After Peppy watch Gwennie carry it to her room and flip through it, pace around the house, her face tight with agony, she know hell was going to burst loose that night. And from where she perch herself, Peppy could hear everything going on.

'So this is what you interested in?' Gwennie fling down the magazine on the floor and start to stamp on it. Eye water was in her voice. 'This sin and nastiness. This is the example you setting for the younger ones? Well, it can't go on inside here. You have to go or change your ways.'

'Alright then, I will go.' And Peppy could hear the same sureness of self she been noticing about Rudi ever since her arrival, almost as if him grow ten feet taller since him leave the father's house. And she could tell Gwennie wasn't ready for this response, for her face just turn grey all of a sudden. Rudi help plenty with the bills too. If him leave, things sure to fall heavy on her shoulders.

'The church,' Gwennie tell him, her voice weak, 'that will change you.'

But she never say anymore, for Rudi started packing.

When Peppy reach home from school the next evening, his room was empty, every trace of him gone. And Peppy did have to come to the conclusion that maybe Rudi set the newspaper there as bait so him could move out. For him never put up any struggle, never try to compromise, him just leave. Say him need to live his own life now. She did miss him a little, for even though him was getting more and more estranged, him was still her favourite.

V

The telegram with the news of Aunty Cora's death came two weeks after her reply to Peppy. When Delores give Peppy the telegram the Saturday evening after work, all Peppy could do was just to take it from Delores' hand and sigh out loud. Then she lock up herself in the bathroom and sit down on the floor, back turn to the door.

Out in the living room merry-making was taking place. Delores had several of her friends over from church. Now and again peals of laughter ring out, shattering her solitude inside the dark room. Them never know much about Aunty Cora. Only that she had a big shop where them could get handfuls of paradise plum, icymint and ju-ju during visits. Them know too that she whoop long and loud, but that's all. Them don't know anything about the constant rum drinking to ease her maladys, the arthritis that would render her immobile now and again, the lump that was threatening her life. Delores say Gwennie doesn't know as yet. That she been gone all day.

Lock-up inside the bathroom, Peppy couldn't holler out a sound. Everything seem bottled-up inside. People die like flies up at the hospital where she work. This very morning, the old man she used to talk to on division 86, pass on. When she walk pass his room on her way in, the door was wide open, mattress turn over. By lunch time them wheel in somebody else. The new name was on her dinner list.

She figure it must be Leslie who send the telegram. Only him, George and Peppy call her MaCora. MACORA DEAD 25/5/80 AT HOSPITAL. FUNERAL 3/6/80. She reread it several times, opening and closing her eyes. She reread it again. Peppy think back on the last letter Aunty Cora send. If there was any indication that she worse than usual. But nothing. The last letter was no different from the others. Aunty Cora always complain that she on her last and don't have much longer to go. But then next month a new letter would always come, the very same complaint attached.

'Peppy,' Jeff knock on the bathroom door, 'coming out soon?'

'Go outside and stop bothering me.'

Jeff kiss his teeth and kick the door. Then she hear him sigh and walk off.

The telegram was still in her hand. She imagine Buddy must be happy now. Him get all the land to himself. Peppy's mind run on Aunty Cora's only son and the constant quarrels that occurred between them. Whenever him want to quarrel with Aunty Cora and Peppy was in the room, him use to tell her to please leave. Big people talking. She couldn't bear him. Like father, like son. Him and Leslie piggish alike. Him could barely wait until Peppy leave before roughing up Aunty Cora.

'You change the will yet, old lady?' him use to style her.

And Peppy would always wonder why is it Aunty Cora would never tell him to take his ass and go to hell, why she'd tolerate his out-oforderliness instead, her voice always soft and weak, always pleading towards him.

'Give me more time so I can think it over.'

Peppy could tell that Aunty Cora's heart was heavy. You could hear it. But she know Aunty Cora would do exactly as him want.

'Peppy not you pickney. Send her to her mother. George not you pickney. Send him to his father. Miss Gertie not you pickney, how come she getting land? Babbo, that nasty old drunkard, getting cow? Old lady you crazy! What me get, you only son? Two and one half acre of rock stone! Not even good land, but rock stone, break back, tough dirt that can't grow anything.'

And Aunty Cora never would say anything, almost as if she afraid of him, almost as if she deserve the way him manhandle her. After quarrelling with Aunty Cora, him would step outside, call Leslie and quarrel with him as well, about how him worthless and lazy and won't work the land. Not to mention George. Him hate George and Miss Gertie like poison. When him start on Leslie, Leslie would never say anything. Just sort of hang his head. Careful not to jeopardize anything, for him want Buddy to bring him back to England. When Peppy go back inside Aunty Cora's room, she would always find her sitting up on the bed, hands holding up her jaw, the emergency flask she keep under the mattress, not too far off. And Peppy could do no more than to pray and hope Buddy's two-week visit would make haste and come to an end so him can return to England where the constant drizzle hurt his arthritis and the stressfulness of his job raise his blood pressure sometimes even to the point of stroke.

'Peppy?' Delores this time. 'Coming out anytime soon, medear.'

Peppy sigh out loud. She long for the day when she can have her own room. Sometimes when she think about it, she can't blame Rudi for leaving a tall. As it is now, Delores dictates the hours light must turn on and off, for it bother her eyes. The radio Peppy buy with her first month's paycheck can only turn on when Delores not in the room, for according to her, the boom-boom music Peppy love listening to only disturb her meditation with God.

As the hours fall by, still not a drop of eye water trickle down Peppy's face. And Peppy start to wonder if it have anything to do with the distance that started growing between she and Aunty Cora, after Rudi left and she did have to move back to New Green. For it got to the point where she couldn't bear to listen to the same quarrels between Aunty

Cora and Leslie about cows and pigs and land. She didn't want to hear Miss Gertie complain about her chest and the coughing. She didn't want to hear about Vin's boyfriends. New Green boys just never hold her interest anymore.

She grow tired of the same old conversation with New Green people about hard life, unemployment, drought, sickness. Just about everything and everybody was getting on her nerves. She missed Rudi's friendship and them heart-to-heart conversations. She missed his friends and the unusualness of them lifestyle. Back up in New Green Aunty Cora was starting to restrict her movements as a result of Leslie's eye-watch reporting. 'Now that you turning into a young miss,' she tell Peppy, 'you can't run up and down with the boys and play dominoes as you have a mind. You have to stay in and study your books. Do well in school and set good example. Go to church. New Green people don't take well to this tomboy business a tall.'

Aunty Cora's speedy deterioration and Peppy's pending departure was creating an even wider distance between the two. It got to the point where Aunty Cora wouldn't complain about her bad feelings anymore, almost as if she was afraid to become burdensome. But Peppy could tell, for the rum drinking did pick up. It didn't sit good with Peppy about leaving Aunty Cora to Leslie who constantly rude to her, and Buddy who manhandle her even in his letters from England, and Miss Gertie who live off her like parasite, but nonetheless she still count down the days till the plane ticket arrive.

When Peppy crawl under the sheet that night she was still numb. Gwennie come into the room later on and shake her up. 'You see the telegram?'

'Yes,' Peppy answer, shutting up her eyes and trying to fall back asleep. Those were the only words exchanged between she and Gwennie ever since the stir-up not too long ago. For since then, the two of them been walking around one another even more.

The funeral was the following week Sunday. Monday come and Tuesday pass, and still Peppy don't hear word mention about going back home for the funeral. As much as she like to rely on herself, she never have the money to purchase her own plane ticket. She have it hard asking Rudi, now that him paying his own rent and bills. She couldn't ask Delores either, for with Rudi's absence things fall heavy on her shoulder and she make it a point of her duty to remind everybody about that fact, too. She never ask Gwennie either, for them only go around

185

and come around one another. And Peppy never have the gall to break the pattern.

Wednesday night roll into Thursday, and by Friday she decide well then, maybe she won't be able to see Aunty Cora for the last a tall. Maybe she won't get a chance to see them lowering her in the box. She won't be able to sit up with the men while them drink rum and beers and dig the grave. She won't be able to walk behind the pall bearers as them carry the box on them shoulders. She and New Green people won't be following behind and singing 'Nearer My God To Thee'. She won't be able to watch as Pastor Longmore sprinkle dirt on top of the coffin as it roll down inside the hole and say 'Ashes to ashes and dust to dust'. No, all of New Green will get a chance to bury MaCora except she.

And the eye water still didn't come. June pass and then July, and still she wait for Aunty Cora's letters. July turn into August, and letter come for Gwennie from Grandma, and Delores get letter from her friend down Mile Gully and still nothing from New Green. September, Peppy enter her last year, Jeff start eleventh grade and Rosa move up to middle school. Delores was just as steep in the church, Clive no longer called and Rosa was no longer missing him. Gwennie start a computer literacy course up at the community college two nights a week, and Walter's immigration papers move from on top Gwennie's bureau to inside a box in the corner of her closet along with all the passports and alien cards.

That same September, Craig move in with Rudi for two weeks, only to move back in with his mother the middle of the third week, complaining that she the only person him can live with. Dave finish the Youth Corp up at Springfield and then join the Air Force and Peppy get one letter from Vin.

Vin say she doesn't know where to begin, but is a good thing Peppy never came to the funeral for her belly would burn her to see her Aunty in that fashion. Bloat-up, Vin say, black and blue, you couldn't even tell if it was Miss Cora or not. Them couldn't wheel the coffin inside the church, for it was smelling too bad. Them did have to leave it outside. Pastor Longmore did have to race through the service so the men could hurry up and bury it. The body was spoilt, Vin say, spoilt rotten. Five days she lay down cover up in a blood-up white sheet waiting, waiting for the refrigerator to empty so them can put her in. Every day Leslie go and beg the guard, do sir, put his grandmother on ice, take out one of those that already frozen. Everyday the guard promise yes, him would try, but look at the line of people waiting to put them dead on ice, as well.

It was Marlon, Leslie's little boy, Vin continue on, and Miss Cora alone at the house when she first come down with the sickness. Miss Gertie and Leslie fight again and she claim that as much as she love her Cousin Cora, she can't live with Leslie. It happen around seven in the evening. Aunt Doris was up there earlier, taking care of Miss Cora. Miss Cora's been in plenty pain over a week now. But it happen after Aunt Doris leave the evening. Miss Cora get up to go to the toilet and it wasn't urine that come out, but blood. And she call out to Marlon, boy, go and call Leslie, this business don't look good a tall.

She died up at the public hospital the next day. Aunt Doris say she can't figure out how come Leslie never bring her to a private hospital, for the few nurses and doctors at the public hospital, no matter how wonderful them training, just can't take care of the long line of sick people that need attention. But Aunty Doris figure it out last month after the will read. She never have a penny. Miss Cora will out everything to Buddy. You name wasn't even mentioned, Peppy. Leslie never even get an orange tree. Buddy run George off the property, telling him to go and look for work.

Peppy was outside on the back steps when she get the letter, the woollen sweater keeping her warm from the cool September breeze. She don't like staying inside the house when Gwennie home, for a heaviness seem to always come over her. It remind her of when she used to live with Walter and him would come home drunk. And everybody, no matter how happy and glad they were before, would suddenly turn gloomy and wilt by the time Walter's car pull into the carport. From where she sit down, Peppy could see Windsor Street and the people passing. Now and again she catch bits and pieces of a conversation.

When she was through reading the letter, Peppy fold it up and step inside the house. And the hollering that started never included any eye water. She open up her mouth wide instead and bawl out as if she cut her finger, or a piece of board fall on her toe. And when she holler out, Delores run over first, and then the rest of children start to gather around. But Gwennie never come.

And them watch Peppy as she crouch over in the middle of the room, the letter at her feet, her back to them, her two hands holding her belly. At first them could tolerate the bawling, but then it change. One by one them back out the room, hands fold over ears, face furrow-up, them own belly cringing, for the sound was desperate, was gut-wrenching, was sad, and them just couldn't bear to hear it anymore.

187

VI

Graduation day, even before anybody inside the house started stirring, Peppy wake up early, pick up the piece of paper with the speech she and Dorothy spend long hours writing, and step inside the bathroom, locking the door behind her. From in front the full-length mirror she practise the speech over and over, making sure that back was straight, her head sit down on her neck in good angle, her mouth round up and stretch out as it pronounce each word and each syllable and she not looking down on the paper at all times, but out at the audience.

Peppy got five tickets total. One she give to Dorothy, since them grow close over the years. From the day she went over Dorothy's house and expressed interest in the plenty pictures Dorothy have frame up in her little studio and darkroom she build in the basement of the house, Dorothy not only show Peppy how to use the 35 and 14 millimetre cameras she have, but for one whole month she lend them to Peppy alongside several rolls of film, for she claim Peppy have good eyes for colour and image.

She send a ticket to Rudi, as well. She wasn't sure if him would be able to drag himself from Craig. But him call and say him would try, for him long to see her. Over six months now. She was hoping maybe she'd see him Christmas day. But when him phone and ask Gwennie if him could invite Craig, she point blank tell him no, not over her dead body, that kind of nasty living not going take place in her house.

She also invite Del, if she can manage tear herself way from Bible Study that evening, Mr Taylor, the man who run the After-School-Study Programme at the University and Merle Hennahan: twenty-three-year-old Merle who finish college one year early and worked for Mr Taylor in the programme. She can't quite remember the occasion that brought she and Merle together, but without fail, every evening Merle drive her home in the little maroon Volkswagen she call Betsy and, on days when Gwennie working late, invite Peppy to her studio where she live with her small hairless, six-inch dog, Nagasaki.

Merle don't have plenty furniture in her house, she still have her mattress on the cold tile floor, but she have plenty artefacts on her wall from her travels to West Africa and China and two months in Ireland where her father's line of family come from, no mention about her mother. Evenings when Peppy don't have plenty homework, she spend them with Merle. And sometimes during the warmer months, them sit down outside in the park and read and play with Nagasaki. Cooler months, them watch movies in theatre houses, or drink coffee and mint tea at cafés close to Merle's house. She never have any tickets left over for Gwennie. She wasn't sure her mother would come anyway. Plenty evenings she wanted to ask her, for Merle say she must try, but she was too afraid Gwennie would tell her she don't have the time, for she working late all this week, and by the time she reach home she exhausted.

The small auditorium where them keep the graduation ceremony was full. And from where she take her seat up on the stage, next to the principal and the Deputy School Superintendent and Assistant Principal, and City Hall representative, Peppy could see everyone coming in. Those graduating, and those bearing close resemblance to them. And as them walk in, some with hair pile high on headtops, others in suits, trousers iron thin, feet stepping high and faces proud.

From her seat, Peppy could see the lights flickering on and off in the lobby as more people crowd into the auditorium, women stepping tall so the spike heels won't arouse attention. Then the lights were off, and the room hush over, and she hear one or two coughing and clearing of throat and rustling of paper.

The Deputy Superintendent, with his hair scoop to one side to cover the balding, take his place at the pulpit, hands rubbing together behind him. Him take a sip of water them put from the plastic cup next to him, rinse his mouth and then swallow. And after the Deputy Superintendent grin with the crowd and apologize for the Superintendent who wanted to come and congratulate these bright young ladies and men, but unfortunately, important out-of-town call kept him away. And after him continue hoo and haw about the impact these bright young faces will have on the world, the representative from City Hall never have anything different to say. The Principal was just as bad with his speech about being the good shepherd, and how he's helped to mould and make these young sheep who come into his fold four years ago better human beings.

Peppy's mind didn't linger long on the Principal's speech, for it was her time next, and already her stomach was starting to flutter. So she tried concentrating on soft music, quiet afternoons and dim lights so her belly would settle back to normal. And then it was her turn, and she could hear the clapping and loud cheering from the faces below. She take her place at the pulpit, smile at the crowd as if she's been doing this business for several years, clear her throat in the microphone even though no phlegm lodged itself there, sip a little from the cup even though her throat wasn't dry, straighten out her folder with the speech and fix her eyes to a corner at the back of the room.

First she start off with the importance of education, and how where she come from, it was education that make you or break you. For is those with the education that get the good pay and is them who get the promotion and is them that gain the respect and is them who make the influential decisions. Feeling more and more relaxed with the audience, her eyes start to search out Merle. And at first she didn't see her, for plenty curly-brown hair people were in the audience. But then she spot her, for only Merle alone have a lock of hair that fall crossway her face in that special way, causing her to constantly shake back her head and remove the hair from out her eyes. And her eyes search out Dorothy who she'd expect to see in the very front row, camera around her neck, mouth shouting out 'Bravo, Bravo,' for Dorothy loud that way. She see glimpses of Rudi in his white jacket, Mr Taylor, Del in her puke-green suit, but no sign of Dorothy.

And even when her speech draw to a close, and she wish her class good luck as them set out on the world, Peppy never hear any of the clapping and cheering that was just as deafening as when she started out, for she still couldn't glimpse Dorothy. And she wonder why Dorothy didn't call to say she wasn't well, or that she was going out of town. For she could've given her mother the ticket. No, them don't get along, but still, this is a special occasion, and after all Gwennie is her mother. And Peppy wonder what was running through Gwennie's mind now, when she find out Peppy graduating and that she wasn't invited. And although a little part of her felt guilt, it didn't linger long, for there was a chuckle forming itself inside her throat.

So as the Principal call out names and children walk up one by one to pick up diplomas and scholarship cheques and shake his hand, Peppy find herself going up several times to pick up various awards, for she was a hard worker, so her rewards blossomed out.

After the ceremony conclude, and people started filing out the auditorium and little pockets of crowd started forming out in the lobby, Peppy make her way over to where Del was poised with her Instamatic camera. And after a series of photo taking, Del hug her up and tell her congrats. Merle come over too, with a handful of roses, and Mr Taylor with a package underneath him arm, face beaming from corner to corner.

190

And then Rudi in his white suit came over, and started hugging her up tight. But behind the hugging she could feel his eye water wetting up the back of her neck and hear him whispering to her over and over. 'I didn't know,' him say, 'I didn't know a tall. I feel so ashamed. All this time I was so preoccupied with other things, I didn't know you was doing so well. Me and you used to be so close. Share every little thing. Now you making long speech that sound so good and winning so much and I don't know what's going on anymore.'

And she was a little bit embarrassed, for some of her classmates started to gather around ready to congratulate her on getting away with so much scholarship money, and here was Rudi laying crossway her shoulder crying during this period of merriment. And so in all her embarrassment Peppy never notice Gwennie hovering in the background not quite certain if she to join the circle or wait till them go home. Peppy's eyes meet Merle's at same time, and all of a sudden she wish she was back at Merle's little one-bedroom apartment, wrap up safe underneath her heavy quilt, with Nagasaki's cold nose press close against her chest. But Peppy brace herself and introduce Gwennie to Mr Taylor. Then to Merle. And Gwennie was very polite. She engaged herself in small talk with them about the size of the auditorium, the excellence of the acoustics and the amazement of everybody about Peppy's achievements.

Then Merle squeeze Peppy's hand and tell her good night. Mr Taylor take leave as well, and Del too, for she did have Young People's meeting to attend. Then it was Rudi and Gwennie and Peppy. Rudi cry excuse. Him was going go pick up the car and bring it around to the front. Then it was Peppy and Gwennie. And Gwennie's face seemed older and tired. Her jawbone wasn't as tight. She losing weight it seems, the purple frock she have on with the white embroidery at the collar wasn't flattering, it just hang off. But to tell the truth, Peppy wasn't sure if that was her natural weight or not, for from that day in the kitchen, Peppy and Gwennie's eyes never connected again, going on two years now.

And Gwennie open her purse, take out a white envelope and give Peppy. And the heat that pass from Gwennie's finger to Peppy's as them accidentally touch was so hot, it cause Peppy to pull back same time, dropping the envelope.

'Sorry,' she mumble and bend down to pick up, for she didn't want to stand up there with Gwennie. She wanted to leave and go home, she was tired, the day was long. Down on the ground, she didn't take notice of what was inside the envelope, she think instead of the dreams about her father that don't come anymore, Aunty Cora's body, bloat-up and black. Then she hear Gwennie clear her throat from up above, so she straighten up herself and tell Gwennie thanks.

'The University you going,' Gwennie say to her, her face composed, eyes cover over expressionless, 'I use to do day's work for a man that teach there. Stevens. Nelson Stevens. I think him teach English literature, so many books about Dickens and Thackeray and Brontê were in the house, it have to be.

'You will like Nelson Stevens,' Gwennie continue on. 'His wife not as pleasant, but him easy to talk to, kind gentleman. When you start school I will give him a call.' Then she pause, waiting for Peppy to respond. But Peppy never have anything to say, her fingers were twined up around the envelope, her back tense. 'The students at the University used to call the house all the time,' Gwennie continue on, face pensive. 'Sometimes him even invite them over, young children, gal and boy alike, young like yourself, and them would sit down in the study and chat with him about politics and geography and social studies. Them the courses you must take plenty of,' Gwennie tell her, 'teach you plenty about world affairs, and allow you to hold a point in long conversation.

'Them did have a young baby.' Gwennie's face was far off, and a youthfulness and calm came over it. 'Well, not so young now, about Rosa's age. Cheryl was her name. The wife didn't know a thing about baby caring, not one blast.' Gwennie chuckle.

And as Gwennie go on talk about Nelson Stevens' wife, Mary-Jane Stevens, and how she did have a child-care book in every room, perhaps so she can lay her hand on one in cases of emergency, Peppy couldn't understand this peculiarness that come over her mother. Imagine two good years and not a word pass between them. Peppy sigh. Her mother was so cheerful now, her face almost peaceful. Aunty Cora used to say what don't happen in a year, happen in a day. And Gwennie was still on the subject of Mary-Jane Stevens when Rudi came back inside to tell them the car was ready and waiting outside. The auditorium was empty by this time.